Praise for Sharon

Sharon Ward's IN DEEP is a stellar, pulse-pounding debut novel featuring a female underwater photographer. A heady mix of underwater adventure, mystery, and romance.

> — Hallie Ephron, New York Times bestselling author

Such a great book...Instantly immersive...

> — Hank Phillippi Ryan, USA Today Bestselling author of 13 thrillers

Pack your SCUBA fins for a wild trip to the Cayman Islands. *In Deep* delivers on twists and turns while introducing a phenomenal new protagonist in underwater photographer Fin Fleming, tough, perceptive and fearless.

> — Edwin Hill, author of *The Secrets We Share*

How much did I love In Deep? Let me count the ways. Fin Fleming, underwater photographer, is a courageous yet vulnerable protagonist I want to sip Margaritas with. The Cayman Islands are exotic and alluring, yet tinged with danger. The underwater scenes and SCUBA diving details are rendered in stunning detail. Wrap that all into a thrilling mystery and you'll be left as breathless as - well, no spoilers here. You must read it to find out!

— C. Michele Dorsey, Author of the Sabrina Salter
Mysteries: No Virgin Island, Permanent Sunset, and
Tropical Depression

Breathtaking on two levels, Sharon Ward's debut novel IN DEEP will captivate experienced divers as well as those who've only dreamed of exploring the beauty beneath the sea. The underwater world off the Cayman Islands is stunningly rendered, and the complex mystery involving underwater photographer Fin Fleming, especially the electrifying dive scenes, will have readers holding their breath. Brava!

— Brenda Buchanan Author of the Joe Gale
Mystery Series

In Deep is a smart and original story that sucks you in from page one. Edge-of-your-seat suspense, a hauntingly realistic villain, and a jaw-dropping twist make this pacy read unputdownable until the very last word.

— Stephanie Scott-Snyder, Author of When Women
Offend: Crime and the Female Perpetrator

Sunken Death

Sunken Death

A Fin Fleming Sea Adventure Thriller

Sharon Ward

Sunken Death: A Fin Fleming Thriller by Sharon Ward

Covers by Milagraphicartist.com

ISBN eBook: 978-1-7350511-7-8

ISBN Trade Paper: 978-1-7350511-8-5

ISBN Hard Cover: 978-1-7350511-9-2

Printed in USA

First Edition

Jack, the best husband in the universe.

Foreword

Thank you to everyone who embraced Fin Fleming. I hope you enjoy Sunken Death just as much.

As before, many of the restaurants and dive sites in this book are real places. I've actually eaten there or been diving there. But if anything bad happens in a place, rest assured, I made it up.

I made the mistake of letting Harry die in In Deep, and I heard you loud and clear. It won't happen again. Rosie, the Atlantic Pygmy octopus Fin (and her readers) love so much is hereby declared immortal. Despite the species normal 12-18 month life-span, Rosie will never die.

Recreational divers—don't forget that Fin and the other divers in this book are pros. They engage in risky diving behaviors. Do not emulate them. Obey the safety rules you were taught during training, and never dive outside your levels of comfort and experience.

The wall Fin loves to dive on at Rum Point is still not real, and as far as I know, there is no epidemic of needle sticking in the Caymans.

Chapter 1
Renaming the Maddy

Every sailor knows it's bad luck to rename a boat, but sometimes a girl's gotta do what a girl's gotta do. So, like millions of semi-superstitious sailors before me, I was about to put my boat through an ancient renaming ritual simply because I couldn't see myself captaining a boat named after my mother.

Seafaring folk have always been a superstitious lot, and to avert the horrible curse that supposedly arises from renaming a boat, early sailors developed this ritual to fool Neptune, the god of the sea, into thinking a renamed craft is an entirely different vessel.

I don't believe in Neptune, and I don't believe in bad luck, but I think a little bit of good luck can make up for a lot of stupid. And obviously, it's far better to be lucky than stupid—or cursed.

So here we were, standing on the boat's deck, tied up in the marina at the Madelyn Anderson Russo Institute for Oceanographic Exploration—RIO for short. The early afternoon Cayman Islands sunshine was golden, sparkling off the clear blue water around us. We were here to rename the boat I'd recently inherited from my late stepfather, Ray Russo.

"Miss Fleming, are you sure you've removed all traces of the boat's old name? Keys, logs, life preservers, maps, maintenance records, tee shirts—anything and everything must be removed before we start the renaming ritual." Stewie Belcher wore his usual Hawaiian shirt and cargo shorts, but he had added a purple stole over his shoulders for the solemn occasion.

As one of my stepfather's oldest friends, Stewie was not happy that I was renaming my boat. After coming to grips with the part he'd played in Ray's death, Stewie had checked himself into rehab. He was back now—clean and sober—and even though he was glaring at me in disapproval, his blue eyes looked clearer than I'd seen them in years.

I sighed. "Please, Stewie. Call me Fin like you usually do. Or Finola if you're feeling formal. And yes, I'm sure every trace of the old name has been removed." I pointed to the boat's transom, where my friend Dominic Vernon had painted over the boat's old name last night. The transom was blank, a pure white expanse awaiting the end of the ritual we were about to begin. "Everything has been checked and double-checked."

"You have the tag with the new name?" he asked.

"Yes. Here it is." I handed him the small metal tag he would use in the renaming ceremony.

Stewie had gotten ordained in some crazy church and performed the ritual the first time the boat had been rechristened. Ray had renamed her the *Maddy*, after my mother, Madelyn Russo, when he married her twenty-five years ago. Changing the name again felt like the end of an era, and a sad reminder that Ray was no longer with us. The times I'd spent with him on this boat were the happiest and most peaceful times in my life. Hence the new name: *Tranquility*.

Sailors can be a superstitious lot, but they're not the only ones who worry about being cursed. Most of RIO's employees were oceanographers and dedicated scientists, but they would no more rename a boat without going through this ancient ritual than they would fake their own research data.

It wasn't that any of us truly believed it was bad luck to rename a boat or skip the ceremony. Some of us just felt it was prudent not to tempt fate, and all of us thought it was a good excuse for a party.

I looked at my mother. "You sure you're okay with this, Maddy?" Like everyone else at RIO, I called her by her nickname. I always had, ever since my childhood aboard RIO's research vessel *Omega*. "This boat's been named after you for a long time."

She nodded. "Yes, it has. But Ray chose the old name. It's your boat now, and it shouldn't be named after your mother. *Tranquility* is a good name."

Stewie nodded and began his intonations. "Oh, mighty and great ruler of the seas and oceans, to whom all ships and we who venture upon your vast domain are required to pay homage…" He droned on through the lengthy ritual.

When he finally dropped the metal tag overboard, followed by a liberal pour of champagne spilling into the sea, I knew he was nearly finished. He ended the ceremony with "…we offer these libations to your majesty and your court." He followed that with exhortations to the four winds, asking for fair breezes and safe ocean passage. The last words were followed by another spill of champagne.

When the second bottle was nearly empty, he poured the rest into a champagne flute and handed it to me. "Drink up."

I sipped and handed the glass to my mother, who took a sip before handing it off to my father, Newton Fleming. He passed it to Oliver Russo, a young man we thought of as Ray's son, even though my parents and I knew he wasn't related by blood. Oliver passed it to Gus Simmons, my late stepfather's other best friend of many years.

I noticed Gus didn't pass the wine to his wife, Theresa, who was expecting their first child. Instead, he passed the flute to Lauren Forster, the new First Mate on the *Omega*. Lauren passed it on to Vincent Pollilo, the *Omega*'s captain.

The caterers waiting on the dock took this as the sign to pour champagne for all our other guests and all the RIO employees who had gathered to watch the renaming rites. After everyone except Theresa and Stewie, who was newly on the wagon, had taken at least a sip of champagne, the ceremony was over.

As soon as he'd finished the ritual, Stewie walked over to my father, Newton Fleming, and held out his hand. Newton handed Stewie a wad of folding money as payment for his part in the ceremony. When he had the cash in hand, Stewie gulped another glass of water, stuffed a cookie in his mouth, and jammed a sandwich in the pocket of his cargo shorts. He walked over to Lauren, kissed her cheek, and slung an arm over her shoulder. "Ready, Babe?"

We all gaped but tried not to stare. We expected her to push him away or slap him for daring to touch her.

But to our surprise, she smiled at him and kissed him on the lips. "Ready." We were shocked by their display of affection because they were such an odd couple.

Lauren was a tall, voluptuous, and lovely blonde with impeccable credentials. Stewie was lazy, short, fat, and sloppy. Like Stewie, Lauren was dressed in cargo shorts, flip flops, and a baggy Hawaiian print shirt. While some couples end up dressing alike after they'd been together a long while, Stewie and Lauren had already adopted the habit of dressing alike although they couldn't have known each other for more than a week or two. The two strolled off, arm in arm.

The conversation didn't resume until we saw Stewie's old rattle-trap car leave RIO's parking lot. Once they were out of sight, the party was back in full swing for another hour or so. By then, the workday was over, and people started drifting out in small groups.

Liam, my sort of boyfriend, and Oliver, my sort of brother, began carrying aboard the life preservers, logbooks, coffee mugs, and other items emblazoned with the boat's new name. Once they had everything aboard, Liam left for his shift at the Ritz and Oliver went back to running RIO's dive shop.

Maddy, Newton, and I put the new things away while we

4

waited for my friend Dominic Vernon, the best marine artist in the Cayman Islands, to arrive. He was scheduled to take the *Tranquility* to dry dock to paint the boat's transom with her new name.

The next time I looked up from my work, it had been more than an hour since the guests had departed. The caterers had long ago removed the last of the champagne, finger sandwiches, and cookies we had served. Dominic still hadn't arrived, and he didn't answer his cell when I called.

Maddy bit her lip. "I have a conference call scheduled with some West Coast donors. I've gotta get back to my office. I hate to leave..."

"Don't be silly. You're the founder and executive director of the Madelyn Anderson Russo Institute. You have more important things to do than hang around here with me." I didn't look up from where I was sorting maps into the *Tranquility*'s built-in cabinets.

"Nothing's more important to me than you. But I don't want to miss this call. Donors." She turned to walk away.

"Don't worry. I'll stay with Fin until Dominic gets here." My father stowed the last life preserver in a locker beneath the galley table and smiled at her back. I could feel how much he still loved her even thirty feet away from him.

"Want a coffee, Fin? I don't know about you, but I'm beat from drinking champagne in the sun." He poured water into the coffee maker and flipped the switch before settling at the table.

"Sure." I joined him in the galley. I wasn't used to drinking alcohol during the day either. Or drinking much at all, for that matter. When I got stressed out, I don't drink. I go diving.

Newton and I stayed on the *Tranquility* chatting until the sun touched the horizon. "Where could Dominic be? He's usually so reliable," I said, remembering the terror I'd felt waiting for Ray to appear during his deep freedive last year. Dominic's lateness was an uncomfortable reminder of that helpless feeling, and I tried hard to shake off my foreboding.

"Maybe he got mixed up and thought you were bringing the

boat to him. Think we should float on over there and see what's up?" Newton stood and stretched. I climbed up to the flying bridge to start the engines.

When I turned the ignition key, the engine whirred and whined without catching. I tried again. "Sounds like there's something caught in the propeller," I said. "I'll go look." I slipped out of the shorts and t-shirt I wore over my bathing suit and took the keys out of the ignition to prevent any accidents while I was underwater.

I stepped onto the bow of the *Tranquility*, slipped my mask over my head, and put the snorkel in my mouth before doing a giant stride entry into the water. Underwater, I looked along the length of my boat and caught sight of a tangle of rope and what looked like a mass of debris caught in the propellers. I surfaced, took a deep breath, and swam underwater toward whatever it was.

The water was clear as glass, so I was still at least fifteen feet away when I realized the debris was a body. The face was swollen and bloated, and the eyes were wide and staring. I could see the rope pulled tight around his neck.

It was Dominic.

I shot to the surface. "Newton. Call the police."

Chapter 2
DS Scott Comes By

NEWTON and I waited in the *Tranquility*'s cabin, clutching our coffee cups in shaking hands. I looked up from the clouds of steam rising from my coffee to see DS Scott, the Deputy Superintendent of the Cayman Islands Police, strolling across RIO's lawn.

It had been less than three minutes since we'd called the police. I was surprised at how quickly he'd arrived, and even more surprised at the leisurely pace he was taking as he approached us. I rubbed my arms against a sudden chill. I hadn't seen DS Scott since the day of my last arrest.

Newton reached over and took my hand. "It'll be fine."

I nodded. My father is a lawyer, although he doesn't practice law. In real life, he heads up an investment firm that concentrates on eco-friendly and green initiatives. Even so, he had done a good job of keeping the police off my back after Ray's death, and I was grateful to him for that.

Until a few months ago, Newton had been out of my life since I was five years old. I hadn't seen him even once in all the intervening years. So far, our renewed relationship had been a lot of two steps forward and one step back events.

But I knew having him do all the talking meant that at least this time my lamentable tendency to take the blame for every bad thing that happened wouldn't get me into trouble.

DS Scott didn't seem in a hurry to reach us. He might have been out for a late afternoon stroll with the pace he was keeping. His head swiveled to each side, taking in everything around him. As always, his eyes were focused and intense. My palms started to sweat, even though I had done nothing wrong.

He ambled down the dock and stopped next to my boat. "Permission to come aboard, Captain," he said.

"Welcome," I said. "Would you like some coffee?"

He kicked off his shoes and hopped onto the deck of my currently nameless boat. "No, thanks. I have some news."

"Do you want me to show you the body?" I asked.

He did a double take. "Body? What body?"

Now I was confused. "The one we called the police about. Dominic Vernon. He's under the boat. Isn't that why you're here?"

He shook his head. "No, like I said, I came to give you some news. But that can wait until we figure out what's up. Where is the body?" He looked around the cabin, as though he thought Newton and I might have been sitting at the table with a dead person.

"Underwater. Caught in the mooring lines. I didn't touch anything after making sure he was dead." I realized my statement could be misconstrued, and I shot a pleading glance at my father. Newton was gazing out the window and apparently had neither seen nor heard me. *Thanks for taking the lead here, Newton.* I'd have to dig myself out of the mess I'd already made.

"I don't mean I made sure he was dead. I mean I determined whether he was still alive when I found his body. He wasn't, so I surfaced, and we called you. Otherwise, I would have already begun a rescue effort."

"I appreciate the clarification," he said. If I didn't know for sure the man had no sense of humor where I was concerned, I would have sworn I saw his lips twitch as though he were suppressing a laugh.

Newton tuned back into the conversation. "I'm Miss Fleming's lawyer, as you may recall from the last time we met. Please address your questions to me."

DS Scott sat on the daybed opposite the galley table. "Yes, I remember. Let's get started. When was the last time you saw this Dominic Vernon alive?"

"Yesterday. He was fine when we left him at his marina around four. Newton and I arrived here together around eight this morning to prepare for the renaming ceremony. So, Dominic must have died between four o'clock yesterday and eight this morning."

DS Scott walked to the stern of the Tranquility and touched the outside of the transom. "Do you know what time Mr. Vernon painted the boat?"

Newton took a sip of now cold coffee, grimaced, and put the mug aside. "When we arrived this morning, the first thing we did was check to make sure it had been painted. The paint was dry, so Dominic must have done the work either late yesterday afternoon or early last night. He was supposed to be back for the renaming rite at two o'clock today, but he never showed up. Now we know why."

My father rose to refill his mug. "We've been on the dock full time since around one, and before that we were on and off the dock several times and didn't see him. From that, I conclude his death occurred sometime between last evening and eight this morning."

The policeman nodded and wrote something in his notebook. He reread what he wrote, then flipped the notebook shut and slid it into his breast pocket.

Two police divers were approaching us along the dock. "I think the rest of your team is here, DS Scott. The body is underwater, although not down very deep. Can I get you or them anything? Tanks? Weights? Lights? We have everything you might need right here in the shop. That way they won't have to bring all that heavy equipment from the parking lot."

"That's very kind of you. I'll leave you to sort things out with them while I watch since I'm not a diver myself."

Although I couldn't remember their names, I knew the two divers from training classes I'd taught at RIO, so we greeted each other cordially. They were grateful for my offer to supply them with tanks and weights because it saved them from lugging all the heavy stuff to the dock from the distant parking lot. Oliver was still working in the tank shack, so I sent him a text asking him to bring several scuba tanks, an assortment of weights, and a couple of powerful underwater flashlights to my boat. While I waited for Oliver, the divers went below to check in with DS Scott and don their dive skins.

Just as the divers emerged onto the deck, Oliver arrived with the tanks and other equipment I'd requested. "Everything okay out here?" he asked.

"Yep. I'll fill you in later when the dive is over."

He nodded and walked away.

"Do you want me to dive with you?" I asked the police divers.

"No thanks. If you could just tell us where the body is and wait up here in case we need anything, that would be great," said the taller of the two divers.

I suggested they enter from the empty slip next to mine, or off the bow of the boat instead of from the dive platform near the rear transom to avoid getting tangled in the mess of ropes I had seen. I offered them a dive knife from my own gear bag in case they needed to cut the ropes to free Dominic, but they refused.

I imagined how awful it would be to see Dominic like that, and I wanted to give them whatever comfort I could offer, so while they were gearing up, I called the manager of RIO's café and asked her to send soup and sandwiches for the divers, with fruit and cookies for dessert. Juice and water, because diving makes you very thirsty —but carbonated beverages can cause stomach cramps and gas during a dive. Then I put on a pot of coffee for them. I had a feeling they'd be diving several times this evening.

Each diver had clipped a small underwater camera to their buoyancy control devices, also known as BCDs, and I knew they would take a lot of pictures before they brought Dominic up. Other than the pictures they took, there would be very few clues at the crime scene. The sea washes everything clean.

Chapter 3
Sorrow

DS SCOTT HAD SUGGESTED we wait in the RIO building while his team worked, so Newton, Oliver, and I were sitting at the small round table in Maddy's office. Maddy was at her desk. None of us was doing any talking.

It took about half an hour before the flashing red lights of an ambulance arriving on the RIO grounds alerted us that the police were ready to remove Dominic's body. We were wondering whether we should go back outside when DS Scott poked his head in the door of Maddy's office.

"Dr. Russo, we'll be removing the body now, but I'd appreciate it if you and Fin could join us just for a moment. Let us know if you observe anything unusual."

"Of course," Maddy said. She grabbed a sweater from the back of her chair, and we all followed DS Scott back outside.

The divers had placed Dominic's body on a black body bag laid out on the dock near the *Tranquility*.

"He looks peaceful. Like he just went to sleep. No rope burns on his hands. It doesn't look like he tried to get untangled at all."

DS Scott was staring at me with what looked like approval,

although I thought that was unlikely. "Very astute observations," he said. "Anything else?"

I shook my head. With the reality of Dominic's death right there in front of me, I couldn't think clearly or find the words to speak.

"Okay then. Dr. Russo, if you and your family have another moment, I'd like a few minutes to talk to you. I have some news I wanted to share."

Maddy nodded. "Of course. Whatever you need."

DS Scott led us all into the galley of the *Tranquility*. He sat in the captain's chair, while the four of us sat at the galley table.

DS Scott's expression was bleak, and he looked like the words he was about to speak pained him. "It's about Lily Flores Russo. She recanted her confession, claiming she made it while suffering from nitrogen narcosis. She said none of her confession was true. In the absence of any physical evidence and without a confession, we had no case against her. All charges have been dropped, and she was released from custody this afternoon. I wanted you to hear this news from me. I came here to warn you to be careful."

I gaped at him. "But she's a psycho. A killer. She wrecked our lab and trashed my boat. There must be something you can do." My hands were shaking, but whether from fear or fury I couldn't say.

Newton took my hand and squeezed. "It'll be okay."

Oliver stood up. "Fin's right. It won't be okay. Lily's crazy, and she'll try to ruin everything." He brushed tears from his eyes.

Maddy's face was as ghastly pale as her famous white-blonde hair, but her voice was steady. "Thank you for letting us know. Is there anything we should know or do?"

"I'll have extra patrols keeping watch on the RIO grounds, your condo, and Fin's house. For now, that's all we can do." DS Scott cleared his throat. "But there is something else related to Dominic's murder. If you could keep people off the dock for the next few days while we complete our examination, I'd appreciate it."

The dock is a key part of our business. It's where we moored the boats used for our research team, our dive classes, our glass bottom boat tours, and our Stingray City trips, and it's the jumping off place for our shore diving business. Not to mention it's where most of the staff keep their personal watercraft. It was essential, yet Maddy didn't hesitate. "Whatever you need. Please just keep me informed on your progress."

DS Scott smiled sadly at her. "Will do. We'll work as fast as we can. I'll leave Officer Miller here to watch the dock. Goodnight." He turned and left my boat.

We were all in shock, too stunned by Dominic's death followed by the news of Lily's exoneration to speak. Oliver's hands were clasped in front of him, and he stared at his knees. He kept opening his mouth as though he'd been about to say something, but then changed his mind. I was pretty sure I knew what was coming.

Despite occasional bouts of teenage brashness, Oliver had a sensitive side. I knew he struggled with Lily's part in Ray's death. Even as a child, before his mother lied to him about Ray being his father, Oliver had idolized Ray. He'd been devastated by his murder. But Lily was his twin sister, and he loved her.

Finally, Oliver cleared his throat. "I'm sorry about Lily being free. That must be awful for you guys. And since Ray wasn't really my father, I'll understand if you don't want me around anymore."

I put my hand on his. "From the moment he learned of your existence, Ray was your father in his heart. And he always knew he wasn't your biological father, any more than he was mine." Because we knew Ray had loved him like a son, we'd immediately accepted Oliver as part of the family.

"I'm so sorry for the trouble we've caused you all…"

Newton reached over and put a hand on his shoulder. "You didn't do anything, so you have nothing to be sorry about. You're not responsible for Cara's or Lily's actions."

I could sense Oliver didn't want to look at us—afraid of what he might see. "She's my twin sister, and she's crazy. My mother is crazy. For all you know, I might be crazy too."

"You're not crazy, and we love you," Maddy said. "No matter what. And Newton's right. You're not responsible for your sister. Or your mother."

"I'm not Ray's real son, you all know that. There's no reason you have to include me in your family."

"Yes, there is," I said. "You were the son of Ray's heart, just the way he always said I was the daughter of his heart. You're Ray's real son because he loved you as a son, so you are part of this family. Forever. No matter what." We had only known Oliver a short time, but we had come to love him.

Oliver brushed new tears from his eyes. "Being with you all like this means so much to me. I never had a normal family."

Newton started laughing. "I wouldn't be so sure you have a normal family in us, either. But you can be sure we'll always love you. You have a home with us forever."

Oliver swallowed hard. "Thank you. You can't imagine how much it means to me."

"Um...," I said. "I've been living on my boat practically full time. Most of my clothes and personal items are here. I've got to pack up and get the stuff I'll need for the next few days."

"Need any help carrying your stuff?" Newton asked.

"No thanks." I gathered my belongings. My family and I had just stepped onto the dock when I saw Liam racing across the lawn. As always when I saw him, my heart fluttered, and I had to stop a moment to admire the view.

He's tall, with broad shoulders, long legs, and shaggy blonde hair. As much as I like looking at him, I enjoy talking with him even more. He's smart, articulate, and well-read. He makes me laugh all the time. To top it off, after we'd been diving together several times, he'd mentioned he holds a Master Scuba Diver certification. Liam is the whole package, and then some. I only wished our relationship was moving a bit faster.

"What's going on?" he shouted as he trotted past the ambulance and police cars to join us.

I stepped forward and put my hand on his arm. "Dominic's dead, Liam. He was found under the *Maddy*. I mean, the *Tranquility*."

Liam paled. "Dominic, dead? How? What happened?" He and Dominic had been acquaintances rather than friends, but still, it's upsetting when someone you know dies unexpectedly. Especially someone as young as Dominic, who had just celebrated his thirtieth birthday.

"We don't know what happened yet." I hefted the duffle bag in my other hand. "I was just getting my things. I'll be staying at my house on Rum Point while DS Scott completes his investigation."

"I see. Well, I'll get my stuff too." Officer Miller had been keeping watch on the dock, but now he followed Liam onto the *Tranquility*.

Newton tightened his lips and clamped his mouth shut. I could tell he thought Liam had been living on my boat with me—which wasn't the case. Liam and I were friends, and we were taking teeny, tiny baby steps toward making our relationship more than that. We both said we wanted to move ahead, but we hadn't gotten very far down the path yet.

But Newton didn't know the state of our relationship, and he clearly thought Liam and I had been sleeping together on the boat. He wasn't sure how to react to the idea. He was trying hard to be a good father, and we'd frequently discussed what that meant when your daughter is a grown woman, and you hadn't bothered to check in on her in more than twenty years. He'd confessed that he had a hard time remembering I wasn't a little girl anymore.

I had to laugh at his relieved sigh when Liam came off the boat carrying nothing but a paperback book he'd been reading.

Liam waved the book in the air. "This is a great story. I've been looking forward to finishing it all day. Couldn't wait for my shift to end. I brought your book too." He winked at me as he handed me the most recent volume of Ray's ship's logs that I'd been reading.

"Ready to go?" I asked.

He nodded. Like many of the island's divemasters and hospitality workers, Liam didn't own a car. Instead, he traveled everywhere by bicycle. Tonight, he left it in the parking lot at RIO. I dropped him off at his place, a small staff apartment on the grounds of the Ritz. He shared it with several other Ritz employees.

Once at my home on Rum Point, I had trouble settling down. Dominic's death and Oliver's pain had both hit me hard. Alone and at loose ends, I decided to do what I always do when I need to work out my feelings. I went to the breezeway and gathered my dive gear for a solo dive.

Chapter 4
Rum Point Dive

AFTER PARKING my Prius in the lot at the beach at Rum Point, I set up my regulator, the air delivery device that connects to the tank and goes into the diver's mouth for breathing. I wiggled into an old black dive skin.

I usually wore the RIO branded skins from the annual documentaries, but they all had the RIO logo on the shoulder, and my name on the leg. Sometimes people recognized me because they saw my name, and today I wanted to be anonymous. I clipped a small redundant air supply to my buoyancy control device, and then I checked the BCD's pockets to make sure everything I might need was there.

Flashlight. Check.

Extra snorkel. Check.

Scuba sausage. Check.

Dive knife. Check.

Underwater slate and pencil. Check.

Weights. Check.

Retractable line. Check.

Satisfied, I donned my BCD for the short walk across the sand, carrying my mask and fins in my hands. At the water's edge, I had a moment of doubt. This had been the location of one of Lily's many attempts on my life. Maybe it wasn't such a good idea to dive here alone, now that she was free again. Then I shrugged and donned my mask and fins. I couldn't live my life in fear, and I wouldn't let Lily control my actions.

I waded backwards into the warm water. When I was waist deep, I turned and dove.

I used my snorkel to swim to the ropes that marked the edge of the designated no boats area. Then I switched my snorkel for my regulator and sank beneath the waves. The giant orange and blue sea fan corals swayed rhythmically, dancing in time with the ocean's music. There was a very faint surge today, and the rocking motion of the water was soothing.

I let the water carry me, my hands folded loosely at my waist, holding onto my pressure gauge so the hose wouldn't dangle and get caught in the delicate coral formations. The brilliant corals were lined up along both sides of a sandy stretch that led like a runway straight to the edge of the reef, where it dropped off to form a sheer vertical wall, like an underwater mesa. As I swam along at a leisurely pace, I scanned the sand below looking for any sign of a stingray—my favorite sea creatures.

Out of the corner of my left eye, I saw the telltale outline of a stingray's wings in the sand, and I smiled. The stingray's hooded eyes followed my path, but she didn't swim away from me. I was sure this was Suzie-Q, a new stingray who had moved into the area after the death of my beloved Harry. I knew she was female because she lacked the pelvic fin extensions known as claspers that marked male stingrays, and because she was quite a bit larger than the typical male.

Like Harry, Suzie-Q didn't like me to get too close, but she usually didn't swim away unless I got within touching distance. I don't know how she knew how long my arms were, but if her past behavior was any indication, she knew to within a centimeter or less when I was in range. Then and only then would she burst from her hiding spot and sail away to a new location.

I'm a visitor to the underwater world, and I hate to disturb the undersea life. I let her be and dropped over the rim of the reef, sinking down to about seventy-five feet where I knew several green moray eels made their homes.

Moray eels look fearsome, with their sharp teeth and gaping mouths, but their jaws are open to help them breathe, not necessarily to be ready to pounce on the unwary. Even so, it's a good idea to avoid wearing anything that glitters while diving, and not to feed them or tease them in any way. They have very poor vision, and they will bite.

I stayed back a respectful distance, hovering in mid-water to watch the morays as they surveyed the area in front of their dens. When one eel ducked back into his cave, I figured I had outstayed my welcome, so I swam on, rising slightly in the water to stay within a safe dive profile.

As I crested the reef rim at about 50 feet of depth, I passed by a large tiger grouper patiently hiding in the coral, watching for prey. His mottled skin made it easy for him to disappear into the intricate coral formations. He was about two feet long and plump, so I knew he was well fed, but if something edible passed by, he would lunge out to swallow it, usually in a single gulp.

A green sea turtle rose over the wall and cruised along the sand path looking serene and wise. He saw me watching and veered off. He was soon lost to sight among the larger corals. I passed over Suzie-Q still buried in the sand, her hooded eyes following my path.

I looked at my pressure gauge and realized it was time to head back to shore. I kicked along slowly, thinking about Oliver and his obvious guilt about Lily—and his longing for a family.

Oliver's mother had put him through a lot of emotional highs and lows during her effort to get her hands on Ray's treasure, the Queen's Tiara. First, when Oliver was a child, she'd told him his father was dead. Then she'd told him his father was Ray Russo, a man he had idolized his entire life. Later, Oliver found out that wasn't the truth either. The realization must have broken the sensitive heart he hid under his tough-guy, late-teens façade. No wonder Oliver was shattered. He'd lost Ray all over again.

I understood his desire for a family. I was self-aware enough to know that a lot of my problems stemmed from my own desire for the same thing.

My biological father Newton and I were trying to forge a relationship, but much of the time, our relationship was still more cordial than loving. I couldn't imagine ever feeling about him the way I'd felt about Ray. Even though Newton and I were both trying, I missed Ray's humor and his love. He had been the best father a girl could ever hope for, and I felt his loss every day of my life.

Chapter 5
A Valuable Discovery

WHILE UNLOADING the hatch of my car after the dive, I realized the photo boards from Ray's funeral were still in my backseat, even after all these months. I hadn't had the heart to touch them before this, but now I was ready. I dumped my tanks, BCD, regulator, and dive skin in my backyard rinse tank, and while my gear soaked off the saltwater residue, I brought the photo boards into my home office, putting them in a corner behind the door.

I sat at my desk to call Carl Duchette at *Your World*. We were scheduled to meet later in the week to discuss ideas for my upcoming photo spread in his magazine, but I wanted to postpone our meeting for a few days because of my family's shock at Dominic's death.

As usual, the minute I picked up my phone, my next-door neighbors started blasting calypso music at deafening volume. How did they always know when I was about to make a call? I needed to shut the office door to block out the sound before I called Carl.

Aside from preventing him from thinking I'd called from the middle of a limbo party, I wanted quiet to consider how to frame my request. Because of his friendship with my late stepfather, Carl had offered me this once-in-a-lifetime opportunity to provide a by-lined ten-page spread of underwater photographs to his magazine, and I didn't want him to think I was ungrateful. But I also felt I owed it to Maddy and Oliver to be here while they worked through Oliver's pain.

When I started to shut the door, the full-length mirror on its back reflected Ray's photos, which were upside down. The most recent one I'd taken of Ray—the one where the tattoo on his hip showed—was in front, and I was shocked to see in the mirror that the tattoo was not an abstract design as I'd always thought, but a set of geographic coordinates. Because the numbers and ordinals had been artfully stylized and integrated into the design of flowers, birds, and mystic symbols, they didn't stand out as longitude and latitude numbers. In fact, unless the image was upside down and reversed, the numbers weren't recognizable as numbers at all. Could this be what Ray had meant when he'd told Stewie I had the treasure map?

An idea blossomed in my mind. It was a way to pay tribute to Ray, ensure that Stewie and Gus got their shares of the Queen's Tiara treasure—if it still existed—and to give *Your World* a dynamite feature for my debut. If I created a photographic record of the search to uncover Ray Russo's fabled treasure, it would be sure to make a huge splash for the magazine.

And for me. My ex-husband had stolen my best work and then accused me of plagiarism when I claimed it as my own. Done right, this photo montage could put my derailed photographic career back on track.

I grabbed the photo board and raced back to my desk to look up the location of the coordinates. Picking up a pencil and my atlas, I decoded the location. It turned out to be a spot near Belize, but in the middle of nowhere in international waters. There was nothing on my charts to indicate any reason why a ship might have floun-dered there.

Even so, I was sure I had found the location of Ray's treasure. It wasn't on the usual treasure routes, but it was a strong possibility as the location. Why else would Ray have tattooed those coordinates on his hip?

I was growing more excited by the minute as I contemplated talking to Carl. I'd have to be careful to present my idea as a treasure hunt, not a sure-fire treasure recovery trip. The semantics wouldn't make much difference in how I'd plan or execute the trip, but the words I chose might make a big difference in Carl's expectations for the finished piece.

My heart leaping with excitement, I picked up my phone again.

He answered on the first ring. "Duchette here."

"Carl, I'm not going to make our meeting next week. I'll be away for six weeks or so, working on behalf of *Your World*. I've found what I think is the location of Ray's lost treasure, and I'll be going after it. I'll keep a complete photographic log of the expedition, and you'll have the exclusive. That is, if you want it…"

He didn't even pause to think about it. "Of course, I want it. I can't wait to read about your treasure hunt and see the pictures. Let's get started on the publicity campaign right away."

"Er…Carl, it would be better if we keep the expedition a secret until I return. The idea of treasure will bring out all the crazies, and we'll have hordes of people following us, messing up the dive sites, maybe even finding the Queen's Tiara before I do."

Carl wasn't going to be deterred from his idea that easily. "I think you're going to have to deal with that, Fin. I need time to build awareness for this spread. It could turn out to be the biggest thing we've published in years."

But I knew that any publicity before the expedition returned would ruin the story and make the photography difficult or impossible. I had to play hardball on this point. "No publicity until the expedition returns. If that's a showstopper for you, I'll do your shoot on something else and find the treasure on my own. I'll give you first dibs on the footage when I get back, but I don't want to deal with all the crazies any publicity would unleash. And you'll have plenty of time to build buzz about the spread, I promise. No one will see those images until you release them."

There was a moment of silence. "You're as tough a negotiator as your father. OK. Now I need to talk to Maddy about sponsoring the RIO documentary again this year. I'd like to offer my financial and logistical support. Maybe you can find a way to feature *Your World* on a banner or something, so we're in all the shots for the shoot and the film. Do you think that will work?"

I was the daughter of two very shrewd businesspeople, and I knew the value of partnerships and using other people's money. "Sure. Great idea. I can handle that contract for you too. I was thinking you'd also sponsor custom wetsuits with the *Your World* logo on the right shoulder, a logo banner inside the *Tranquility's* cabin, maybe decals on the tanks. Stuff like that. I think that package would be within your price range."

I named a figure I thought he could live with. I heard him suck in a breath at the number, but after a pause he agreed.

"Great. And the best thing is, we can use the same dive skins and tank logos for the RIO documentary since you want to sponsor that too. You'd just have to add in the cost of a banner for the *Omega*, some more hats and mugs. Maybe sweatshirts or logo tees for the crew. I think we can put both packages together for..." I named another number, nearly double the first. You'll be sharing the platinum sponsorship with Fleming Environmental Investments, my father's company. How does that sound?"

"Great, Fin. It all sounds great. You've saved me a trip."

"Super. I'll finalize the expedition plans next week, as long as you agree there's to be no publicity before the expedition is over. Does that work?"

"Works for me."

Carl sounded smug, and I wondered if my sponsorship suggestions had been in his plan all along. With *Your World's* logo plastered all over every piece of equipment, I wouldn't be able to sell the shots to anyone else even if I wanted to—which I didn't. Ray had taught me to value my integrity and my friends and family above all else. I would never sully his memory by double-dealing his friend.

But I was so excited by my success I had to tell someone.

Chapter 6
Recovery Team Meeting

NEWTON WAS JUST FINISHING a conference call when I arrived at his condo. When he put down his phone, I reeled off the terms of the two deals I'd just negotiated, the words tumbling out of my mouth so fast it was surprising he understood me. I could tell he did though because his smile grew wider as I continued.

"Nice job," he said when I paused to take a breath. "I couldn't have done better myself." He stood up and gave me a hug. "I guess the apple doesn't fall far from the tree."

I groaned at the old saw he'd uttered, but his obvious pride in me was as soothing as rubbing a rich lotion over a dry patch of skin. I felt at least six inches taller at hearing his words.

"Let's celebrate," he said. "I'm sure I have some champagne around here somewhere."

"Can't. Gotta get working on the expedition plan." Now that I was faced with pulling together the logistics for such a complex project, I felt overwhelmed. It would have been complicated enough to plan the treasure hunt by itself but combining it with the complexities of filming RIO's annual documentary more than doubled the number of details.

As usual, I was trying to take on the entire responsibility myself instead of calling on people I trust to manage some of the details. Memories of how cocky I'd been planning the project that ended with Ray's death was igniting panic, and I paused to take a breath and gulp back a sob. I would have to do much better this time.

"I can help…" he said.

I interrupted him. "Newton, this is a complex undertaking. There's hiring the crew, mapping the route, figuring out food and water needs, equipment requirements, contingencies. Given what happened the last time I was in charge of planning a project's logistics, I need to double check—no, triple check—every detail."

Newton put his hand on my shoulder. "I'm not a diver, but I know how to put together a project plan and figure out the required resources. We can work on it together if you want. Or we can call in another diver who's done this lots of times before. Someone like your mother, for example. I'm sure Maddy would love to help—and you'll need to consult with her whenever the two projects overlap anyway. And Gus has done this before. You'll want Liam, of course, and I'd like to include Oliver too, since he's part of the family. We'll be a team on the expedition, so why not start out as a team?"

My mouth dropped open. He was right. I had fallen back into my old behavior, thinking I had to do everything perfectly—and by myself. It had led to disaster when I planned Ray's freedive last year. Even though there was nothing I could have done to stop his murder, the fiasco resulting from my cascading mistakes had made it even harder for me to ask for help since then.

"You're right. I have to learn to stop taking everything on myself. I need to delegate more." I sighed. I'd thought bringing in more people would slow the project plan down, but Newton made me see it would speed things up if I had experienced people to work with.

But even though Ray's treasure had stayed hidden for more

than twenty years, I couldn't help thinking if I didn't get started right away, someone else would find it and ruin the idea for my photo spread. "I can't afford any delay."

Newton nodded. "I'll make the phone calls to get the team together while you take a moment to breathe and get your thoughts in order. Then you can decide what to do. Maybe we can celebrate later. Deal?"

I nodded. "Okay. Call Maddy, Liam, Gus, and Oliver. They'll be the core planning team." I trotted down the hall to Newton's gleaming kitchen to ask the chef to bring out some snacks and drinks for the upcoming meeting.

I had just returned when his doorbell rang. Without waiting for anyone to answer, my mother breezed in. Newton had bought his condo in the same complex where Maddy lived, so she was only a few steps away. I gave her a hug and we sat at the table to begin working.

Before we started, she held up a hand. "I have to say I'm against using the treasure hunt as the topic of your assignment. Ray never wanted that treasure found or brought to the surface. That's why he never brought it back himself. He said it was cursed. As I recall, sorrow, betrayal, and death by drowning were the terms of the curse. Maybe we should rethink this. How about tracking the migration of the endangered Right Whales as an alternative?"

The plight of the Right Whales is desperate for sure, but it's been covered many times. It wouldn't make the same splash as the hunt for sunken treasure. On the other hand, Right Whales fit in well with the theme of RIO's documentary and the investment goals of Newton's company, one of our primary sponsors. And third, people always love to see whales. I weighed the alternatives, but knew I still wanted to do the treasure hunt for my assignment.

"Look at it this way, Maddy. Everybody has done Right Whales. It won't set your documentary apart from the competition, and that means RIO probably won't receive the same level of donations and funding as it has in the past. I don't mind adding a short segment on the whales to the documentary—in fact, I think it's a great idea. But if you really want to make a splash and earn enough to keep RIO going for the next year, in my opinion the treasure hunt should take center stage."

Maddy thought it over for a few seconds before making her decision. "You're right. We need to do whatever it takes to secure RIO's financing for next year, so the treasure hunt it is. Although Ray was so afraid of that curse…well, never mind. No such thing as a curse."

Then she pulled her PC from her tote bag and connected it to a cable on Newton's desk. Instantly, the contents of her screen were projected on his creamy white walls. "Here's the project plan from last year's *Save our Seas* documentary. Since we never finished it, we can use the same story board and a lot of the footage, but we'll eliminate the freedive, for obvious reasons, and replace it with the Right Whales. What do you think?"

"Perfect. I already talked to Carl about sponsoring both projects, so we've got my filming costs covered, and he's agreed to be a platinum level sponsor on the documentary too." I went on to explain where we'd be showing the *Your World* logo and the price he'd agreed to pay.

I'd been negotiating similar contracts on her behalf for years, so she wasn't surprised that I'd taken the initiative to close the deal. But she was extremely pleased with what Carl had agreed to pay as one of the lead sponsors. We wouldn't be skimping on anything in the budget for this year's documentary.

"Nice job, Fin. Even Ray couldn't have gotten us a better deal." She smiled when she said it, but I saw the pain of losing her husband mixed with the motherly pride in her eyes.

Maddy turned back to her computer to walk us through the documentary's plan, but before she could get into it, Newton's doorbell rang again.

"Ah, they're here at last," he said. He opened the door. Liam and Oliver walked in and took seats at the table.

"Sorry we're late," Liam said. "I had to find someone to cover the rest of my shift at the Ritz and then pick this guy up." He laughed and pointed to Oliver over his shoulder. "Pretty crowded on my bicycle with both of us."

"Sorry. I should have remembered to send a car for you two, but at any rate, we hadn't started yet, so it's no problem."

The doorbell rang again, and Gus Simmons walked in. Gus had been the director of dive operations at RIO until his heart attack a few months ago, just before Ray's death. Now he worked for my father's investment firm as a divisional VP, focused on ocean and environmental concerns.

Now that we were all there, I told them about finding what I thought were the treasure's coordinates obscured in the tattoo on Ray's hip. I didn't tell them the exact location, only that it was several day's boat travel away, and pretty far from land. That meant we would need to carry several weeks' worth of provisions and equipment with us. We could restock as needed by helicopter or by taking one of the smaller boats to the mainland, but we'd want to minimize that to pare down expenses. "And," I reminded them, "Ray recorded them in the days before satellite GPS. The coordinates cover a large area—almost seventy square miles. We don't know for sure the treasure is even there. I'm just guessing the tattoo concealed the coordinates…"

"Pretty good guess in my opinion," said Gus.

I smiled at him. "Yes, I think so too. But it's been more than twenty-five years since Ray found the Queen's Tiara, and anything could have happened in all that time. Someone else might have recovered the treasure or storm currents could have moved the ship so far that we never manage to locate it. We won't know for sure what we'll find until we find it."

"True enough," said Maddy. "Now let's get on with making a plan."

Newton pressed a button on a remote control and the silk drapes on the floor to ceiling windows closed automatically, shutting out the stunning ocean view, but making it much easier to see the projections from Maddy's PC.

Since not everyone was familiar with the storyboard and project we'd had for last year's unfinished documentary, Maddy went through all the major milestones and steps we'd marked as potential problems or risks. We knew that we wanted the search and recovery of the treasure to be the key scene this year, but we didn't know when or even if we'd find the treasure.

We weren't having much luck solving that problem until I had a thought. "We can still make it about finding the treasure. We'll have footage of every dive anyway, so even if we don't know exactly when we'll find the treasure, it won't matter. We can cut in with quick, close-up interviews with each of the principal divers back on the boat if we need to make the segment longer or more dramatic. We can tie it into the 'save our seas' motif by showing the divers picking up underwater trash on breaks or helping any creatures we find in distress. And worst case, if we somehow miss it, we can recreate the 'discovery' of the treasure for the camera."

"OK, that works," Maddy said. "It's settled. Let's start working on the crew roster and equipment list."

Gus looked uncomfortable. "What about the curse?" he asked. "Sorrow, betrayal, and death by drowning. Will you be telling the crew about that?"

Maddy bit her lip. "Why? There's no such thing as a curse. The curse is just a legend, not a proven scientific principle."

Gus said, "Ray believed in the curse. You know it's the reason he never retrieved the treasure. He would have told them."

"Well, I don't believe in it. And if anyone wants to be part of the RIO team, they'll dive where and when I tell them to. Curse or no curse."

It wasn't like Maddy to be so uncaring about her team's welfare, so I knew she wasn't fully confident in her decision to retrieve the treasure against Ray's wishes. I also knew she wouldn't go back on her word once she'd made a promise to me. She'd have to find a way to resolve her dilemma on her own, so I said nothing.

"Gus, do you want to take on your usual dive equipment manager role?" she asked.

"Sorry, Maddy. I won't be joining the crew this year. My health is still not what it was, and Theresa needs me at home. Remember, we have a baby coming." He smiled, and his whole face lit up. "Plus, I have a terrific new job. Thanks to you."

Maddy nodded. "I get that. Oliver, would you be willing to take on the dive equipment manager role? Make sure we have tanks filled when needed, do basic equipment repairs, keep track of spare masks and other gear? You'll have big shoes to fill, but since Gus won't be diving with us this year, we need to find someone else."

Gus nodded along with her words. "I think Oliver would be great in the job. I hear he's done super work at RIO's dive shop."

Oliver looked stunned at the offer. "Yes, I can definitely do it," he said when he got over his surprise. "I'd love to."

He was only nineteen years old but asking Oliver to take on the role wasn't as much of a stretch as it might have seemed at first. He'd been running the on-site dive shop at RIO almost single hand-edly since Gus's forced retirement. He'd proven to be a fast learner and a hard worker. He and I had already started working on his Advanced Scuba certification, and I'd been planning to ask him to dive with my search team. I hoped he'd be able to handle both jobs, and I made a note to discuss it with Maddy later.

"Settled. Okay, on to the next key role," I said. "Liam is a certi-fied Master Scuba Diver, so he'd make a perfect liaison between the team on the *Omega* and me on the *Tranquility*. And he'll be a key member of the treasure search team."

Maddy swallowed the tortilla chip she had been chewing. "Per-fect. I approve of your choice."

We went down the roster of scientists, oceanographers, biologists, dive masters and others on the payroll at RIO, deciding who should become part of the 125 person crew. This expedition would by no means be a pleasure voyage. Even at 225 feet, the *Omega* would be crowded and most people, with the exception of Maddy and the *Omega*'s captain, would be sleeping in an open space crowded with berths.

We needed to be sure everyone we brought along could deal with that while also doing double or even triple duty, and we had to balance the need to attract new donors to support our future research with the requirements of the contracts we had with *Your World*—and stay within our budget.

We came to the last name under discussion. "Stewie Belcher?" I asked. "He's back from rehab, and he seems to be staying sober. He always felt that he deserved a share of the treasure from the Queen's Tiara because of his long partnership with Ray. And he's skilled at diving, equipment repair, search and recovery, site mapping…" I trailed off. Any advanced diver would offer those skills, so it came down to a matter of trusting Stewie again after his betrayal and weighing our misgivings against doing what we knew Ray would have wanted us to do.

Gus cleared his throat. "Ray did promise us both a share of that treasure if he ever decided to retrieve it. He discovered it during our partnership days, so even though we weren't with him when he found it, we all felt that Stewie and I were legally entitled to a share."

I nodded. "I know. So, we'll be splitting the rewards seven ways —you, Stewie, Liam, Oliver, RIO, Newton, and me." Agreed?"

"My share goes to RIO too," Newton said.

We all agreed, and we decided that since Stewie was in line for a share of the treasure, he should be included in the expedition roster. His specific duties would be defined later.

We drafted a memo to the people on the list, advising them of the dates and asking them to let us know if they would be unable to join us and to immediately request any special equipment or accommodations they might need on the voyage.

Maddy sighed. "I'm beat. Let's regroup tomorrow in my office to flesh out the equipment list and figure out how we'll replenish supplies for the trip. Sound good?"

Chapter 7
Dancing

LIAM and I left Newton's condo together. "Are you free this evening?" he asked when we reached the parking lot

"Just so happens I am free," I said. "What did you have in mind?"

"Dinner. Dancing. Mass quantities of margaritas."

My heart skipped a beat at his gorgeous smile.

"Sounds like a plan. Count me in."

"Are you ready to go now? I'm starving."

"Me too. Let's go," I replied.

He blushed. "Do you mind driving? I came on my bicycle and…"

"Sure. I'll drive." I had no idea what he'd been about to say, but regardless, I had no problem driving. In the past, I'd seen him drive one of those small, open-air utility vehicles so beloved by Cayman Islands divers, but I'd since learned that whenever he needed a car, he borrowed it from a buddy he worked with. I had no idea how much he earned as a valet at the Ritz, but it couldn't be much. It probably wouldn't stretch to cover the cost of a full-time car on Grand Cayman.

We jumped into my Prius for the drive to a nearby ocean-front bar, Pinocchio's. A long pier jutted out into the water, and several boats had tied up to it while their owners enjoyed themselves at the bar. We walked across the crowded restaurant and sat under an umbrella at a table in the corner of the outdoor seating area on the edge of the sandy beach. I inhaled the fresh salty air and felt my body relax.

Liam signaled to the waitress, and she took our order. Within minutes, we had a couple of frosty margaritas, a platter of tortilla chips, and a bowl of spicy salsa in front of us. We sipped our drinks and smiled at each other. Simply being with Liam made me happy.

I glanced back at the bar and noticed Stewie and Lauren Forster sitting together at a table, both dressed in their ubiquitous cargo shorts and brightly printed shirts. They had drinks in front of them, but they were just staring into each other's eyes and ignoring the drinks. I was incensed to see Stewie in a bar, with what looked like a cocktail, after just getting sober at rehab. Maddy had paid for his stint in rehab, and I was irate that he had relapsed so quickly.

Lauren looked up and noticed me staring. She smiled and gave a little wave before nudging Stewie. He waved too, then drained his glass. They rose and came over to our table.

"Imagine seeing you two here," Stewie said. "I wish I'd known you were coming. We could have had dinner together."

"That would have been nice. But then you couldn't have had that cocktail," I said, not bothering to hide the edge in my voice.

"I didn't have a cocktail," he said, letting a little bit of heat enter his voice. "I had a virgin colada. With an umbrella."

Lauren nodded. "That's true. I can vouch for that."

I felt my face flaming. "My mistake. Sorry I doubted you, Stewie. So maybe next time we can have that dinner together."

"Good idea," Lauren said. "Well, see you at RIO." She took Stewie's hand, and they left the restaurant.

'I guess it's really true. They are dating." I sipped my drink.

"Looks that way," Liam said, running his finger through the condensation on his glass.

The look on his face was pensive, almost forlorn. It was not like Liam to be quiet or sad. He was almost always upbeat and cheerful. I didn't know what to say to this different persona, so I stayed quiet.

A few minutes later, he finally spoke. "Thanks for suggesting me for the liaison role," he said. "I didn't expect to be included in the expedition, and I was worried you'd forget about me while you were away."

"The expedition will only be a few weeks long, and you're not that forgettable," I said, dipping a salty chip into the rich salsa.

He smiled and took my hand.

We ordered food, and while we were waiting, a trio of musicians set up on the tiny stage inside the covered area of the bar. We were close enough to enjoy the music, but far enough away that the sound didn't inhibit our conversation.

"When did you learn to dive?" I asked him. "You've clearly had a lot of experience. And it's not easy to get the Master Scuba Diver certification."

"I learned back home," he said. "In Australia. I dove the Great Barrier Reef a lot. There's some easy diving on the reef, although unlike here, there's not much in the way of shore diving. After a time spent diving on day trips, I graduated to liveaboard diving, and eventually worked my way around the world, moving from one legendary dive site to the next on my vacations. I was bound to get better eventually." He grinned at me, and my heart melted. "After I quit my last job in Australia, I ended up on Grand Cayman. I think I'll stick around for a while. I like it here."

"I'm glad you landed in the Caymans," I said, smiling back at him.

The waitress brought our food, and we chatted about our various dive adventures while we ate. When we'd finished, we ordered more drinks and watched the band playing. Some of the other patrons were dancing on the miniscule dance floor and even in the aisles around the bar. Liam was tapping his toes under the table. "Would you like to dance?" he asked after a minute.

"Sure," I said, rising. I was terrified to admit I didn't know how. There's not much call for dancing on a research vessel, where I'd spent most of my life. I'd done my higher education on an accelerated schedule, leaving little time for socialization. But it looked like most of the bar patrons who were dancing were just swaying to the beat. It couldn't be much different than letting the ocean surge carry you forward. I could do that, so I figured I should be able to do this too.

Liam was a great dancer. I was comfortable swaying in the crowd, occasionally taking a step to one side or lifting my arms over my head so it looked like I was trying. It seemed to work. At least nobody pointed and laughed.

The sun was setting, and the bar was shrouded in shadow. The bartender flipped on the colored lights and tiki torches, but it was still dim. As the night grew darker, the crowd grew thicker. The dance floor was packed.

After we danced to a few more songs, Liam said "Let's sit the next one out. It's getting crowded here."

I nodded, and we headed back to our table. We turned our chairs, so it was easy to see the luminous ocean or the throbbing crowd just by turning our heads a few inches one way or the other. The music was too loud now to make conversation easy, so we sipped our drinks and watched the moon rise along with the bar patron's spirits, just enjoying each other's company.

About a half hour later, we saw a young woman, maybe nineteen or twenty years old, dancing with a man who looked to be in his late thirties. She was beautiful, graceful, and danced like nobody was watching, as the old saying goes. The man moved in close to her and seemed to be whispering in her ear. Then he took a step back and stopped dancing.

Within a few seconds after he retreated, the girl swayed on her feet and started to collapse. The man caught her in his arms and supported her as he walked her off the dance floor. We lost sight of them in the crowd.

I craned my neck to see if I could tell where he took her, but she was gone.

Meanwhile, the music continued. Now another lovely young woman was dancing with a different older man. Like the other guy, he moved in close to her, then stepped back. A few minutes later, she too buckled at the knees and collapsed. Her partner caught her before she hit the floor. He scooped her up and started carrying her out of the bar.

"Liam," I said. "Something's going on. We can't let that man take her."

Liam looked at me and put his hand on mine. "You're right. Let's go."

We rose and walked up to the man who was still working his way through the thick crowd. Liam stepped in front of them, blocking their progress and raised his voice so he could be heard over the crowd. "Where are you taking her?" he demanded.

"My girlfriend," the man said. "She never knows when she's had enough. I'll bring her back to the hotel to let her sleep it off." He smiled.

Liam didn't buy it. "She's your girlfriend, huh? What's her name?"

"Uh, Toni. Her name's Toni."

"Let's see if you guessed right," Liam said. The girl had a sparkly phone case dangling from her wrist, and it was the type with a credit card slot at the back. Since the man was using both arms to hold the young girl under her knees and shoulders, he didn't have a hand free to stop Liam from grabbing the case.

Liam twisted the wrist strap and deftly removed the cards from the slot. He shuffled through them until he came to her driver's license. "Mary Lou," he said, reading from the card. "She's not your girlfriend. Fin, call the police."

The man looked panicky for a moment, then he thrust the girl toward Liam. Surprised, Liam took her to keep her from hitting the floor. The man didn't wait to make sure she was okay. He turned and ran out the front entrance of Pinocchio's.

I ran out after him, and I could just see him as he jumped in a nondescript car that had been idling at the curb. The car sped off before I got a look at the driver, and the crowd in front of the entrance was too thick for me to get the license plate number.

Liam brought the girl to our table and placed her gently in one of the empty chairs. I stayed with her while he went to the bar to get her some water, but it didn't matter. She was passed out cold.

A few minutes later the flashing red and blue lights from the road told me—and all the other patrons—the police had arrived. The crowd thinned by more than half in the few minutes before DS Scott entered the bar. I waved him over to our table.

Liam handed him the girl's ID and credit cards and told him what we'd observed. "She's the second woman to collapse tonight while dancing with an older man. Both times, the woman fainted a few moments after the man had moved in close to her and then backed away. It looked suspicious."

"We thought these guys might be needle sticking unsuspecting women, so we intervened. The second man was just about to leave with her. We stopped him and asked who she was. He claimed she was his girlfriend, but he hesitated when I asked him her name. I saw her ID on the outside of her purse, so I pulled it out and checked. He'd given me the wrong name, so Fin called you. When he saw that we were on to him, he dropped her into my arms like she was a hot potato and ran out of here." He looked at me. "Did you see any details about the car?"

"Nothing. Sorry." I didn't tell him that I couldn't tell one car from another. Boats—sure. Cars—not a chance.

DS Scott thanked us for our actions and called for an ambulance. While we waited, he turned to us. "That was quick thinking.

You two might have saved her from a horrible fate or even saved her life. Good work."

"Will you be able to help the other woman that was taken earlier? What made the women faint like that? Were they drugged?" I asked him. I shivered at the thought of being drugged and taken away by a strange man for who knew what purpose.

DS Scott quickly lost his smile. "Most people now know better than to leave their drink unattended when they're around strangers, so the old trick of dropping Rohypnol—roofies—in a drink doesn't work so well anymore. The latest thing is 'needle sticking,' where they get in close to someone in a crowded spot and give the target a quick jab with a needle. It can be fentanyl or some other fast acting drug in the syringe, and it's so quick the mark often doesn't even notice they've been stuck. But they pass out almost right away, and who knows what happens to them after that?

"I'll shut this place down for the night, and the bad guys will know to stay away for a while. But unless she gets lucky, I don't know how we can help the other woman you saw until she wakes up and contacts us." For a moment, I thought I saw tears in his eyes.

"Anyway, thanks to your quick thinking, we saved at least one woman tonight. You should be proud."

By the time the ambulance arrived, the bar was almost empty. We waited around until the young woman had been taken away, then we left. I dropped Liam back at RIO to pick up his bicycle and drove home alone to my house on Rum Point.

Chapter 8
A Diving Argument

EARLY THE NEXT DAY, the team finalized the logistical details for both expeditions. To give us time to get our provisions and all the assorted bling *Your World* was expecting to see in the pictures, we settled on a planned departure date in about a month. I left the meeting eager to begin contacting our suppliers and negotiating the contracts for food, water, fuel, and all the other necessities of life at sea. I put in calls to all the key vendors. Then all I had to do was make sure they delivered.

But as RIO's marketing director as well as chief photographer, I was also responsible for designing the logo for the documentary. I would need to get Carl's approval on my design ideas before ordering the banners, tee shirts, wetsuits, mugs, hats, stickers and all the other items where we would be using the logo.

I pulled up the proof of the photo that had the tattoo of the coordinates on Ray's hip. I had an idea for incorporating some of the design elements into the documentary's logo. I isolated one of the mystic symbols and did an image search on the internet. I didn't expect the results I got.

According to the Wikipedia article I consulted, the symbol was an ancient warning. Supposedly, anything that bore the symbol was protected by a powerful curse. According to the article, anyone who took possession of the items it protected without the owner's permission would suffer from a life of sorrow and betrayal, ending in death by drowning.

The story reminded me that Ray had been betrayed by Stewie and Lily, and he had died by drowning. I shivered, and quickly shut down my browser. I didn't want to know any more about the curse. I knew enough to know that given its history, I wouldn't use it in the documentary's logo. I shut down my browser and started my design project over again.

By the end of the day, I had three designs I liked. I emailed them to Carl for his comments and suggestions and advised him of our planned departure date before shutting down my computer. It had been a long day, and I was exhausted.

I walked down the dock to the *Tranquility* and hopped aboard. I needed to dive to wash away the stress of the last few days. I was below decks when I heard Liam's deep voice from the dock.

"Ahoy, Captain. Requesting permission to board."

I poked my head up. Liam and Oliver stood on the dock, each carrying a dive bag bulging with gear.

"Permission granted," I said. "Are we going diving?"

Liam stowed the bags beneath the benches along the side of the deck, while Oliver trotted back to the dive shop to grab some tanks. Liam and I followed him at a slower pace, holding hands outside the tank shack while Oliver locked up. The plan was to do an early evening dive at one of the Bullwinkle dive sites.

Either of the Bullwinkle sites can be a challenge for inexperienced divers. The currents can be unpredictable, and for much of the year the boat ride to the site can be uncomfortable due to high winds on that side of the island. But I wanted to get some pics of the vibrant corals the site is known for, and Oliver was excited to see the famous swim-throughs and coral canyons.

Once at the site, Liam and Oliver hooked us up to the mooring ball while I held the boat steady. When the boat was secure, the dive preparations began.

First, we fastened our tanks into the Velcro straps on the back of our buoyancy control devices and connected our regulators to the tanks. Then we doublechecked our gauges and made sure everything we might need was in the BCD's vest pockets. When all the preparations were complete, we did giant stride entries off the platform and began our descent.

The top of the coral is only about twenty feet below the surface at this site. Because I wanted to photograph the coral using natural light, I planned to spend the early part of the dive around that depth and join up with Liam and Oliver later in the dive.

Sea water diminishes visible colors as you descend. Even with bright sunlight above, the water absorbs red at about ten to twenty feet, so I'd clipped a flashlight to my buoyancy control device to use to reintroduce colors if the sunlight wasn't penetrating far enough this late in the day. I also had a strobe light attached to my camera, one with enough power for shooting at any depth.

The water at this dive site is about fifty feet deep at its deepest point, and Oliver and Liam planned to go deep in the early part of their dive, swimming through the coral caverns and emerging from the swim-throughs—large openings formed by the coral. I would meet up with them after those few minutes of shooting the hardy corals in the shallower parts of the reef.

The reef top was home to some majestic elkhorn coral, so called because its shape resembles the antlers on elk and moose. The magnificent coral came in an array of beautiful colors, reds, burgundies, and greens among them. I took several shots of the most dramatic formations, then as the light faded, I turned on my strobe and descended along the reef looking for Oliver and Liam.

I saw Liam hovering outside the opening of a wide swim-through, waiting for Oliver to emerge, so I swam in his direction. A few seconds later, Oliver popped out and gave Liam the okay sign. The three of us swam together along the coral fortress, peering into nooks and crannies to observe the sea life living there.

We saw tiny shrimp in most of the crevices. Some shrimp shrank back at our approach, but most of them ignored us and went on about their business.

Oliver found a Caribbean Spiny Lobster peeking out of a nook formed by a coral overhang. At first, the only visible part of the lobster was the last few inches of his long, thin antennae. They looked like sea grass waving in the current. Caribbean lobsters lack the large claws of their North American lobster cousins, so they use the antenna to fool predators into overlooking their presence. The sharp spines on their shells are their only protection, making the camouflaging effect of their antennas an important part of their defense system.

After admiring the lobster for a short while, we turned back to the boat. We followed each other up through one of the swim-through tunnels, emerging on the reef about ten feet above where we had gone in. We made our way back to the top of the pinnacle and spent our five minute safety stop swimming along the top of the coral.

Back on the boat, Oliver pulled some sandwiches he'd brought from RIO's café out of his dive bag, and I poured water into the RIO-branded mugs I kept in my boat's galley. We were starved after the long day and the dive, so the sandwiches tasted like a feast. We munched in companionable silence until it grew dark, then we headed back to shore.

———

I was up and going early the next day, sitting at the desk in my office watching the sunrise while sipping a cup of coffee when Newton walked in.

"Seen the news yet today?" he asked.

"Nope. I try not to ruin my day until the sun's all the way up," I said. "What's happening?"

He turned his tablet toward me, and I saw the headline. "Daughter of famed ocean explorer launches search for fabled treasure."

I put down my coffee and grabbed the tablet so I could scan the rest of the article. The information had come from a press release issued by *Your World*. It even included a quote from Carl Duchette.

"Ray never researched the wreck's history, so he didn't know who the treasure originally belonged to. But he found it in open ocean so under international laws, it's available for salvage. He'd thought the pieces—especially the tiara—were so opulent that its unknown owner must have been a queen. He called the treasure the Queen's Tiara, describing it as one of the most exquisite pieces he'd ever seen. Shortly after he found and abandoned it, Ray told me he believed the treasure was cursed. Not wanting to risk the curse's promise of "sorrow, betrayal, and death by drowning," he never brought any of it to the surface. Now we're ready to retrieve the fabled pieces, and I can't think of a better person to do it than Ray's stepdaughter, Fin Fleming, who is also the daughter of world-famous oceanographer Madelyn Russo. *Your World* is proud to sponsor Fin's expedition, and I'm certain our readers will be delighted by her upcoming photo montage of the expedition."

I gaped at Newton, stunned. "He promised no PR until we got back. How could he do this?"

My father knew me well enough to know there was no sense in talking to me until I got over my fury. "You'd better call Carl and straighten this out. Call me if you need me to step in." Newton turned and left my office.

I was so angry that I thought about going diving so I could calm down before I made the call, but then I realized I wanted Carl to know I was angry. I didn't like being lied to, and since the contract wasn't finalized yet—we had a handshake deal, but the paperwork was still with his legal team—I was free to take the treasure hunt and the documentary sponsorship wherever I wanted. While I was formulating the words to express my anger, the phone on my desk rang.

I recognized the caller ID as coming from the *Your World* offices, and I thought about not answering. After a few rings, I relented and picked up the phone. "Fin Fleming here. How may I help you?"

"Hold please for Carl Duchette," said a vaguely familiar male voice. A few clicks. Then I heard Carl's voice.

"Fin, I don't know what to say. I am so, so sorry. I don't know how this happened. I know we had an agreement, and this press release looks like I blatantly violated it. That wasn't my intention. Just a case of miscommunication with my staff."

"I'm not at all happy about this, Carl. I've got a good mind to take the photomontage and the documentary sponsorship to your competitor. What do you think of that?"

He sighed. "I wouldn't blame you. This is a colossal mess, and I'll have to find a way to fix it. I told Stefan…"

"Wait. That wouldn't be Stefan Gibb, would it?'

"Yes. My new assistant. How did you know?"

"He's a snake. I hold him at least partially responsible for Ray's death." I told the story of how Gibb had abandoned his post during Ray's freedive, leaving the winch that measured the depth of Ray's dive plate open to his killer's evil adjustments.

"So, Carl, if Gibb is on your team, you can count me—and RIO —out. We want nothing to do with him."

Carl paused. "As you wish. I didn't know. I was quite clear in my instructions that he was to hold the release until I gave him the go ahead. I see now that he must have deliberately sent the press release out to cause trouble for you. He's off my team as soon as we end this call."

I thanked him, and we agreed to continue with the deal we had negotiated, but I still wasn't happy. How was I going to lead the expedition now when we were sure to be followed by every would-be treasure hunter within a thousand miles?

I looked out my office window and saw several strange boats circling the bay. The treasure hunters and pirates were descending on us already.

Chapter 9
Replan

I CALLED a meeting of the core project team for later that morning to figure out the new plan. We met in Maddy's office. Newton, Oliver, Maddy, Gus, and I were already seated when Liam burst in, out of breath and looking rushed and harried.

"Sorry," he said. "I had to get someone to cover my shift, and my supervisor wasn't happy."

Newton nodded. "We can't have a key member of the team being late all the time. I'll have a word with him after the meeting to let him know we may need you at a moment's notice. He'll have to deal with it. I'll cover the cost of the extra manpower if he feels he needs to staff up to cover for your absences…"

Maddy interrupted. "I have a better idea. Liam, can you stay after the meeting so we can chat?" She smiled at him.

Liam looked at me with raised eyebrows. I shrugged. I had no more idea than he did about why Maddy wanted to talk to him.

We discussed the issues around finding a new date and whether it would be better to depart right away before more scavengers arrived or to delay our departure for months, hoping the treasure seekers would get tired of waiting and leave. Everybody on the team had a different opinion about the best date and the reason for choosing it. We were getting nowhere, so I told them I would figure out a new date and send it to them for their approval. They agreed, and the meeting adjourned.

Shortly after the meeting broke up, I was in my office juggling my wall calendar and several weather maps trying to find another date that would be as good as the one that we had originally chosen for the expedition. I knew we'd selected the optimum date the first time, so it annoyed me that we'd have to abandon it. But since the press release Stefan Gibb had sent out included our planned start date, we either had to leave right away, or wait out the unauthorized treasure hunters who were bound to show up at the first whiff of gold. It could take months for them to lose interest, and we didn't have time to waste.

The trick to planning the expedition's timing was to go late enough in the year that we'd miss tourist season, but not so late that we'd hit hurricane season. I also wanted to avoid thimble jelly fish spawning season, major religious holidays for designated crew members, and school vacations. We needed at least three to four weeks to complete the mission, and the list of dates that wouldn't work was a lot longer than those that would.

I sighed in frustration.

From behind me I heard Liam's voice. "Can I help?"

"Thanks, but I know you have to get back to work. I'll figure this out and then let you all know what the options are."

"I don't have to hurry back to work, and there's something I want to talk to you about. Do you have a few minutes?"

"Sure. I'm not getting anywhere with this anyway. What's up?"

"Maddy offered me a job. I want to know how you feel about me working here."

"Really? She offered you a job. We don't have valet parking at RIO."

"I'm a lot more than a valet," he said. "Didn't you ever look me up on the web?"

56

"No, never. I'd rather get to know a person face-to-face than look at curated profiles. So what's the job?" I was truly puzzled about what Maddy had in mind.

He blushed, turned his head away. "CFO. Replacing Ray."

At first, I didn't say anything.

Then, "Are you qualified for that job? Ray had an MBA, and he understood our business. It's not a job just anyone can do. He won't be easy to replace." I felt like a jerk as soon as the words left my mouth, but it was too late to recall them. And I didn't want Ray replaced. I wanted him back.

He looked stunned. "You really don't have any idea who I am, do you? Weren't you even curious? You never looked me up at all?"

I shrugged. "Why would I? What would I have seen?"

"Maybe a lot. For one thing, I founded Oh! Possum software. Hottest video game of the last several years. I led the company from zero to eleven billion. Sold it for a lot of money." He turned away. "So, yes. I'm qualified to be CFO. Some might even say I'm overqualified."

"But you're just a valet." I was confused.

"Not anymore," he said. "And I never was *just* a valet. It was a temporary gig, and I had my reasons for working at it. You never even cared enough to ask."

I could see the hurt in his eyes before he turned and left my office.

Chapter 10
A Celebration

I SAT AT MY DESK, playing with my electronic pencil, and feeling bad about the conversation with Liam. He'd obviously been hurt that I had no idea of his background, but I truly believed in getting to know someone face-to-face, not making judgements based on internet info that might or might not be accurate.

But my comment that he was "just" a valet had to have hurt. Liam had always been so much more than his job to me. He was smart, funny, well-read, caring, thoughtful, a great diver—the list of his good points went on and on. So far, I hadn't come across any bad points or red flags. He was clearly too good to be true.

It was a big change from the way things had been with Alec, my ex. With him, it had been all drama, all the time. I enjoyed being with Liam, and we were taking things slow in our relationship. So slow I wasn't sure we had anything going on that could even be called a relationship. But whatever it was, I enjoyed it and didn't want to lose it. I sighed and tried to get back into my work.

An hour later I heard Liam's voice from outside Ray's old office. He was talking to Eugene, RIO's head of maintenance, and Stanley, the junior member of the maintenance crew. They were talking about rearranging the furniture. This might be a good time to make amends.

I walked down the hall. "Got a minute, Liam?" I asked.

"I was going to move the furniture..." he said.

"No, you weren't," said Eugene. "That's my job. Go talk with Fin in her office and by the time you get back, Stanley and I will be done here."

"Thanks, Eugene. Thanks, Stanley." Liam clenched his jaw as though walking with me was a punishment, but he went along to my office. "What?" he said, after shutting the door.

"I'm sorry that you expected me to know who you are, aside from being the nice man I met when he parked my car. But wouldn't you rather be with someone who likes you for who you are instead of wondering if I like you for who you used to be, or for your money, or some other irrelevant fact I might have gleaned from the internet? Because I do like you, Liam. I like the man I've come to know because of who he is, no other reason."

He stared at me for a minute. "I like you too. And you may be right." He paused. "You are right. I'm glad we got to know each other this way. I left the high tech world behind and hid away here where nobody would connect me with Oh! Possum for exactly that reason. Thank you for reminding me."

"Great," I said. "Now let's take the afternoon off and celebrate your new job. I assume you're not officially on the payroll until at least tomorrow morning, right? So, you can leave any time you want?"

He laughed. "Luring me into playing hooky already? You're a very bad influence, Miss Fleming."

He took my arm and we walked down the hall and outside to the *Tranquility*. I started the engine and we cruised to Nelson's, a nearby outdoor restaurant that had a private dock for patrons who arrived by boat.

The claim to fame at Nelson's was that they played continuous reruns of the beloved TV show, Sea Hunt. The series had run from

1958 to 1961, and divers everywhere cited it as one reason they got into the sport.

Even with 155 episodes to play, the constant repetition of a finite number of episodes could get monotonous, so the owner broke it up with occasional underwater movies and reruns of television documentaries from RIO and the Cousteau Society.

We were seated near the bar at a beachfront table under a huge red umbrella that wore the Stingray Beer logo. When the server asked what we wanted, I ordered a pitcher of margaritas and three platters of every appetizer on their menu.

Liam looked astonished that I'd ordered so much food. "Hungry?" he asked.

"Not especially. But we're celebrating."

When a team of servers brought the food out, I asked them to offer it to all the patrons in the bar, and to buy a round of drinks for the house.

"What's the occasion?" asked the server originally assigned to our table.

I squeezed Liam's hand. "My friend just got offered a great job, and we're very excited about it. We want to share our happiness."

"Sure thing. Congratulations, man" he said to Liam. He passed our request on to the rest of the wait staff, and they began circulating with the food and taking drink orders.

I poured us each a margarita from the pitcher and toasted Liam. "To the new CFO of the Madelyn Anderson Russo Institute of Oceanography. I know you'll be great at the job."

He smiled at me and sipped his drink. The band started to play a slow song, and we got up to dance. I stepped into his open arms, and he held me close. Things were so easy with Liam, unlike the crazy antics of my rabid weasel ex-husband, Alec Stone.

After our slow dance, the band started playing faster music, so Liam and I drifted back to our table. The bar was packed with writhing, twirling bodies, all gyrating to the beat. I noticed one very pretty blonde dancing with a much older man. He leaned in close to her, and I froze.

Not again. It couldn't be.

A few minutes passed, and the tiny blonde buckled at the knees. Her dance partner scooped her up and headed for the exit. I jumped up from my seat and ran after them. "Suzie," I called. "Wait for me." When I caught up to them, I tapped the man on the shoulder. "Where are you taking my friend?" I asked.

He looked surprised. "She said she was here alone, so I was taking her to the hospital. Here. You take her," he said, thrusting her into my arms. Behind the man, I saw Liam on his phone, heading to the parking lot.

"Thanks," I said to the man's back. As soon as I'd taken her, he'd raced out of Nelson's, but I knew Liam would be outside keeping an eye on him. Staggering a bit under her weight, I went back to our table with the woman in my arms.

The flashing red and blue lights outside were barely visible in the bright sunshine. Two policemen and two paramedics came inside. I waved them over to the table. The EMTs quickly assessed the woman, strapped her to a gurney, and raced away.

Liam and DS Scott came in from the parking lot and sat down at our table. "Fin, you have a way of being in places where trouble happens. If I didn't know you so well, I'd be suspicious, but as it is, all I can do is offer advice. Be careful. They may have recognized you and Liam from the other night, and they'll be on the lookout for you." He rose and walked out of the bar.

With the excitement over, the bar patrons went back to drinking, throwing darts, and dancing. The band came back to play, and soon, they had the crowd in a frenzy.

"I'm so sorry your celebration was ruined," I said to Liam.

He smiled. "Nothing's ruined. I got the bad guy's license plate number, so they'll find him fast. We saved someone. And I'm here in a beautiful spot with a beautiful woman. What more could I want?"

The band launched into a slow song, and he held out his hand for me to dance. At first, I felt bad that we were here dancing and having fun when that poor woman could have been kidnapped or worse. Then I realized that we'd done everything we could for her, and possibly saved her life. Why shouldn't we dance? I took his hand and we melted into each other's arms on the dance floor.

A few minutes later, the song ended, and the band announced they were taking a break. Liam and I returned to our table. The bartender turned on the TV over the bar, and the familiar sounds of the RIO documentary theme song floated across the beach to my ears.

I turned, just in time to see twelve-year-old me fall off the gunwale of my stepfather's boat and split my lip on the deck. Next came me at eight, eating raw fish and spitting it out, all over my grimy t-shirt. Then me at three vomiting over the wrong side of the boat during a storm. Chickenpox at four. Ten years old and slipping out of my too-big BCD when I stepped into the water for a dive. There I was at eleven, squealing and crying as a stingray swam by my head at Stingray City.

Someone had put this reel together and taken pains to include every one of Fin Fleming's most embarrassing moments. Twenty-five years of slips, spills, pratfalls, and drool. The people at the bar were roaring with laughter. I was mortified.

Someone watching at the bar must have noticed me sitting at the beachfront table, because soon everyone was whispering and pointing. I heard a vaguely familiar voice. "Yes, that's her."

I looked in the direction the voice had come from and saw Stefan Gibb standing at the bar watching me, a nasty smile on his face. "Like my fan video?" he asked.

He turned and walked away while I was suddenly mobbed by people asking for my autograph, all talking about their favorite of my many embarrassing moments from the vintage RIO documentaries.

I was signing napkins and t-shirts, a frozen smile on my face while humiliation seared my cheeks. The crowd showed no sign of thinning out. Even the people who had already received an autograph stayed put, kibbitzing with the others, reliving their most-loved—and my most embarrassing—moments from out of my dorky past. Stefan must have left the blooper reel on an endless loop because every time I looked up there was another example of me looking like an idiot.

After a few moments, Liam took my arm. "Miss Fleming has to go now. Thank you all for coming. She appreciates your support, and she loves you all. Right, Fin?" He turned me toward the dock and the safety of the *Tranquility*.

I stumbled after him. When we got aboard, he took the keys and started the engines. "Wave at them," he said. "Smile."

I didn't need a reminder to show the fans I valued them. Maddy had drilled this behavior into me as a child, and by now, keeping a pleasant smile on my face in front of fans was automatic, no matter what I was feeling inside.

When we were away from shore, Liam turned the boat back to the RIO marina. We tied up to my slip and sat side by side on the bow. Liam had his arm over my shoulders, holding me close to him and stroking my hair. I was shaking at first, but gradually the tremors tapered off and finally, they disappeared.

"Why did he do that? Why does he hate me so much? First the press release and now this." I couldn't understand why Gibb seemed to have a vendetta against me.

Liam kissed the top of my head. "Well, you did get him fired. Twice, if I'm counting correctly. Once from the RIO staff after Ray's dive and then again yesterday from the *Your World* team."

I sat up quickly, but he pulled me back to nestle against his shoulder. "I'm not saying he didn't deserve it either time. I'm just saying he may see things differently than you do. Maybe he thinks you're the one with the vendetta."

I looked up at the brilliant blue sky. "I never thought of it from his point of view before. But he's wrong. I'm not out to get him. I just want him to stay away from me. And why was he in New York at *Your World*? That feels like deliberate stalking. And why come back to Grand Cayman after he got fired? I'd have gone someplace new. And that so-called fan reel must have taken a lot of time to put together. Why? What's in it for him?"

"I don't know, Sweetheart," Liam said, this time kissing my forehead. "But you're safe here with me."

Chapter 11
Goodbye to Rosie

LIAM and I went back to my office to finish picking out the new date for the expedition to leave. Now that I'd had time to calm down, the second-best departure date was obvious, except it meant we would have to leave in a few days. Maddy called a meeting of the entire expedition team and told them about the change. Everyone on the original list committed to being ready at dawn the day after tomorrow.

We swore everyone to secrecy regarding the new date. Even Ray's old friend Stewie Belcher, unreliable at the best of times, made a solemn promise not to tell.

I spent the rest of the day calling our suppliers and arranging for fresh food supplies, fuel, water, and other necessities to be delivered sooner than our original request dates. When I called the manufacturer of our custom dive skins, he said they had plenty of the skins we used for our documentaries on hand. Thank goodness he only needed the names of the crew and the logo artwork by the end of the day today so he could do the embossing and make the delivery happen on time.

I called Carl Duchette next and told him he needed to choose the logo design ASAP. He hemmed and hawed and finally told me to select the one I liked. I sent my choice to Maddy, Newton, Liam, and Oliver, and they all selected the same design I liked as their top choice. That simplified matters since we didn't have to engage in the usual endless rounds of discussion. I immediately emailed the design files and the list of the expedition crew to the supplier and crossed one more worry off my list.

It was well after dark when I dragged myself out of the RIO office. I started toward the parking lot before deciding to spend the night onboard the *Tranquility*. I was too tired to drive home. I'd make a run out to Rum Point tomorrow to pick up the clothes and personal items I needed for the journey.

As I walked out to my boat, I noticed that nearly every slip in our marina was filled, and I didn't recognize many of the boats. I hoped they didn't belong to people who planned to follow the expedition in search of the sunken treasure, but I knew they probably were.

The next day passed in a blur of last minute details and decisions. I didn't even have a moment to eat all day, but by nine that evening everything was under control. I was about to head to my car when I remembered I hadn't said goodbye to Rosie, the Atlantic Pygmy octopus I'd been studying and training as part of my doctoral thesis.

Rosie is tiny—her entire body including her complete arm span only measures about five inches. She's shy and prefers to hide in a shell or behind a rock in her aquarium. And she's smart. Give her a whole pile of unrelated objects, and she'll invariably select the one that matches the picture on a card I hold up for her, showing she has enough intelligence to understand abstractions. I adore Rosie.

She's very affectionate toward me too, and often flashes a rosy, pink color when she sees me or to thank me when I feed her. I don't really have a handle on how she perceives the passage of time, but I like to think she misses me if I don't visit every day. And now I'd be gone for several weeks. I had to stop by to see her before I left.

The RIO research lab is huge, because we house aquatic creatures from the very small—like Rosie—to much larger specimens. We don't keep whales, dolphins, seals, sharks, or pelagic creatures that don't do well in captivity. Research is our primary reason for existence, and we employ a large staff of scientists, so we need the space for their experiments.

The lights in the room are on all the time and they're always dim so we don't startle the sea creatures. After Oliver's twin sister had practically destroyed the lab a short time ago, we'd added security cameras and an alarm system, although we still employed human guards for the lobby, offices, and public areas. The research lab is just too critical to our mission to risk losing it again.

I approached Rosie's tank quietly so as not to startle her. She peeked out of the opening in her shell home. When she recognized me, she oozed over to her pile of objects, ready to work with me.

But I didn't want to work tonight. I just wanted to say goodbye. I washed and rinsed my hands thoroughly so I wouldn't introduce any harmful bacteria into her environment, then I stuck my fingers in the tank. Rosie propelled herself through the water and grasped one finger with her tentacles.

She wrapped herself around my fingers and explored the skin of my hand with her suckers and the sensitive tips of her tentacles. After a few moments, I disentangled myself from her embrace and whispered "Goodbye, Rosie. I'll be back soon."

On my way to the parking lot, I saw even more strange boats in our marina. All the marina's slips were full, and we even had boats tied up to the mooring balls further out, where we sometimes took our dive classes for their checkout dives.

My greatest fear had come to pass. We were surrounded by treasure hunters, waiting like sharks to follow the scent of money. I'd have to think of a way to throw them off our trail.

Chapter 12
A Pleasant Evening

LIAM AND OLIVER were sitting in Liam's borrowed car in front of my house when I got home. I leaned in their driver's side window and caught the heady smell of jerk chicken. I could tell by the scent it was hot and fresh, and my mouth watered in anticipation. "You brought it from Chicken! Chicken!" I said with delight, referring to my favorite family-run chicken place on West Bay Road.

"Yep. With all the fixings. Can we come in?" Liam waved the bag gently, so the tantalizing smell filled the air.

"The chicken is certainly welcome," I said. "I guess you guys can come in too." I laughed so they'd know I was teasing, and we bustled up the walk.

As always when I entered my home, a sense of peace stole over me. I loved my house and everything in it. I relaxed, and a small smile crept onto my face as we went to the kitchen.

Liam started parceling food onto my large, brightly colored stoneware dishes, while Oliver pulled sodas from the fridge. We sat at the table and ate until every bite of the food was gone. Then we cleaned up, and my visitors got ready to depart. We had an early start planned for the morning.

Liam and I were saying goodnight in my foyer, while Oliver waited discreetly in the car. "Do you have everything you need for the trip? You can put your bag in my car with mine and I'll load it onto the *Tranquility* in the morning when I arrive," I said.

"It's already on the *Sea Princess*. Maddy asked me to captain her boat for this trip. I guess Newton and I will be bunking on the *Sea Princess*. Maddy will be staying in the owner's suite on the *Omega*."

The *Omega* is RIO's primary research vessel. At 220 feet long, the ship is nearly twice as large as Cousteau's famous Calypso and carries a crew of up to 125 people. It's a floating research lab complete with a dive tank filling compressor, dive scooters, enough dive equipment to stock a medium sized dive shop on land, a film lab, and manned and unmanned underwater rovers and other underwater conveyances. The ship had always been the heart and soul of RIO, as famous in its own way as Maddy and Ray.

I was disappointed that Liam wouldn't be traveling with me, at least during the day. On the other hand, I wasn't sure our budding relationship could handle the stresses of being together twenty-four hours a day in a confined space with little privacy. Maybe in this case, the adage 'Mother knows best' was true.

Or she may have just been looking for a way to keep Newton at arm's length. His love for her was painfully obvious to everyone, and although she liked him, she'd made it clear that he had no chance of getting back together with her.

The next morning, I was up and on the road before my neighbor's rooster had even thought about crowing. I'd already called Liam, Maddy and Oliver. I had an idea, and I couldn't wait to see if it worked.

Chapter 13
Setting Sail

THE DOCK WAS CROWDED when I arrived. The café staff was there, passing out free coffee and donuts, and I grabbed one of each as I walked to the *Tranquility*. I took a sip of coffee and started her engines, revving them up in a way that would have made Ray cringe. The noise was loud enough to wake everyone sleeping on the boats in the nearby slips.

I was gratified to hear more engines start up as Liam, Maddy, Newton, and Oliver boarded the *Tranquility*. I quickly outlined my plan. "Oliver, I'm sorry, but you'll need to spend most of the morning ferrying people and equipment out to the *Omega*. Can you do that?"

He bit back a yawn. "Sure thing. Got a list?"

I handed him the list of equipment and crew that needed to be on board the *Omega* before we could leave. "Bring a few members of the crew back and forth on each trip, but make it different people each time, okay? Switch off shirts and hats—whatever you can think of that will make the passengers look less memorable. I don't want the watchers to know this bustle isn't for real."

I linked our phones and sent him the contact info for the last few key suppliers who were supposed to deliver today. "Check on the deliveries, and don't be subtle about it. Walk around the dock while you talk. Wave your arms in the air. Try to look exasperated, but under no circumstances say or do anything to upset the suppliers. The act is just for the people watching you, and you need to make sure they believe we don't have everything we need yet. I want it to look like chaos. Got it?"

"Got it," he said with a mock salute. He hustled out onto the dock, phone to his ear. His words drifted back to me. "There's been a change in plans. We need that stuff today. Now, if possible. We hope to leave within the hour. Noon at the latest if you can't deliver like you promised." He waved his arm in the air like he was frustrated at the slow response of whoever he was talking to.

Since it was unlikely any of our suppliers were open this early in the morning, I assumed he was talking into a silent phone, but I had to admit his acting was great. I saw several people poke their heads out of their own boats, and immediately duck back inside to prepare for departure.

Meanwhile, I called Stewie at his home. He was the only member of the expedition team who wasn't already on the dock. His phone rang for a long time before he picked up. He coughed. When the coughing subsided, he said "What?"

"Can you go to the offsite storage locker on your way in and get the banner for the documentary and bring it to the marina at RIO? I want the one we used last year on the *Omega*. And the little pennant flags we used last year on Rio One and Rio Two? I want them all hung ASAP."

He groaned and started whining. "We don't have the new banners yet. The old banners have last year's logo..."

"Not a problem, Stewie. Just do it, please."

I knew the people watching us wouldn't know that we were using last year's banners, since we'd never released the documentary because of Ray's death during the filming. But I wanted it to look like we were making our usual departure preparations, so any banner we could hang on the boats would do at this point. I'd be able to swap the old ones out for the correct ones as soon as they arrived. They would be fine in the meantime as long as the new ones were in place before we started filming.

Liam and Newton went out on the dock to ask Oliver to run them out to the *Sea Princess*. Oliver randomly selected three more people who were on the dock to join them and then he loaded a couple of boxes onto one of RIO's small Zodiacs. He started the engine while still pretending to be talking on the phone and sped off. I shut off the *Tranquility*'s engines. All was going as planned.

Maddy and I watched Oliver pull up next to the *Sea Princess*. Liam got off first and helped Newton board. As soon as they were off the Zodiac, Oliver raced off toward the *Omega*. The crewmembers he'd brought with him climbed aboard and then lowered a winch to lift the freight he'd carried onto the *Omega*'s deck.

When the freight had been stowed, Oliver held the boat steady while a few people climbed down into the Zodiac. Then he zoomed back to the dock, turned right around, and brought more people and boxes to the *Omega*. He 'talked' on his phone while the crew boarded. This return trip, he stopped at the *Sea Princess* on the way back to drop someone off and pick Newton up. I'd asked him to create chaos, and he was doing a masterful job.

Still grumbling, Stewie arrived with the requested banners and flags. Oliver paused in his travels to help Stewie decorate *Tranquility* with the jaunty pennants, then he dropped Stewie at the *Sea Princess* to help Liam string more flags.

Oliver repeated variations on his performance until noon when the custom dive skins were finally delivered. They were silver Lycra with blue adornments. The RIO logo was on the right shoulder, and the *Your World* logo on the left. They were personalized with each wearer's name printed on the right leg, and the logo for Fleming Environmental Investments, my father's company, was printed on the left leg. Even with all that advertising, they still looked sleek and futuristic. I was pleased with my design.

Once the crew had everything settled on board the *Omega*, we would be good to go. Stewie, Liam, and Oliver unfurled the large banner off the *Omega*'s sides, where it flapped gently in the breeze. The sign on the banner read "SOS: Save our Seas." Last year the logo had showed a freediver, but Oliver had hastily covered that part with white paint. We'd hang the new banner with this year's logo as soon as we unpacked it.

Oliver called my cell to let me know everyone was on their assigned vessel, and all the freight was stowed. A crowd had gathered on the dock and RIO's nearby lawn to watch our little show. They must have thought we were the most disorganized bunch of people in the world. But that was my plan. I wanted them to see chaos. It would distract them from what was really going on. I didn't want them to realize the trap I had planned for them until it was too late.

I took out the emergency bullhorn to make a speech, making it squeal on purpose. The crowd covered their ears and groaned as I spoke. "Thank you all for coming. As you know, we're about to embark on an expedition to try to recover the legendary Queen's Tiara. We appreciate your support as we undergo this perilous journey. Please wish us well."

I put the bullhorn away and started the *Tranquility*'s engines. I waved at Liam as I backed out of my slip, and he climbed the ladder to the flying bridge on the *Sea Princess*. In another few seconds, *Omega*'s engines started with a mighty thrum.

I took the lead as we left the harbor. Liam and the *Sea Princess* fell in behind me, and *Omega* brought up the rear. As soon as it was clear we were underway, all the boats in the marina started up and sped after us.

I motored smoothly out to sea, turning to head past Bodden Town, passing by Ocean Frontiers, and around Colliers. I went by the Reef Resort and continued past Babylon, a favorite dive site of mine. Then I headed straight out to sea, to Hightop, a rarely dived site that Maddy and Ray had set the moorings on. Hightop was too far out to sea to be popular with most dive operations, so the three moorings were usually free.

As expected, one of Rio's sleek black Zodiacs was moored on the first ball. I'd asked Gus to tie up to it early this morning so there wouldn't be any free moorings after Liam and I arrived. It was essential to my plan that no other boats could be legally moored.

Gus waved as I passed him, and I waved back. I pulled up to the second mooring and grabbed the ball to tie off the *Tranquility*. Out of the corner of my eye, I saw Liam at the third mooring securing the *Sea Princess*. I heard the rattle of *Omega*'s anchor chains as the crew let the anchor down. We were all in place.

Omega was the only vessel with a permit to anchor here. There were no other moorings nearby, so our followers would have to head back to shore soon or risk running out of fuel. Plus, I had an unpleasant surprise waiting for those who decided to stay.

Chapter 14
A Clean Getaway

I PUT down the radio after talking to my old friend Officer Ebanks of the Cayman Islands Coast Guard. They were now on their way to clear out the followers, treasure hunters, and looky-loos. After a few minutes, I saw the first cutter come into view from the west and recognized Officer Ebanks' voice over the loudspeaker. "This is a restricted anchorage area, and you must have a permit to anchor here. If you are not tied up to an approved mooring, please have your permits ready for the officers when they approach your vessel."

Rather than risk a fine for illegally anchoring or mooring, about one third of the boats peeled off and headed back to shore or to nearby dive sites to check for open moorings. Earlier, I'd made sure most of those were taken by the personal boats of the RIO team members who weren't making the voyage on the *Omega*, so the treasure hunters would be forced to move even further away. I had no illusions they'd give up on following us, but with luck, they'd be far enough away that they wouldn't see us depart or be able to catch us if they did.

I pulled out my binoculars and saw another Coast Guard vessel approaching from the southeast. The two cutters began working together to corral the remaining vessels that had been following us. One crew member climbed aboard each boat to check papers and look for contraband. Then another cutter approached from behind the first, and the captain of that boat waved his hat in the air. That was our prearranged signal. It was now a Coast Guard operation, and the unauthorized boats would be required to stay in the area until the Coast Guard allowed them to leave. Within seconds of the last cutters arrival, I heard the *Omega* hauling in her anchor chain. She pulled away, gaining speed quickly.

Liam and I both unmoored our boats and left, following the *Omega* at top speed.

A few of the treasure boats tried to follow us, but the third Coast Guard vessel blocked their departure. When I glanced back, Coast Guard officers were boarding another one of the follower boats and another officer was on the Zodiac that Gus was captaining. They were having a genial conversation, but the whole point was to make it look like they were detaining him and not showing favoritism toward RIO boats.

Within minutes, another cutter arrived and pulled up to a few of the remaining boats to drop off officers to examine the boats' documentation. Maddy had pulled in a favor to coordinate this operation, and Newton had provided the funding for what the sailors were calling a training exercise. Most of the officers on board the Coast Guard boats were off-duty, helping us out because we had trained many of them and we had close relationships with them. The whole thing was my idea—an elaborate sting, set up to enable us to get underway without being followed.

Our three boats headed out to sea for about ten miles before we all made wide, arcing turns to the southwest as we rushed toward the location where we hoped to find the treasure. Our goal for today was not to get all the way to the coordinates Ray had left me, because it was too far to make the trip in a single day. Instead, the goal was to put enough distance between us and our pursuers that

80

they wouldn't be able to find us in the vast ocean expanse. If our friends in the Coast Guard could keep the treasure hunters penned up long enough, we had a good shot at it.

After about four hours of travel at top speed, my 300-gallon tank was low on fuel. I assumed the *Sea Princess* was running on fumes as well. I called a halt to the day's travel. We had covered about half the distance to the destination.

After the *Omega* dropped anchor, I pulled the *Tranquility* up to her stern and made fast to the cleats. The crew scurried over with a fuel hose to refill my tank from the giant on-board reserve tank. When I finished, I moved aside, and Liam and the *Sea Princess* took my place.

When both the *Tranquility* and the *Sea Princess* were anchored, Lauren brought the *Omega*'s Zodiac tender over to bring Newton, Liam, and me to the *Omega* for a team meeting. It looked like we'd made a clean getaway from the treasure hunters, since we hadn't seen any sign that we'd been followed. We agreed that we would stay anchored here over night and resume travel in the morning. Meeting adjourned, Lauren pulled the Zodiac's keys from the voluminous pocket of her cargo shorts and took us all back to our respective boats.

We were ready to go before sunrise the next morning. We took off, heading to our destination, which was in international waters, several miles off the coast of Belize. We arrived mid-afternoon, and again, the *Omega* anchored before refueling the two smaller boats.

Vincent Pollilo, the *Omega*'s captain, Liam, and I each scanned the ocean bottom with our vessels' on-board sonar and saw nothing that looked like a wreck, so I suggested we do a quick dive to take stock of the terrain below. The dive party would consist of Maddy, Liam, Oliver, and me. Stewie was assigned to sit out the dive on the *Sea Princess* and assist in case we ran into any trouble on the dive.

Lauren brought me and my photography equipment to the *Sea Princess*, then ferried Newton to the *Omega* where he planned to spend the rest of the day working. Then she brought Maddy,

Oliver, and our silver dive skins with the new logos on them back to the *Sea Princess*. It was like that old riddle about needing to get chickens and foxes across the river in the fewest number of trips, but Lauren did a great job of working out the logistics. While I waited for everyone to arrive, I set up my cameras and lights. I wanted to capture some of this dive prep as well as the dive itself for the *Your World* spread, and some of the video might even make its way into the documentary.

I took a few minutes of video of Oliver and Maddy approaching on the Zodiac, then some shots of Liam and Oliver slipping into their RIO-branded dive skins. Then I filmed Maddy putting her distinctive long white-blonde hair in a ponytail to keep it out of her face during the dive.

After that, Maddy, who was a great photographer in her own right, used her personal video camera to take some footage of me gearing up. When she finished, she handed her camera to Stewie to keep safe while we were diving. I picked up my own underwater camera, and the four of us entered the water and began our descents.

Chapter 15
Search Diving

ALTHOUGH WE WERE ONLY a little over 800 miles from the familiar dive sites of Grand Cayman, the underwater terrain here was different. Both Belize and the Cayman Islands have designated much of their surrounding waters as protected marine parks, so they both have vibrant coral and abundant marine life. Belize is home to three of the four true atolls in the world, and to the second largest barrier reef in the world. At 186 miles long, it's second only to Australia's Great Barrier Reef. The barrier reef provides a little extra buffer from wild ocean currents, so the corals are lush and healthy, and the atolls attract a variety of pelagic life as well as typical reef fish. And here, in the pristine international waters, the terrain was even more spectacular.

We reached the reef-top at about fifty feet and began following an open path toward the drop off. The sandy bottom on the path was home to a group of garden eels standing upright, back ends in the sand, their whole bodies waving in the currents as they fed on passing plankton. There might have been over a thousand of them, all about five inches tall and looking like blades of grass swaying in a breeze. As always, I was mesmerized as the shy eels ducked back into their burrows at my approach. Seeing row after row of garden eels disappear into the sand is one of the most incredible underwater sights to see. I took several still shots and a few minutes of video of the adorable creatures.

When we reached the reef's drop off, we decided to split up to cover more ground. Normally, this wouldn't be a good idea because two of our divers would start out swimming with the current. That can be dangerous. Divers should start their dive moving against the current so it can provide a little boost on the way back in case they're tired. But Maddy and Liam, strong swimmers both, went with the current, while Oliver and I went against the current and followed the reef to the right.

As Maddy and Liam swam away, I took a few photos. I signaled to Oliver to swim ahead of me and to stay above my depth. I took a few shots of him swimming, making sure to get the incredible, vibrant coral in the frame with him. Then I put my camera aside and concentrated on looking for signs of a wreck.

We had covered quite a bit of ground without seeing anything that bore further investigation—other than the sea life, which was spectacular. We saw several large Nassau groupers, which was heartening because they are an endangered species. Hundreds of small blue-head wrasse, each about ten inches long and shaped like cigars, were flitting about the reef, creating an ever-changing pattern of vibrant color.

But both Oliver and I stopped dead and stared when the pair of giant manta rays swam past us out in the blue. Each one had a thirty-foot wingspan, and they were an awe-inspiring sight. When they had disappeared into the distant murk, Oliver and I looked at each other with wide eyes. I'd seen mantas many times before, but the sight never failed to stun me. At least I'd had the presence of mind to snap a few pictures as they cruised past us, their white bellies glowing in the dim sunlight filtering through the water.

It was time to start on our way back, so we headed up to the top of the reef and swam along the corals that lined the sandy areas, looking for anything that could be the missing wreck, but we had no luck.

I looked to the anchor line and saw Liam and Maddy approaching it from the other direction, so I signaled for Oliver to follow me back. We all ascended along the line, stopping at fifteen feet for a three-minute safety stop. Rather than just hang there, we all swam across the reef top continuing our search, but we still didn't see anything promising.

After our safety stop, we climbed aboard the *Sea Princess*. Stewie was sitting with his back against a couple of life preservers, snoring in the sunshine. This wasn't the first time I'd wondered why we kept him on the payroll.

While Ray had been alive, their friendship kept him safe from censure, and Maddy felt a sense of loyalty to Ray's wishes. As far as RIO's payroll was concerned, it was her decision. But the treasure hunt was my baby, and I needed to know I could count on him to be doing his job.

He startled awake when he heard our tanks clanging as we put them in the tank rack. "How was the dive?" he said, rubbing his eyes.

I gave him a hard stare. "We were lucky enough not to run into any problems, since our tender was taking a nap instead of paying attention."

As usual, my words rolled off his back, but he was smart enough to know he needed to keep Maddy happy. He opened the cooler and brought my mother some orange slices and water, like she was a tourist on her first dive trip instead of one of the most famous ocean explorers in the world. The rest of us helped ourselves as we usually did.

We sat in the sunshine on the benches while our surface interval elapsed. A few minutes before it was safe for us to dive again, Liam started the boat and moved it about a quarter of a mile east. He re-anchored, and we all went to the boat's transom to gear up for another dive.

I helped Oliver into his buoyancy control device and checked that his tank was secure, and the air was turned on. Then I handed him his fins and gave him an arm for balance while he put them on. He stepped into the water, and the rest of us followed within a few seconds.

We descended slowly along the anchor line, scanning the surface below for anything we thought might be a wreck. Once again, we saw no signs of any wreck during the dive, although the underwater landscape was spectacular and the sea life abundant. It was a pleasant dive, and I was sorry when Oliver ran low on air, and we had to return to the boat.

This time when we surfaced, Stewie was awake and helped us board by taking our fins and BCDs as we climbed the ladder. We decided to break for lunch before our next dive, even though it was still early in the day. Diving uses a lot of calories because your body works hard to stay warm underwater. And although it feels easy, a diver is using a lot of muscle power to move through water, which is much denser than air.

After lunch, Maddy and Oliver took our empty tanks back to the *Omega* for refilling. When they returned, Newton was in the Zodiac with them. As he came aboard, he tripped and lost his balance. Liam reached out to steady him. "Careful, Mate. We don't want to have to rescue you out here. It's a big ocean."

Chapter 16
Finding The Wreck

THE COORDINATES RAY had left us corresponded to an area of more than seventy square miles, so we knew it could take days or even weeks to cover it. All we could do was keep looking, so we moved the boat again, another quarter mile east and geared up to dive. Knowing Newton was aboard, Stewie was on his best behavior, helping everyone with their tanks and offering a steadying arm when we put on our fins. Except for Oliver, we were all experienced master divers and didn't need this kind of help, but I was glad to see Stewie at least trying to be useful.

This time Liam and I buddied up and swam east, while Maddy and Oliver went west. We drifted along the reef top, swimming slowly, and examining anything that looked like it might once have been part of a ship. Although I'd checked to see if I could find out more about the wreck's history, there were no records of a ship lost in the area, so we weren't sure exactly how old it was, but from Ray's description, we thought it was probably at least a hundred years old. In that length of time, a wooden boat could have deteriorated almost beyond recognition. With any luck, corals might have grown on it before it rotted away, helping it to retain a vestige of its original shape and making it easier for us to pick it out from the rest of the reef.

I was down at about eighty feet when I saw something up ahead. An arching triangular shape reminiscent of a boat's hull protruding slightly from the wall. It was covered in lush coral growth, but still, I suspected we had found the wreck faster than we could have expected. I swam toward it.

Above me, Liam saw what I was heading for and swam down to join me. It didn't take us long to be certain it was a boat. It looked as though the ship had sunk, landed upright in a crevice in the reef, and stayed there. Although the boat was completely encrusted by algae and coral, we could swim the boat's length from bow to stern, because the coral had left a gap of about three feet along the sides, almost like an aisle. The coral had grown together over the boat, blocking out the light from above, so the wreck sat in what amounted to a cave in the reef.

I pulled Liam back out along the wall and indicated I wanted to photograph him as he "discovered" the boat and swam along its length in the crevice. I turned on my camera's strobe lights to film him. He understood what I wanted, and slowly swam along first one side of the boat, then the other. He stopped to peer into each of the open portholes as he passed, but he didn't try to enter, even when he came to a large open spot in what had once been the boat's hull. He was camera savvy enough to hover outside the opening long enough for me to get several shots of him there. I needed plenty of pictures for the photo montage contract with *Your World*.

I mapped the location on my underwater slate and fastened a florescent yellow plastic tie to the nearby coral, so I'd be able to easily find the wreck again. I also swam up above it to take pictures from other angles, so I'd know what it looked like if I approached from a different direction.

I was excited. Now that we'd found a wreck, we had to take the time to explore it. It was possible it might not even be the same wreck that Ray had found so long ago.

In any case, I needed to take a lot of pictures to flesh out both the *Your World* story and the RIO documentary before we could bring back the Queen's Tiara and the rest of the treasure. I'd heard stories about these items for most of my life, and I couldn't wait to see the fabulous piece and the rest of the legendary lost fortune.

By now we were at the turnaround point for air, so Liam and I headed back to the anchor line. We met Maddy and Oliver at the bottom and the four of us ascended as a group. I was so eager to tell Maddy the news that I could hardly wait out the obligatory three-minute safety stop.

I was bursting with excitement by the time we were all on board and had removed our gear. While Stewie was passing out orange slices and water, I breathlessly told Maddy and Oliver what Liam and I had found.

I was practically jumping up and down. "This must be it," I said. "At long last we get to see the treasure. I never understood why Ray didn't want to talk about it, but now we'll find out."

Maddy was quiet for a minute, pensively sliding the solid gold doubloon pendant she wore long its chain. Ray had given her the necklace instead of a ring when they'd married. "This coin was the one thing Ray brought back from the treasure. He always said it was better if it stayed lost. He said the tiara was cursed. It would bring only sorrow, betrayal, and death by drowning to anyone who tried to claim it. When people kept after him to retrieve it, he started telling them the treasure was just a tall tale he'd made up. After a while, even I forgot it was real. Maybe we should respect his wishes and leave it where it is. I never thought we'd actually find it, and I wonder if we should abandon the recovery effort in deference to Ray's wishes."

Newton chimed in. "It's a little late for second thoughts, Maddy. You're under contract to *Your World*. So is Fin, for that matter, and even if you think RIO can weather the scandal of reneging on the terms of the deal, at this point in her career, Fin can't afford to be in breach."

Maddy glared at him, and even though they were both astute businesspeople, for the first time I could see how her spiritual nature would clash with his lawyerly thought processes—leading inevitably to their divorce so long ago. They were the best of friends and respected each other, but they weren't soul mates the way Ray and Maddy had been.

I bit my lip, unsure what to do. I was counting on support from Maddy's team and resources and supplies from the *Omega* for my expedition. If she withdrew now, I'd be unable to continue working to raise the treasure even if I chose not to drop the project. I didn't have the upfront money to pay the crew, or the resources to keep them fed and comfortable.

"Don't worry, Fin. If RIO pulls out, I'll provide whatever you need to complete the terms of your contract." One thing about Newton—he was never afraid to throw his considerable wealth at a problem. He didn't realize how annoying this habit could be.

Maddy glared at him. "I didn't say I was pulling RIO out. I said I had some concerns." She drew herself up to her full five feet of height. "Oliver, would you run me back to the *Omega*, please?"

I knew she hated confrontations, and she hated it even more when Newton stepped on her authority. Retreat was her usual first step when dealing with anger, but she always came back to address the issues after she'd had a chance to cool down. Surprisingly, her laid-back approach usually ended with her getting her own way, even if she had to restart the discussion two or three times before it was resolved to her satisfaction.

Oliver jumped to his feet to help her onto the small runabout he'd been using to ferry people and equipment between the various boats. "Let me just grab the empty tanks."

"I'll help you, Mate." Liam picked up a couple of tanks by their valves and handed them down to Oliver, who secured them in the small inflatable's tank racks. When all the tanks were on the tender, Oliver took off for the *Omega*.

Stewie pulled a can from his personal cooler and quickly stuffed it into a koozie before I could see the label.

"I'm done for the day." He walked along the gunwales to sit on the bow where he couldn't hear our conversation.

I sat on the nearby bench, head down, thinking about how I could pull this off without the *Omega*'s support. Liam sat beside me. "Don't worry. I'm with you," he said, taking my hand. "One hundred percent. Whatever it takes—even if I lose my new job." He grinned wryly.

"I know you don't need a job, but if it comes to it, you'll have a spot at Fleming Environmental Investments anytime you want," Newton said.

"Thanks. I'm happy at RIO, and I think Maddy will get over this if we don't make a big deal about it. She's just feeling disloyal to Ray's memory, that's all. She'll come around."

The sound of a boat's engine nearly drowned out his last words. I stood and saw a sixty-five-foot catamaran approaching at a rapid clip. I crossed my fingers that it was just a sport fisherman coming home after a day at sea, but the boat slowed down as it neared our position and came to a stop about a half mile away.

I heard the clink and rattle of an anchor, and I groaned. "We've been found."

But it was worse than I had feared. Once the catamaran's pilot was convinced the boat was secure, he stood on the bow and waved his hat in the air. It couldn't be.

But it was.

Alec Stone, my ex-husband, was here.

Chapter 17
Betrayal

NEWTON TURNED TO ME. "What's he doing here?"

I shrugged and watched in dismay as Alec dove in the water and began swimming toward the *Sea Princess*.

At a half mile away, his boat wasn't very close to us, but he was a strong swimmer. As a dive instructor, he was required to be able to swim a mile in about twenty-five minutes, so it wasn't long before he was standing on the transom. "Got a towel?" he asked me?

"Nope. Sorry," I said. "What are you doing here? And how soon will you be leaving?" Then we all watched in disbelief as, without being asked, Stewie brought Alec a warm, fluffy towel and some ice water.

"Thanks, Stewie." Alec dried his face and took a sip of water. "Wow. I needed that."

Stewie must have noticed the thunderous expressions on our faces because he turned and hurried back to his perch on the bow before we could confront him with our suspicion that he had given Alec the coordinates of our position. Otherwise, how could Alec possibly have found us so quickly and so precisely?

Alec smiled, perfectly comfortable with our discomfort.

"Well?" I said when it became apparent that he had no intention of telling me why he was here.

"I was just cruising, heading for a few days of dives in the Great Blue Hole. Imagine my surprise when I saw your little expedition anchored here. Is this where the treasure's been all along? Or are you still looking for the wreck's site?"

"None of your business what we're doing. And you're still miles from the Great Blue Hole. You'd better get a move on." I suspected Alec was trying to find a way to use me to further his own career again.

"I'll take that." Newton took the towel from the bench where Alec had dropped it and threw it down the stairs into the cabin. He divested Alec of his water, dumped the contents into the ocean, and carried the cup below.

Liam took Alec's arm and pulled him to his feet. "Sorry we don't have a boat to ferry you back. But you got here on your own, so I'm sure you'll be okay on the way back. Ocean's that way, Buddy." He flicked his thumb over his shoulder toward the boat's transom.

Alec's behavior had been unpredictable for the last several months, and he'd thrown tantrums and had violent outbursts unlike anything I had seen while we were married. He scowled at Liam, and for a minute I thought he would resort to violence here on the boat. The two men glared into each other's eyes until at last, Alec turned away and dove off the side. I sighed with relief that he was gone.

It was obvious to everyone that Stewie had contacted Alec and leaked our location. When Alec had swum out of earshot, Liam jumped up on the gunwales and headed for the bow. "Stewie. A word please."

I put my hand out and caught his arm. "Let me. I've known him longer, and he's part of my team."

As RIO's new CFO, Liam outranked me, so it was within his

right to be the one to chastise Stewie for the breach of security protocol. But he stepped down and let me pass.

I sat down beside Stewie on the bow. "Did you tell Alec our position?"

Stewie's struggle between self-preservation and honor showed in his eyes. Eventually, honor won out. "Yes," was all he said.

"You knew we wanted to keep the wreck's location secret, didn't you?"

"Yes."

"Then why shouldn't I fire you right now? Send you back to Grand Cayman without a job?"

Stewie looked taken aback by my question and tone of voice. Even I was surprised.

"I'm sorry. I wanted to be part of the team, and since Ray's death, you all treat me like dirt." Stewie's voice cracked.

"That's because we can't trust you to keep your word," I said. "This latest betrayal makes it even harder."

He looked at me, tears in his eyes. "Don't you think I hate myself for the part I played in Ray's death? It eats at me every day. Please let me stay on. I'll earn your trust again. I swear it."

Against my better judgement, I said. "Last chance, Stewie. Your very last chance." Then I left the bow and rejoined Newton on the rear deck.

While I'd been talking to Stewie, Liam had climbed the ladder to the flying bridge. Our eyes met, and I nodded to him. He nodded back and picked up the radio, but I couldn't hear what he said.

A few minutes later, Oliver headed our way in the *Omega*'s tender. As soon as Oliver had tied up to the boat, Liam said, "Stewie, your ride's here. Are you going back to the *Omega*, or will you be joining your buddy Alec?"

Stewie didn't look at Liam as he shuffled past. "*Omega*. At least then I can be with Lauren."

I could see Liam wasn't happy with the answer, and neither was I. Stewie had a long history of betraying everyone around him—

everyone except for Ray. He'd never knowingly have done anything to hurt his oldest friend, although we all knew his irresponsibility had contributed to the tragedy of Ray's death.

Leaving Stewie loose on the *Omega* wasn't a good idea at all, especially if he'd be hanging out with Lauren. She was a key member of the crew, and he had a way of overhearing things he wasn't meant to hear. Being on the *Omega* meant he might have access to information he could feed to Alec. If Alec was paying him for inside info, we had no hope that Stewie would keep anything he learned to himself.

But we had hired him on for the expedition and although we might have liked to, we couldn't just leave him in the middle of the ocean either. We were stuck.

Then I had an idea. "Hold up a minute, Oliver, will you?" I turned to Liam and Newton. "Let's put Stewie in solitary on the *Tranquility*. I'll stay with Maddy on the *Omega*, and you—Liam and Newton—can keep sharing the *Sea Princess*. That way we can isolate Stewie and maybe keep him from doing any more damage."

"Are you sure you want him alone on your boat, Fin? Who knows what mischief he could get into?" Newton looked worried, and I couldn't blame him. He'd dropped big bucks on refurbishing the boat after it had been trashed not too long ago.

"I'll keep the keys with me," I said. "And we'll bring him prepared food, so he won't have to cook or make a mess. He'll be happy as a clam to have us waiting on him. Nothing to do but sit in the sun." I looked at Liam. "When this is over, we need to talk to Maddy about putting some conditions around Stewie's continued employment."

"Agreed." Liam said. "But in my opinion, he belongs in the brig, not on your boat." His face looked like thunder.

Newton stepped forward. "Why don't I stay on the *Tranquility* with him? That way I can keep an eye on him, make sure he doesn't step out of line."

That was a surprise. My father liked his alone time, losing

himself in quiet contemplation. He hated noisy environments, especially while he was trying to work, and Stewie chattered non-stop about nothing. And Newton was a neat freak. Even more than random noise, he hated it when things were out of place.

Liam gave Newton an approving nod. "Thanks, Mate." Then he turned to Oliver. "Please take Stewie to the *Tranquility* and leave him there. And if you would, bring the keys here to Fin. Both sets please."

This was a huge sacrifice Newton was signing up for. "Stewie's a slob as well as a backstabber. And he talks constantly. He'll make you crazy."

Newton nodded. "Yep. But I'll survive. And I'll feel better if there's someone there keeping an eye on him."

When Stewie had left, Newton began nonchalantly making dinner. He'd put some chicken parts in a marinade earlier, and now he put them in a pan to sear while he made rice and green beans.

"Can I help?" I asked.

"No thanks. Why don't you make some drinks and relax? You and Liam have had a busy day. And anyway, I like to cook."

This was news to me. I'd never seen my father cook anything except burgers on a grill. But then again, I hadn't had a chance to see him do much of anything because until recently, I hadn't seen him for more than twenty years.

Liam, Newton, Oliver, and I had dinner together, and when we were done, Oliver brought a plate over to Stewie on the *Tranquility*. Now we were sitting in the leather recliners in the main cabin of the *Sea Princess*, sipping our after-dinner lemonades. I yawned, and that set Liam and Oliver to yawning as well.

"Do you want me to take you over to the *Omega* now, Fin? You must be tired." Oliver looked pretty beat himself. He wasn't as used to a full day of diving as the rest of us were.

"Not yet. I'm too comfortable." I smiled and stretched out in my comfy chair, listening to the conversation but too tired to join in.

Chapter 18
Another Arrival

THE NEXT THING I KNEW, I could smell coffee brewing and the sun was shining on my eyelids. I must have fallen asleep and stayed asleep all through the night. At some point, someone had covered me with a light blanket. I opened my eyes and saw Liam just emerging from the cabin below. Newton had already come back over from the *Tranquility* and was watching the coffee brew, but Oliver was nowhere to be seen.

"Good morning, Sleepyhead," Liam said as he passed my chair to get to the coffee. He poured three cups, handing one to Newton before bringing one to me. He sat in the chair next to mine and took a sip. "How are you doing today?"

"I feel great." I sipped my coffee.

"Good," he said. "We need to figure out a plan."

"Don't worry about Stewie. We can take care of him when we get back to RIO. And I'll know better than to ever include him on an expedition again."

He nodded. "That's a good idea. But Stewie's not the problem right now. We have more company."

I put down my coffee and rushed to the deck. There were three ships clustered together about a half mile to a mile away. One was Alec's catamaran, which I'd expected to see. The other two were strangers I didn't recognize. Worse yet, I noticed one of the strange boats was flying the Jolly Roger—a pirate flag.

Many party and recreational boats fly the Jolly Roger without understanding its significance. In a sunny marina or launching from a bar's pier, the flag is of no concern. But way out at sea, in international waters, the Jolly Roger takes on a much more sinister vibe. Since we were known to be looking for sunken treasure, I feared we were looking at an actual pirate ship rather than a party boat.

"Uhoh," I said. "Do we know who they are?"

Newton came on deck, his feet bare. He handed me the coffee mug I'd left below. "Not yet. But we will. I called Gus and he's tracking the registration numbers."

"We have to keep them away from the wreck. They'll spoil everything," I said.

"We won't let them near it," said Liam. "Maddy and Oliver are on their way over and we'll make a plan."

A few minutes later, Oliver tied the tender to the back of the boat. Maddy climbed aboard and then Oliver stepped on deck bearing a basket of freshly baked blueberry muffins. He was welcomed aboard with shouts of joy. We were happy to see Oliver, but we were joyful about the muffins. We went below to the galley table to munch and decide on a plan.

Newton was pacing around, making us all nervous. "We should move the boats right away. Get them away from the site of the wreck. Keep moving—that's what we'll do. It'll throw them off track…"

"No, it won't," said Maddy, crushing the crumbs on her plate with her finger. "We can't go too far away, or the wreck will be out of diving range. They'll see us enter the water, and they'll watch for our bubbles when we're under. Pretty soon, they'll know exactly where we're diving. If they're smart, they'll plot our anchor spots and home in on the wreck that way."

"We should still move the boats. Just not too far. Otherwise, they'll know we're already anchored above the wreck. At least if we move away, we can make them work a little bit to find the actual location." Liam sipped his coffee. "Is there something on the *Omega* we can use to throw them off about what we're doing? Like a rover?" He was referring to a type of small sub usually used for deep water exploration.

"We have both a manned and an unmanned rover on the *Omega*. We can dive in the rover. That might work," Maddy said.

"No, it won't. We need to be scuba diving for the documentary, not sitting inside a sub. And we'll have to be on scuba to be able to go inside the wreck to retrieve the treasure. And for *Your World*, I need pictures that don't look like they were taken from behind glass," I said.

Oliver stood to clear the plates. "Won't we be too far away to get much bottom time if we're not anchored right above the wreck? It's down deep, so our bottom time will be limited enough as it is. If we have to swim a long distance, we'll use up our air and our bottom time just getting to the site." He brought back the coffee pot and refilled our mugs.

There didn't seem to be a solution that would throw the pirates off the scent and still let us achieve our objectives.

Then I had an idea. Or rather, I put everybody's ideas together into a plan. "How's this sound? First, we go somewhere else, so they don't realize we've already found the wreck. I'm thinking the Great Blue Hole. It's nearby, and an amazing dive site, so it's believable that we'd go there for the documentary. When we come back to this area, we move the base of operations a good half mile east of here—right about where those other boats are anchored now. Then every time we dive, we send out three teams of divers. One team in the rover. That'll make them think the treasure is deep. Maybe too deep for them to follow." I sipped my coffee.

"But we also do regular scuba dives, and we launch them from the *Omega*. Three or four times a day, we send out a team of four divers, two women and two men, using regular scuba tanks. These divers are very overt about their entries and exits. They scatter around wherever they're diving, like they're doing search patterns along the reef, but always heading east from the *Omega*."

I laughed at this next part. "And while the pirates are watching the decoy divers, and checking out the terrain to the east, we do our entries from the far side of the *Omega* and head west. We all use rebreathers, so we don't have any bubbles, and we use the underwater scooters to get us back and forth from the wreck fast, so we don't use up all our air. The only hard part will be coordinating getting back on board the *Omega* without them seeing us."

Everybody stared at me for a minute, thinking it through. "Brilliant," Liam said at last. He lifted his coffee mug in a toast, and we all clinked our mugs. Our plan was in place.

Just then the radio squawked. Gus was calling Newton from Grand Cayman. "Hey, Boss," he said. "Got the registration on those boats. They're both leased. The cabin cruiser is leased to a company called Flowers Corporation. I'm looking into who they are. The other one is leased to a Noah Dylan from Austin. Trouble is, the guy doesn't exist. I'm working it, but that's all I've got for now."

"Good work, Gus," Newton said. "Keep on it."

"Hey, Gus," I said. "While we have you, any news on those guys doing the needle sticks at clubs? I'm worried about them being on the loose," I said.

"You and me both. But no news. They picked up the guy you and Liam caught at Nelsons, but he isn't talking. The big boss is still running wild and free."

"Nobody's safe while they're out there."

"That's true. But at least you got one bad guy off the street. Good work there. Need anything else, Newton?"

"Nope. Thanks, Gus. Just keep on it," Newton replied.

Chapter 19
The Great Blue Hole

WE ALERTED the *Omega*'s crew and the research team that we were moving the boats to a new location. The news that we were heading to The Great Blue Hole spread like wildfire, and everyone was excited that we were all to have free time once we were anchored in our new spot.

The Great Blue Hole off the coast of Belize is ranked among the top ten dive sites in the world, and everyone who'd ever been diving in this mysterious spot was excited to be going back. Anyone who hadn't been there before was thrilled at the opportunity to add it to their dive logs. In case Alec had more spies on his payroll, we told the crew we were there to film for the documentary.

Theory has it the hole formed when the glaciers retreated about 100,000 to 150,000 years ago at the end of the Ice Age. Rising water levels filled the existing limestone caves and caused the reef to collapse, creating an almost perfect circle. The formation is part of the Belize Barrier Reef System, and at a little under 1,000 feet in diameter and more than 400 feet deep, many scientists and oceanographers believe the Great Blue Hole to be the largest marine sinkhole in the world.

Because it's such an extreme contrast with the light turquoise water just a few feet away, when viewed from the surface, the dark blue color of the water in the hole adds to the mystery of the site.

Inside the hole, divers see lush coral growths, many looking like icicles hanging from the eaves of a house in winter or the stalactites in a cave. Nurse sharks often make their homes in this quiet area, or deep inside the original caves, most of which remain unexplored. Caribbean Reef sharks patrol the area, along with dark-colored midnight parrotfish and brilliant purple tang who munch companionably on algae and coral substrate. In short, the Great Blue Hole is without question, one of the world's best dive sites. And we were on our way.

Maddy and I had been to The Great Blue Hole many times, but neither Liam nor Oliver had ever been. Even though we were all beat from so many dives in the last few days, and we needed to rest up for the upcoming marathon of wreck exploration and treasure recovery dives, we decided it would be criminal to be so close to such a stellar site and not check it out. The *Omega* chugged over and anchored along the edge of the hole, in the shallow waters of the reef, with the *Tranquility* and the *Sea Princess* close beside her.

We made our dive plan and then donned our buoyancy control devices and tanks. Although he was working on his advanced diver certification with me, Oliver didn't have it yet, so he was still restricted to a depth of no greater than one hundred feet. Even then, he could only go that deep if accompanied by a dive instructor.

Since I was his dive instructor, I would buddy up with him and make this one of the training dives counting toward his certification. Liam and Maddy would be buddies and dive together, and they agreed to stop at a depth of one hundred sixty-five feet, since oxygen in regular air becomes toxic under pressure at about one hundred seventy feet.

Several other members of the *Omega*'s research staff and crew wanted to dive the Great Blue Hole as well, partly for research but just as much because it's such an interesting dive. The *Omega*'s dive platform was crowded with divers, tanks, gear and the vast collection of jars, bags, and nets the researchers would use to collect samples. Lauren, Vincent, and his team were also deploying the rover to film the depths of the hole, which had only recently been explored by Fabien Cousteau and Sir Richard Branson. Until their expedition, no one had seen the bottom.

Before Oliver and I began our dive, I launched a drone with a small camera attached to fly over the hole. I wanted to capture the wonder of this natural formation and show people the majesty that exists in the ocean. Technically, the dives at the Great Blue Hole shouldn't be part of the treasure recovery expedition, but I was planning to either include some of the images or give Carl a proposal for another photo mélange on the world's greatest dive sites that he could run a few months after the treasure hunt story.

By the time I'd finished and stored the drone in a safe place, most of the other divers had already made their entries and were on their way down. Lauren was standing off to one side. "Don't you want to dive today?" I asked her. "You're welcome to dive with Oliver and me."

"Um, no thanks. I'm not interested. Maybe another time," she replied.

I was surprised by her answer. I couldn't imagine that anyone involved in oceanographic research wouldn't be eager to explore the mysteries of The Great Blue Hole. And she worked for RIO, so she must be interested in the ocean. I couldn't understand her reluctance to dive and her willingness to pass up this opportunity. Whatever. She must have her reasons.

She checked Liam and Maddy off on the diving manifest as they did giant stride entries off the rear platform. As soon as they had cleared the area, Oliver and I went in.

We descended slowly, clearing our ears by holding our noses

and swallowing or blowing gently every few feet. We both carried powerful underwater flashlights because the water in the hole is much darker than usual for a Caribbean dive, even close to the surface. We stayed near the wall, shining our lights to reveal the brilliant colors and stunning beauty of the corals.

At about twenty-five feet down, we shone our lights under a small overhang and saw a nurse shark. The docile shark was not pleased that we had disturbed her nap, so she swam away to find a new hiding spot.

The stalactites dripping from the walls gave the underwater scene a spooky appearance, and Oliver and I smiled at each other. We saw a school of purple tang nibbling on the coral, their scales a brilliant deep color with bright yellow tails. The entire school scattered in unison as soon as we got within a few feet of them.

I was watching Oliver closely to make sure he wasn't showing any signs of nitrogen narcosis. Under pressure, our bodies absorb more nitrogen from the regular air in our tanks than they would at sea level. Below sixty feet, the extra nitrogen can cause hallucinations or giddiness—making divers feel tipsy or causing them to lose their sense of direction. That's one reason newly certified divers are restricted to depths of sixty feet or less. They need to be completely comfortable diving before exposing themselves to the additional risk presented by nitrogen narcosis.

Oliver seemed fine, so we continued descending until we were hovering at about ninety-seven feet. We leveled off and concentrated on the coral and sea life around us.

We looked toward the bottom, and we could see groups of divers shining their flashlights into caves and crevices or collecting water samples or specimens of fish or coral. We couldn't stay too long at this depth because of the risk of absorbing so much nitrogen that we'd need to do a decompression stop, so we began slowly wending our way back to the surface.

We were still at about sixty feet down when a pair of unknown divers swam very close to us. We knew they weren't part of the RIO crew because they wore generic black dive skins instead of the silver RIO branded skins. They followed our every move as we explored the wall of The Great Blue Hole. Their presence felt menacing.

When it was time to surface, they followed us up but swam away when we reached about twenty feet. We hovered at fifteen feet below the dive platform, waiting out our three-minute safety stop that helps to prevent the bends. Liam and Maddy joined us on their ascent, hovering along with us. While we floated, I stared down at the inky depths below, wondering what secrets this mysterious place kept hidden.

Chapter 20
Yet Another Arrival

WHEN WE SURFACED, I saw the pirate ship was anchored inside The Great Blue Hole's perimeter. They had found us again, despite the care we had taken to try to lose them. I realized that the unknown divers who had followed Oliver and me on our first dive must have come from the pirate ship. That made their presence during the dive feel even more threatening.

We were scheduled to be diving on the wreck at dawn tomorrow, so we reluctantly skipped a second dive in The Great Blue Hole and prepared to take the boats to the new site half a mile east of the wreck's location.

By mid-afternoon, we were ready to depart. I prefer the increased visibility of piloting the boat from the flying bridge, so after I hauled in the anchor, Newton and I climbed the ladder. I started the engines, hit the throttle, and waited for the *Sea Princess* to begin moving.

The engines sounded odd. Higher pitched than usual. Different amplitude. I shut the boat off, but I could still hear the roar. Newton tapped my shoulder and pointed his chin toward Alec's catamaran.

It wasn't the *Sea Princess*'s engines making that noise. A small seaplane was coming in for a landing. As soon as it stopped moving, a slim woman with long dark brown hair got out and stood on the plane's pontoon. She dove into the water and began swimming toward Alec's boat. The four men on the nearby pirate ship erupted into whoops and cheers, waving their black tri-cornered pirate hats in the air.

"What's going on?" Newton asked.

"I don't know, but I'm pretty sure that swimmer is Lily. She must be joining Alec on his boat. The two of them are probably up to no good."

Although they're twins, Lily's personality was as different from Oliver's sweetness as whiskey is from mother's milk.

I watched as she climbed onto the catamaran. Alec brought her a towel and wrapped her in it with a hug. The cheers from the pirate ships grew louder, and the hat waving more boisterous. Lily signaled to the seaplane's pilot, and it roared off.

I collapsed into the captain's chair, head in hand. "We're doomed. We can't dive with that witch around."

Newton put his hand on my shoulder. "Maybe. Maybe not. It's possible her antics will distract everyone over there from what we're really doing. And we'll all be extra vigilant now that she's here. In the meantime, I'll contact Gus to see if he's had any more luck identifying who's on those other two boats." He picked up his SAT phone and turned away from the interlopers' boats to make his call.

Meanwhile, my own SAT phone rang. "I swear I had no idea."

I recognized his voice. "I know, Oliver. Don't worry. It'll be okay." I only hoped it would be.

"Thanks for believing in me. We're ready to go. You ready to follow?" he said.

"All set." I started the engines again, and I saw the water churn behind the *Tranquility* when Liam started her engines. Our three boats left the area in a vee formation, with the *Omega* in the lead.

It took a couple of hours to reach the spot we'd chosen. We

wanted to be far enough away from the wreck that the treasure seekers would be drawn away from it, but not so far away that we couldn't easily get back there ourselves. Scooters or no scooters, we wanted to spend as much time on the wreck itself as we could, and every minute we spent traveling back and forth had to come off our allowable bottom time.

Allowable bottom time is a function of depth and time, and the reason it's so important to keep to safe limits is because the human body absorbs more nitrogen under pressure than at the surface. Even though the gas in our tanks is just regular air, compressing it means there are more nitrogen molecules in a given volume of air than there are at sea level. Because the air molecules are closer together, it takes more of them to fill a diver's lungs when they breathe, so there are more nitrogen molecules in their bodies.

Absorb too much nitrogen, and you risk the bends, more formally known as decompression sickness, when the diver surfaces. To ensure that a diver doesn't absorb so much nitrogen that they can't ascend to the surface without making decompression stops to offgas, we limit bottom time on a dive. And since the deeper you are, the more nitrogen you absorb because of the increased pressure, the shorter your allowable dive time.

The calculations are complicated, so most divers today use small computers worn on their wrists or attached to their tank hoses to do the calculations for them. The computers account for variations in depth throughout the dive, so total dive time can be maximized, but there are still strict limits or else the computers go into decompression mode, requiring a series of stops at various depths and locking the diver out of additional dives for twenty-four hours. And if you're locked out, you can't just change to a different computer, because the new computer wouldn't have the right nitrogen load stored to use in its calculations. It simply isn't safe.

We'd be doing a lot of deep dives on this project. The wreck was at eighty feet, so our bottom time would be just a few minutes per dive, and we'd have to spend an hour or so between dives waiting for our nitrogen levels to return to normal. It was a complication I hadn't counted on, but I should have anticipated it. It could add several additional days to our exploration of the wreck since we couldn't stay on it for long. I was mentally kicking myself for the oversight as I piloted the boat to the new location.

After we'd anchored, the five of us on the wreck team went to the *Omega*. Oliver went straight to the dive gear storage area to gather up the equipment we would need to carry out our plan.

Vincent and Lauren were supervising the team getting the rover ready for deployment. Vincent looked crisp and professional in his captain's uniform. Lauren was dressed in what I was beginning to think of as her uniform—baggy cargo shorts and a Hawaiian shirt. She was engrossed in her work and ignored us, but Vincent waved as we passed on our way to the galley to select the body doubles for the decoy dives.

The galley was a madhouse. Sometimes working for RIO, we forget how wonderful diving is because we do so much of it, so the opportunity to just dive with no agenda was prized. Since the underwater terrain here was gorgeous, and the decoy team would be able to just dive for the enjoyment of diving on this gig, Maddy had no shortage of volunteers.

She started by looking for Oliver's double, and she quickly settled on a young scientist named Joel, who was an almost exact body double, right down to the hair color.

Next, she tried to match me up. We didn't have as many choices here, since even though the crew was fifty percent women, most of them were a lot curvier and several inches shorter than me. We finally decided on a scientist named Maya, who had long limbs and a long torso like mine. But since she was quite a bit older than me, her long hair was a stark white, a sharp contrast to my short medium brown hair. We decided we'd wear hoods while diving to hide our hair.

Pleased by the quick successes with her first two attempts to find doubles, Maddy smiled as she continued auditioning other potential divers. Unfortunately, finding body doubles for herself and Liam among the crew was a lot harder than it had been to find them for Oliver and me.

Liam was above average height, with broad shoulders and narrow hips, with distinctive golden blonde hair. After much discussion, we settled on crewman Todd, who was several inches shorter and a bit heavier, but he had a similar build and golden blond hair a little bit like Liam's.

No one among the crew even came close to approximating Maddy's petite ninety-five pound frame. We decided that the three divers she'd selected would have to be the only decoys, so Maddy would not be able to dive with the team. She'd stay conspicuously on deck while the rest of us dove. She was saddened to be off the wreck team, but it was the only way we could make the plan work.

Oliver, Maddy, Vincent, and I discussed how to set up a platform for us to dive from on the far side of the *Omega*. Vincent suggested we use the davits designed for lowering *Omega's* lifeboats, which was a great idea. We would crouch on the floor of a lifeboat while it was being raised or lowered, just in case anybody happened by while we were in the process of coming or going. In the unlikely event that anybody did come to that side of the boat, we wouldn't be visible from below, and Vincent could always make it look like raising or lowering the boat was a drill. He also proposed that he and Lauren take on the responsibility for making sure our equipment was in place and our tanks filled between dives since Oliver, who'd been supposed to oversee equipment, would be diving with us. Our new plan was in place.

The plan was as good as it could be under the circumstances, but I was worried about the treasure hunters—particularly the unknown pirates—ransacking the site before we could get the images I needed and recover the treasure. Until Lily's arrival, we hadn't seen anyone on the pirate ship's deck or heard any sound from the boat in all the time it had been anchored nearby.

Nobody had come on deck when the ship followed us to our new anchoring site, so the captain and crew must be operating the boat from inside the cabin. It was very mysterious. Before the meeting broke up, I asked Newton if he'd heard anything more about who was on the third boat.

"Gus is still trying to find out more about this Noah Dylan from Austin. He doesn't seem to exist. There's no history for the man and no paper trail anywhere, except the one credit card used to rent the boat. But don't worry. We'll figure it out. Meanwhile, I'll keep an eye on them while you guys are diving."

I nodded, but his answer didn't satisfy me. I wanted to know who was on the pirate ship, and why they had followed us out here. I couldn't figure out why the pirate captain would go to all the trouble of making up a false identity. If they meant us no harm, why not reveal themselves?

I didn't like it one bit, and despite his reassuring words, I could tell Newton didn't like it either. The rest of the team seemed comfortable ignoring the problem while Newton and Gus worked on uncovering the identity of the unknown pirate and his crew. Since the other team members weren't worried, I said no more on the subject, but I made a mental note to keep checking in with Newton.

Chapter 21
First Wreck Dives

EARLY THE NEXT MORNING, it was time to try out our plan for disguising our dives. Lauren and Vincent surreptitiously gathered the rebreathers, dive scooters, our BCDs, fins, and masks and stowed them in one of the lifeboats.

When it was time, all the designated decoy divers put on their dive skins and hoods and walked around on deck while Vincent and his team readied the rover. While he was rolling it out of its storage locker, Liam, Oliver, and I scurried from the tank tent to the floor of the lifeboat, where we wiggled into our gear.

Maddy and the decoy divers watched the rover deployment, then the other team of divers entered the water off the *Omega*'s dive platform while one of the crew simultaneously lowered the lifeboat we were in. There was enough activity on the other side of the deck that we hoped anyone watching would miss the action at the lifeboat, especially since the bulk of the *Omega*'s bridge was between us and anyone watching from the other boats.

As soon as our lifeboat hit the water, we donned our masks, grabbed our scooters, and rolled into the water. As planned, we immediately sank down to thirty feet, switched on the battery powered scooters and made a wide arc just to be sure we were completely out of sight before we headed for the wreck.

The underwater scooters we used at RIO are expensive professional models, about three feet long and shaped like small torpedoes. They are sleek and lightweight, battery powered, have a long range, and can go to great depth. Best of all, if necessary, the diver could operate the scooter with one hand, leaving the other free for using a tool or whatever might prove necessary. The scooters are perfect for covering a long distance underwater without using up a lot of air on the journey.

We were at the wreck within minutes. I filmed Oliver traversing both sides of the wreck and peering into the portholes, just as I had filmed Liam when we first found it. Then Liam filmed me, although I probably wouldn't use my own image in either the *Your World* montage or the RIO documentary. But better safe than sorry. You never knew when some forgotten snippet would be exactly what you needed to make a film feel complete.

After he filmed me, I stayed outside the large gap in the wreck's wall to film them while Liam and Oliver shone their flashlights around inside to get a handle on what the interior was like. There were no guide ropes—essential for safety purposes—on the inside, so either Ray had removed the ones he'd used, or they'd rotted away over the last twenty years.

Whenever a diver goes into a confined space or an area with any type of overhead obstruction, they should always use guide ropes or another foolproof method that leads to the exit. Sand and silt may have accumulated on the bottom of the enclosed spaces, and the diver's fins can stir it up, completely obscuring everything in the space. It's usually dark inside an overhead environment, but once the silt has been stirred up, using a flashlight can make it even more perilous. The light reflects off the silt particles floating in the water, making it impossible to see anything at all. Divers can quickly become disoriented and lose all sense of direction, even which way is up and which is down. So, since there were no ropes inside this wreck, we had to install new guides before we went too far in.

To make matters worse, since we were at eighty feet of depth, we would be susceptible to nitrogen narcosis as well as the potential for decompression sickness, both caused by excess nitrogen. We'd be doing several dives a day over the course of several days, so excess nitrogen would build up, making either condition a real possibility. We'd need to take extra care of each other and strictly observe the recommended surface intervals between dives to rid our bodies of the excess nitrogen to prevent a dangerous buildup.

Nitrogen narcosis can sneak up on you if you don't know what to look for, the way sometimes having one more sip of a cocktail can mean the difference between feeling relaxed and being tipsy. I made a note to keep a careful eye on Oliver, who was the least experienced member of the dive team.

While I filmed the process, Liam drove an eye bolt into the boat's hull and tied on the brightly colored nylon rope he'd brought with him. Then Oliver shone his light inside the wreck while Liam went a few feet further and installed another eye bolt into the ceiling of the wreck's compartment. He repeated the process three more times before we had to end the dive and return to the *Omega*. Luckily, we had the underwater scooters, so the trip was quick and easy.

When we arrived back at the *Omega*, I ascended ahead of the others, going slowly, and searching the surrounding area to make sure no other divers or boats were present. At the surface, I stuck my head out just enough to be able to see the area around me. All was clear.

I looked up to see Maddy gesturing for me to hurry into the lifeboat. I gave her the OK sign, sank under, and signaled Liam and Oliver to ascend. We all scrambled into the lifeboat and pulled the weather cover over us. As soon as we were in, the davits began lifting the lifeboat back to the *Omega*'s upper deck.

When the lifeboat stopped moving, Maddy pulled back the

boat's cover. "Hurry up. The other team is on the ladder on the dive platform, ready to come aboard."

The three of us scrambled out of the lifeboat, leaving our scooters and gear inside it, and scurried into the nearby tank filling tent on the *Omega's* deck. It had a roof and opaque sidewalls and was open on each end. The end of the tent didn't quite reach the start of *Omega's* tower, so the few steps we took between the lifeboat and the tent was the only time our ruse was likely to be discovered.

As each of the decoy divers came aboard, they scurried into the tent to divest their equipment. Maya hurried in and stripped off the distinctive silvery dive skin all RIO divers wear when diving on official RIO dives. She slipped on a long tee and some flip flops she'd stored in the tent earlier.

While she was changing, I strolled out of the shack, still wearing my dive skin and hood. I pulled the hood down off my head, letting it pool around my neck to show my brown hair.

Todd, Liam's body double, was standing outside the shack's entry, chatting with Oliver's double. I walked over to Todd, and he handed me a towel. We stood together chatting while Oliver and Joel, his double, changed places in the tent. Oliver emerged shortly after Joel had entered, wearing swim trunks and a T-shirt. Then faux-Liam went inside, and Oliver and I strolled away. The three body double divers had exited one at a time through the opposite end and quickly gone inside the *Omega's* nearby lab, where they would resume their normal duties until it was time for the next dive.

Meanwhile, Vincent and Lauren were on deck making a big show of retrieving the rover from its unmanned dive. The rover's trip wasn't a waste of resources, because it had gone deep to film its surroundings and take water samples RIO would use in its research.

We repeated the whole process three more times that day. Each time, Liam was able to penetrate the wreck a little further.

He was so far in now that I went inside with him to use my camera's strobe lights as illumination while Oliver hovered outside the opening keeping watch. Oliver was a good diver, but even though he was working on his advanced certification, he wasn't yet qualified to dive in an area with an overhead obstruction.

By the second dive on the next day, we had guide ropes set up in the entire area behind the opening. While Liam had been installing the ropes, I had been sketching a map of the ship on my underwater slate. There were doors at each end and stairs leading to an upper and a lower level. The remains of a large cabinet lay on the floor near the far wall. A lantern hung from the center rafter. Piles of trash and detritus were scattered around the floor, and as I'd expected, everything was covered with a fine silt.

Several yellow jacks had made the wreck their home, and two majestic queen angelfish swam in slow circles around the cabin. A moray eel peeked out from beneath the cabinet, and two crabs had made a home above him in its open drawers. Several brightly colored nudibranchs slithered along the floor. Their soft colorful bodies and feathery gills gave them an exotic otherworldly appearance that belied their membership in the same family as the homely sea slug.

I labeled the different areas on my map and noted the location of all the openings and the placement of furniture or artifacts. I took a lot of photos of the sea life and the corals that had encrusted every surface. They weren't treasure, but they'd make nice additions to the project.

After I had enough shots that I was comfortable we could move on from this room, Liam tried to open the door that we thought would lead to the captain's quarters. It opened easily, and I shone the light inside.

It was pitch black in there, but my strobe was strong enough to reach even the far corners. The bright light revealed two doors, one in each corner, both covered with coral growth. Other than plankton, the room was devoid of life. There were no visible openings to the sea outside.

This room looked like it had been the scene of a battle or a robbery. The furniture, what was left of it, was overturned, and pieces of the bed, the desk, and two of the cabinets were strewn about the room. The damage might have occurred while the ship sank, but we would never know.

Liam got busy stringing more guide ropes, while I filmed him. My bright strobe lights had the dual purpose of bringing out the brilliant colors for the film and of providing enough light for him to work. It took two more dives before he had the room roped for safety. Now we turned our attention to the doors, to see what lay beyond.

Liam used the dull side of his dive knife to pop one door open. It opened easily, revealing a small closet. The ragged remains of the captain's belts and boots littered the floor. I photographed the inside and made an inventory of the items I could identify without touching or moving anything, while Liam moved on to work on the second door.

This door did not open easily. I saw Liam working hard to find a knob or handle that would spring the door open. He put his mask up close to the coral encrustation, looking for anything that would give a clue as to how to open the passage.

He finally found a knob and cleared away enough coral from the frame to free the door. The knob turned easily, but the door didn't budge. He followed the outline of the door and saw that metal plates had been attached to the jamb at the top, bottom, and along the sides. This was not standard construction for boats of the era that we'd assumed this ship had come from, so we were mystified about how the plates got there and what their purpose was.

While we were examining the outline of the door, we noticed a raised area in the center of the upper panel. Liam pried around the edges with his knife, and a metal plaque popped off. It was so covered with coral that we couldn't tell what it was for. Liam stuck it in a catch bag he'd had stowed in a pocket of his BCD. To keep his hands free, he attached the bag to a D-ring on his vest.

It was late in the dive, and we were near the turnaround point for our air consumption, which meant Oliver must be even lower, since he used his air at a faster rate than either Liam or I did. It was time to head back.

We left the ship, picked up Oliver at the opening to the wreck, and returned to the *Omega*. We stayed at the anchor line until the other dive team returned, then we all executed our exit plans. By now, we were getting good at this maneuver.

Despite our excitement over the progress we'd made, we decided to take the rest of the day off to give our bodies a little extra time to off-gas the extra nitrogen we absorbed from breathing compressed air during the four dives we'd completed since morning. Oliver ferried Maddy, Liam and me to the *Sea Princess*, and brought Newton over from the *Tranquility* to join us for a debriefing on our progress.

When Newton heard we were through diving for the day, even though it was only mid-afternoon, he was stressed out by what he considered a lack of urgency on our part. "Every day we delay retrieving the treasure is a day those pirates may discover our subterfuge. We need to move faster."

Liam bristled, but I put my hand on his arm as a signal to let me handle Newton. "Our safety is more important than the treasure. And even getting pictures is more important than getting the treasure. We're not in it for the money, or even for the fame and glory. You know we don't plan to keep or sell the treasure. Unless we find out who the rightful owners are, the treasure will be going to some museum anyway. We're here to take pictures that tell a story. And, sure, the treasure might have historical significance, but that doesn't outweigh our lives. Or my contract."

He bit his lip. "You're right. I'm just so darn competitive…"

Even I knew this was an understatement. Newton was a shrewd businessperson, and although he'd started with a pot of money from his parents, he'd parlayed that into one of the largest investment funds in the world, even though he only invested in environmentally sound endeavors. Saving the environment had been his focus long before it became trendy, and he'd been instrumental in supporting and furthering industries like recycling, ultra-powerful energy-efficient batteries, electric vehicles, reusable packaging, and solar and wind power. He was one of the key donors supporting the ocean health work we did at RIO.

"You guys know diving, so I'll stick with what I know best." Newton logged into his computer to check up on the financial doings of the day and to instant message with Gus about the day's business. Oliver and Liam worked together in the galley to clean up the plaque we'd recovered, while Maddy and I went over some of the photos I had taken so far. I marked several as "definite maybe" candidates for the photo montage for *Your World*.

Chapter 22
Pirate Diving

LIAM WAS STILL WORKING on removing the accumulated crud from the metal tablet, so he had it soaking in a pail of vinegar and water to soften the buildup of coral. We were all curious about what its purpose might have been, and what the door led to.

Because of the thickness of the metal plates that held it shut, all I could think of was the door must have led to the brig, but it made no sense to have the brig back up to the captain's quarters. Brigs were filthy and malodorous, so no captain in his right mind would set up his quarters next to one. A brig would usually be in the belly of a ship.

I'd just fired up my computer to do a few internet searches on old sea vessels when Oliver asked if he could take the Zodiac to Alec's catamaran to say hello to Lily.

It was an understatement to say that none of us were fans of Lily, but we all loved Oliver, and after all, she was his twin sister. One by one, we reluctantly agreed he could go.

Alec's catamaran was anchored about a half mile away on the far side of both the unidentified cabin cruiser and the pirate ship.

After Oliver dropped Newton at the *Tranquility*, he had to pass by the pirate ship to get to Alec's boat.

The pirates all came out on deck and waved their black tri-corner hats at him as he passed. We could hear them shouting out to him. "Ahoy, Matey. C'mon aboard. Have a ration of rum with us. You scurvy dog. AARGH." Other stereotypical pirate phrases floated across the water to us. Oliver gave them a friendly wave as he passed, but he continued to the catamaran without stopping. He tied up, then jumped onto the deck.

Lily was waiting for him. She gave him a hug, but I swear I felt her eyes on me as she stared over his shoulder out over the waves. I shivered.

Alec brought Oliver a can of something to drink, and the three of them reclined on the deck for a while. I tried not to stare, but I had a hard time looking away. I'd come to think of Oliver as my younger brother, and I hated the thought of him spending time with two snakes like Alec and Lily.

On the other hand, it looked like Lily and Alec had grown closer since they'd first met. So maybe Oliver thought of Alec as family too, and I had no right to interfere in that. Family was too impor-tant to us both.

Maddy was watching the goings on at the catamaran as well as watching the mystery boat for any signs of life. I could see her casting uneasy glances toward the silent and seemingly abandoned cabin cruiser every few minutes. We were so distracted we weren't making much progress with analyzing the photos.

Finally, over on the catamaran, Oliver got up and jumped down into the Zodiac. He untied the line and started the engine.

"Thank Goodness," Maddy said. "He's coming home safe."

Oliver putted slowly across the waves. As he neared their boat, the pirates waved their hats in the air again, yelling, "C'mon, Mate. Join us for a beer."

I assumed they were either bored with watching us do nothing or they hoped that if they got him aboard, they could trick him into giving them information about what we were doing and the progress we'd made.

I hoped he didn't fall for their scheme, so I was dismayed when he steered the inflatable to their transom and tied up. Through my binoculars, I could see the astonishment and glee on their faces.

They clapped him on the back when he got aboard. Someone stuck a pirate hat on his head and a can of soda in his hand. He sat in one of the deck chairs, and the four pirates sat nearby, still wearing their pirate hats. Maybe they just wanted to keep the sun out of their eyes, but I found the hats unnerving anyway.

Obviously, I couldn't hear what they were talking about, but I got angrier and angrier as I watched first one pirate then another as they tossed their empty drink cans into the ocean. They'd been passing around bags of snacks, and each empty bag followed the cans into the sea.

Oliver stood up, and I could see him gesturing angrily at the garbage they'd thrown into the ocean. One of them made a calm down gesture and then he threw his hat to the deck and jumped into the water to gather up the trash. Oliver relaxed and sat back down, but a few minutes later, he got in his boat and puttered back to the *Sea Princess*.

"I'm going diving," he said when he came aboard. "With Noah, Stefan, Austin and Dylan."

"I know who Stefan is," Maddy said, "but who are the rest of those people?"

"They're the guys with Stefan, and they want to have a little adventure. They're cool."

Maddy and I just looked at each other, but we didn't have any right to tell Oliver what to do with his free time. Neither of us thought Stefan Gibb was cool, and we had serious doubts that any of his friends were either. But legally, Oliver was an adult, so the decision was his.

"Just keep them away from the wreck site," I said.

"Duh! Why didn't I think of that?" he said.

He took the little Zodiac over to the *Omega* to pick up his BCD, mask, fins, and regulator along with a couple of tanks. He waved as he putted past us on his way back to Stefan's boat.

We watched as he reboarded the pirate ship. Stefan hoisted a diver down flag with its jaunty red background and diagonal white stripe. The five men donned their BCDs and tanks, then one by one they did giant stride entries off the back of the boat.

The four of us on the *Sea Princess* tried not to stare at the pirate's boat, but we couldn't look away. The clock slowly ticked on. We tried to estimate what the dive's duration might end up being, but there was really no way to guess. Their bottom time depended on how deep they went, how hard they worked, and how efficient they were in using their air. We knew Oliver's usual air consumption rate by now, but we had no way of knowing the rates of his diving companions, since it was a function of depth, their level of training, comfort in the water, and their physical and aerobic fitness. All we could do was wait for them to reappear.

I was about to put on my dive gear and go after Oliver when I saw the first member of the group emerge. I saw through my binoculars that it was Stefan Gibb. He was quickly followed by the other three pirates. Stefan helped them by taking their fins and carrying their BCDs with the heavy tanks attached, and I saw in this courtesy the effects of Vincent's training from Stefan's time in the *Omega*'s crew at work.

A minute passed after the last pirate emerged. Then two.

There was no sign of Oliver.

I had just finished setting up my gear to launch a rescue dive when Maddy said, "It's okay. He's on the ladder." I exhaled, relieved he was not injured or hurt.

We watched as he stowed his gear in the Zodiac and headed back to us. He waved to the four shipmates as he motored away.

"Well?" Newton said when Oliver had boarded the *Sea Princess.* "Learn anything?"

"Yeah. Those guys are lousy divers, except for Stefan. And if you're diving with grey reef sharks and you're the last diver in the water, a shark may position himself between you and the ladder, apparently just to mess with you. I was scared to death. Finally, I was so low on air that I just went for it, and he swam away. But man, I was scared."

Maddy, Liam, and I had seen this shark behavior before, and it was extremely unnerving even if you knew it might happen. Newton didn't like the water and he could barely swim. He'd never been diving, and he shuddered at the idea of playing chicken with a shark. He stood up from the couch where he'd been sitting and hugged Oliver. "Thank goodness you made it back okay."

Oliver blushed at this show of affection, and I was happy to see Newton taking an interest in him, accepting him as a member of the family.

Liam asked, "Did you see anyone on the mystery boat? I haven't seen any signs of life at all. But someone must be aboard."

Oliver nodded his agreement. "Someone must be there, but I didn't see a soul. I did hear a radio playing very softly when I went by the first time. The music stopped in the middle of a song, like someone had shut it off. I didn't hear anything after that, the whole time I was on the pirate ship."

We pondered the question of who could be on board and what their agenda might be for a few seconds until my stomach growled, loud and long. "Sorry. I'm starving."

"Me too," said Oliver. "Diving makes me hungry."

Newton was sick of his own cooking, so we decided to eat dinner with the crew on the *Omega*. Newton made a couple of sandwiches for Stewie's dinner, and Liam brought them over to the *Tranquility* before taking us all to the *Omega*.

Chapter 23
The Plaque

WE HAD a delicious meal in the galley with the crew and the research staff. The *Omega*'s chef was a master at cooking with limited ingredients, but today he'd gone all out.

While we'd been diving, he'd taken an early morning boat trip to Belize to pick up some fresh meat, veggies, and fruit. Our dinner consisted of roast pork with pineapple chimichurri, baked yams, and sautéed cabbage, with bananas Foster for dessert.

After dinner, we went to Maddy's cabin in the bow of the boat. We sat on the comfortable chairs and the pullout couch to discuss our progress and plan our next moves. We watched as Liam dumped the contents of his pail into the sink of Maddy's en suite bathroom. He rinsed the plaque under running water and scraped at the remaining encrustation to remove as much as he could.

We were surprised by how quickly the thick layer of gunk had given way to the mild acid, and we realized that the plaque was not as old as we'd first thought. When its surface became visible, it looked to be made of modern stainless steel. Liam turned the metal plaque over and we saw the engraving. The words 'sorrow, betrayal and death by drowning' had been etched above the mystical symbol I'd first seen in Ray's tattoo. The symbol Wikipedia said meant a curse of 'sorrow, betrayal, and death by drowning.' I shivered.

Oliver said, "That's a bad sign. Someone sure thought there was a curse on that room."

"It isn't part of the ship's original construction. This piece is much newer than the rest of the boat." Liam held the plaque up to the light, peering at the inscription.

I shivered. "Could Ray have put it there? Did he believe in the curse? Maybe that's why he never retrieved the treasure."

Maddy frowned. "Ray wasn't superstitious—at least, no more than any other sailor. On the other hand, he always said the treasure should remain hidden. He did believe it was cursed. That's why I was so surprised he gave you the coordinates, Fin. And I can't imagine him going to all the trouble of having that sign made and then fastening it to the door in the wreck. It's like he was of two minds about the treasure and the curse."

"When we were first together, he often had nightmares about the wreck. He told me about them once. He dreamed of a woman with long black hair, guarding the treasure, and threatening to hurt people he loved if he didn't set her free."

"That's right," I said. "I remember he had those nightmares sometimes when I was little. I could hear him muttering in his sleep when we were on the boat. Maybe he went back to the wreck later and installed those steel plates."

Liam said, "Well somebody put them up, and not that long ago. Whoever it was went to great pains to be sure whatever is inside that room could never get out. The door was sealed shut with a bunch of heavy steel plates just like this one."

Newton stood up and stretched. "We're not going to figure this out until you get inside that room. I think we should all get a good night's rest and tackle this again in the morning. Would one of you take me back to the *Tranquility?* I don't like leaving Stewie alone too long, and I can only imagine what mischief he'll get into if he gets too bored."

We all said goodnight, then Liam, Oliver, and Newton headed off to their assigned boats, while Maddy and I stayed in her cabin.

Chapter 24
The Dream

MADDY HELPED me pull out the bed on the sleeper sofa. I could have gone to the crew quarters, but the owner's suite was so much cozier and more private that there was no contest. I brushed my teeth, put on my PJs, and climbed under the covers. Maddy shut out the lights and we were in for the night.

Within a few minutes I could hear soft snores from my mother's side of the room. She'd have been mortified to think she snored, and the thought of her indignation made me smile. She was so strong and competent on the outside, yet still soft and insecure inside. It was a conundrum many women had to deal with. The face they showed the world had to be close to perfect.

I think that's why Maddy and Ray had been so good together. They each accepted the other exactly as they were. Maddy had always been free to show her softer side to Ray, and it had to have been a great relief, given how hard she worked to make it in the male-oriented profession she'd chosen.

I tossed and turned for a few minutes, worrying about whether I'd ever achieve the level of success in my field that she'd reached in hers. I hated the thought that I might be a disappointment to her, although she'd never given the slightest sign that she was anything other than my biggest fan. I thought again about how Alec stealing my best work and selling it under his own byline had set my career back, and my anger surged anew.

I didn't want to disturb Maddy, so I threw on my robe and went up to the deck of the *Omega*. It was late, and the only people out were the two watchmen, one at each end of the ship. They waved as I walked by. I paused midship and leaned on the rail, enjoying the reflection of the crescent moon on the still water.

Then the night got brighter. A light had gone on in the flying bridge of the mysterious third boat, the cabin cruiser anchored a little behind and between Alec's catamaran and the pirate ship. I watched, transfixed, as Lily climbed out of the water onto the boat's transom. A small female figure wrapped her in a towel and hugged her.

The two of them went below, into the cabin of the boat, and someone extinguished the outside light. I waited and watched for an hour, until the light flicked back on. Lily came on deck and dove into the water. She swam back to Alec's catamaran and climbed out.

She stood under the light and waved her arm over her head. The light on the mystery boat flickered once, then went out again.

I waited a few minutes, but there was no further activity. I assumed everyone had bedded down for the night, so I went below and snuggled in my bed. I was asleep within minutes, but it wasn't restful.

I hadn't been asleep for long when I started dreaming. I knew I was dreaming, but it seemed so real I couldn't wake myself. I was in the cabin of the wreck, but it wasn't a wreck yet. It was a beautiful boat, sleek and well-kept, floating serenely atop the waves. Its crew wasn't visible. It was interesting to see how my mind filled in the details of the boat. The brightly colored pennants, so much like the ones I'd hung on the *Tranquility*, were fastened to the rigging, and they wafted through the air on a gentle breeze. The figurehead of a woman on the prow was painted in bright colors. She wore a blue dress, and a jeweled gold crown adorned her painted black hair.

In my dream, I walked toward the boat's stern and down a short flight of stairs. The entryway at the foot of the stairs was so short I had to duck my head to enter the lower area.

I was in the first room we had explored on the wreck. The portholes were in the same locations, and I recognized the lantern hanging from the center rafter, even without its coral crust. The cabinet stood neatly against one of the walls, and a nearby table was spread with a map held flat by four gold doubloons, one in each corner. While I watched, one of the doubloons disappeared, fading from the dream in a wisp of smoke.

I walked down the stairs that I knew led to the captain's quarters. Here too, the room was exactly as I'd pictured it from the wreckage. The bed, tucked in a corner, had been neatly made. I knew that if I'd tried, one of those doubloons would have bounced, just the way a modern-day quarter is supposed to bounce on a properly made military bed. The cupboard door stood slightly ajar, and I could see the captain's belongings hanging there.

The other door, the one that had been welded shut on the wreck, was plain wood in my dream. Solid, and with a bulky brass knob. A few inches above the knob an iron hasp had been fastened to the wood and locked shut with a large brass padlock. There was no key, but as I dream-walked toward the door, the padlock snapped open and fell to the floor.

I reached for the knob to see what was in the room beyond, but my hand stopped a few inches away. I felt a moment of terror, then I heard the snick of the latch, and the door popped open an inch or two even though I'd made no attempt to open it.

I reached out and pulled it the rest of the way open. The walls of this room were plain wood. There were no openings, and no furnishings except a large metal chair like a throne in the exact center of the room. One of the most beautiful women I had ever seen sat on the throne, her hands bound to its arms with iron bands. Each of her wrists had been tattooed with the mystical symbol of the curse. Her feet had been shackled to its legs with iron fetters, completely immobilizing her. Her blue silk dress shone in the soft light that filtered in from the captain's quarters, and a golden tiara sat atop the intricate coils of her raven hair. Her lips were a bright red, and her eyes a piercing blue.

The entire vision was remarkable in its detail, but the most striking detail of all was the tiara she wore. It shone as brightly as the moon on the water last night before I'd gone to bed. A large diamond the size of an egg had been placed in the center, surrounded by smaller diamonds, rubies, and sapphires. Each of the arches of the tiara was tipped with a smaller diamond. The diadem was encrusted with sapphires. I had never seen such magnificence, even in a museum.

The woman in the chair had been watching me as I took in the details. She licked her lips with a pointed pink tongue. "Please, set me free," she said at last. She spoke in Italian or maybe Portuguese or Spanish. I didn't know which one it was. I didn't speak any of these languages in real life, but somehow, in my dream, I understood her words.

I shook my head. "I can't. I don't know how."

"There are keys in the cupboard in the other room. Get them. Please. Set me free." Her eyes pleaded with me, and I found it hard to resist her. I started to leave the room, when I remembered the plaque we'd brought back, and the mystic symbol carved on it.

I turned back to the woman. "Are you a witch?"

She nodded. "Yes. I am a witch. So set me free, and I'll give you anything you want. Friends. Liam. A career. Your father. Ray alive again. Name it, and it will be yours." A tear slipped prettily from her right eye. "Please."

I wondered how she knew my dearest wishes, and then I realized this was a dream—all in my head. Of course, the woman would know everything I knew. "You're just a dream."

"Set me free and you'll see if I'm just a dream."

It was then that I knew for sure that Ray must have been the one who'd put the plaque and metal plates in place. He too had faced this temptation, and he'd recognized this woman in his dreams as evil. Her eyes glittered, no longer soft and dreamy, but hard and cold. "Do it," she commanded.

"No." I turned to go.

"You'll be sorry," she shrieked. "Sorrow. Betrayal. Death by drowning. That's your future. Just like it was Ray's."

As I walked away, I was engulfed in fire. My feet started to melt, and I fell to the floor. I crawled up the steps and slammed the door shut with trembling hands. Fire was everywhere, and I screamed at the searing heat.

A gentle hand touched my shoulder. "Fin, wake up. You're having a nightmare." Maddy's hand was cool.

Her loving touch extinguished the lingering fire from my dream. "Thanks, Mom," I said. She climbed under the covers with me and rubbed my back, just as she had when I was a child. For a long time, I only pretended to go back to sleep.

137

Chapter 25
A Serious Discussion

THE NEXT MORNING, Liam, Oliver, and Newton arrived while Maddy and I were sitting in the crew lounge sipping our coffee. Oliver had made fresh blueberry muffins again. They were still warm, and we fell on them as though we hadn't eaten for days.

Maddy hadn't said anything about my nightmare this morning. Neither had I, although I was still unsettled by my encounter with the witch of the wreck. That uneasiness didn't stop me from eating my share of the muffins though.

Newton split his third muffin in half and inhaled the fragrant steam. "Oliver, I don't know where you learned to bake these, but you'll have to give my chef the recipe. They're superb." He swallowed a small piece and then said, "And I think you should visit the pirates again this afternoon. Get to know them. Act like you want to be friends."

Oliver chewed and swallowed a bite of his own muffin before he answered. "I'd already planned to. I think I can learn more about their plans if I befriend them. And I can say hi to my sister again while I'm there, but mostly I want to go because it gives me a chance to get up close to that mystery boat. I don't like that nobody has shown themselves yet. Whoever it is, they must be up to something."

"That could be true," I said after a sip of coffee. "Someone was definitely aboard last night. It might have been a woman." I told them about my late-night stroll on the deck and seeing Lily swimming to the mystery boat. "Someone welcomed her aboard. Maybe the boat belongs to the girlfriend one of the pirates, and she and Lily are friends. It could be the pirate only goes over there to sleep or when he has to move the boat. Maybe the rest of the time he spends on the Jolly Roger with his friends, and the girlfriend stays alone on the cabin cruiser. Or I guess it could have been a man who welcomed Lily. It was dark, and the boat is pretty far away."

As a team, we hadn't thought about the possibility that the two boats belonged to the same group until I said this. We spent a few minutes discussing the possibility, until Oliver chimed in, "I think we're off base with this idea. Someone was definitely aboard when I went by yesterday. Remember, whoever it was, they shut the radio off. There's someone on that boat, and whoever it is, they don't want us to know who they are. And I can't see Alec letting Lily visit one of those pirates alone, late at night. He's way too possessive for that."

Oliver continued. "It must be someone we know, or someone we'd recognize. Otherwise, why wouldn't they show themselves?"

This was an insightful observation from Oliver. We all paused to see if we could think of anyone Alec wouldn't mind Lily visiting alone at night. He was so jealous, we couldn't think of a soul.

I glanced at Oliver with admiration. He'd seen right through the holes in my theory about the boat's occupant while the rest of us skipped along a dead end trail, oblivious to a key clue we'd already been given. That kid was smart.

Maddy cleared her throat. "I want to dive with the team today. I'm tired of staying on the boat doing paperwork while you three are having all the fun. I want to see the wreck, and the lifeboat ruse is working fine. I'll just hop in with the rest of you. Nobody will think twice if I don't appear on deck for an hour or two."

I nodded. "Fine. Good idea, actually. But how about if we wait until the afternoon dives for you to join us? The pirates sleep late, so Oliver can dive this morning without losing out on his time with them. Then you take over for the afternoon dives, and he can go see Lily and his friends the pirates. His visits will provide some distraction in case they are watching for you to dive."

The team agreed this new plan would work for everybody, so we separated to prepare for our day's work. Maddy went on deck to confer with Vincent, while Liam, Oliver, and I wiggled into our dive skins before racing into the lifeboat. A few minutes later, Lauren delivered our scooters and rebreathers, so we geared up and waited to be lowered.

Once in the water, the scooters brought us to the wreck in less than a minute. When the circumstances of my nightmare floated through my head, I pulled back and slowed down. Right away, Liam noticed I wasn't by his side, and he stopped swimming and turned around to look for me. I sucked in a breath and gave him the okay sign. It was silly to think my dream could hurt me here in the real world. We sped on.

At the wreck site, Oliver once again kept watch outside while Liam and I went in and approached the barricaded door. My heart was thudding in my chest, and I was using up my air at an unaccustomed rate.

Liam had packed a small prybar in his BCD pocket, and he set to work on the panels while I filmed him. Now that the captain's quarters were open to the ocean, more sea life had found its way in. I filmed a small octopus hiding in a corner and a few bright turquoise parrot fish who were checking out the area. In reality, I would have filmed old sandwich wrappers to avoid watching Liam's progress opening the door. The thought of what we might see back there terrified me.

He'd removed three of the five remaining metal plates holding the door closed by the time we needed to surface. For the first time in my life, I was glad it was time to head back from a dive.

When we exited the wreck, my heart skipped a beat because I didn't see Oliver outside the wreck opening. I swiveled around looking for him. When I finally saw him, he was floating prone out over the drop down. He wasn't moving.

I sped over and grabbed his arm. He startled upright and looked at me with wild eyes. I realized he was okay. He'd just been watching a few turtles cavorting down below.

I signaled I was sorry for scaring him and he gave me the okay sign. We all grabbed our scooters and let them ferry us back to the *Omega*'s anchor line where we met up with the decoy group to make our separate ascents.

Back aboard the ship, I asked Liam if he would mind if I started training Oliver on diving in an overhead environment during our next dive. It would be something to keep Oliver engaged during the dive, and it might help keep my mind off my growing fear of opening the locked door. Liam had no objections, so I floated the idea by Oliver. He was thrilled and excited by the opportunity, and I realized I had underestimated how bored he'd become keeping watch alone outside the wreck. During our one hour surface interval, I worked with him on the basics of diving in an environment with an overhead obstruction.

When it was time to dive again, Maddy joined us in the lifeboat. She had volunteered to film Liam as he worked on opening the door, so I'd be free to work with Oliver in the outer chamber.

We made our way to the wreck. Maddy and Liam swam quickly through the opening and down the stairs to the captain's quarters. Oliver and I hovered outside the hole in the hull, peering through the opening, and memorizing the landmarks inside the area we'd be exploring, including the layout of the guide ropes Liam had set during our earlier dives.

Oliver went in first, and as I expected, he kicked up a lot of silt as he swam, even though I'd cautioned him to use only the tiniest of kicks while swimming. I reached up and wrapped my hand around one of the guide ropes and followed him in. When he was directly under the lantern in the center of the space, which I had set as his objective, he turned around. Ahead of him now was a swirling wall of silt floating through the water, obscuring every detail. He reared back in shock, letting go of the guide rope he'd been holding as he did.

Because he was in a clear space, I could see a vague outline of his movements through the curtain of silt. His next move should have been to grab hold of the guide rope before he became disoriented, but instead he swam to his right, probably hoping to get around the cloud of floating particles so he could see the entry.

I knew the entry would remain obscured for a lot longer than our air supplies would last, so I reached out with one hand without letting go of the rope. I had a flashlight in the free hand, and I waggled it up and down hoping Oliver would see the light and reach out to me. Instead, he swam nearer to the wall with the door to the captain's quarters. This would have been a reasonable move, because he'd have been able to pick up the guide rope there, but he was still kicking up a lot of silt. Soon we'd both be engulfed in the cloud.

I stretched my arm out and touched him with the flashlight. He grasped my hand, and I pulled him toward me. I lifted his hand to the guide rope and slid it in the direction of the exit. Then I followed him outside, where we waited for Liam and Maddy to join us.

They were experienced enough to expect a silt cloud when they came up the stairway from the captain's quarters, so they'd both grabbed the guide rope before they swam up the stairway. They easily made it to the exit, emerging at least three or four minutes before I expected them to.

We returned to the Omega for lunch. Oliver and I sat apart from the rest of the team so I could review the lessons learned from this morning's dive. Oliver recognized right away that he had created a dangerous situation with his careless kicks. He could have easily endangered the lives of the whole team. Just before we were ready to go back to the lifeboat for our afternoon dives, Oliver apologized to Liam and Maddy for his folly in rushing into the wreck and possibly putting them in danger.

The plan for the rest of the day was for him to wait until our dive was well underway to visit Lily and the pirates. Because we hadn't seen or heard from them since breakfast, we'd also asked him to check in on Newton and Stewie on his way by.

I didn't like the idea of Oliver being on his own with the pirates. Or with Alec. Or especially with his own twin sister. But he was an adult, and technically not my responsibility. What could I say?

Chapter 26
Attack of the Thimble Jellyfish

THE FIRST AFTERNOON dive went well. Liam was very close to being able to remove the final metal plate, but we didn't want to push our bottom time on this dive. Maddy and Liam were enjoying the anticipation and they were more than willing to hold off on opening the door.

On the other hand, I was dreading what I would see when we opened it. I hadn't been able to shake the lingering terror of my nightmare.

Once back on the *Omega*, we agreed to skip our last dive of the day and wait until morning to open the door so we could keep an eye out for Oliver in case he needed us.

After our usual routine of switching places with our body doubles in the tank tent, I wandered across the deck and looked out over the clear turquoise water. As expected, I saw the *Sea Princess*, the *Tranquility*, the pirate ship with our Zodiac tied to it, the mystery cabin cruiser, and Alec's catamaran. Nothing had changed, but I couldn't shake off my uneasy feeling.

Newton and Stewie were sitting together on the deck of the *Tranquility*, but I couldn't see what they were doing. Alec and Lily were sunbathing on the catamaran's canvas deck. There was no sign of life on either the mystery cabin cruiser or the pirate ship.

Then I realized that the lack of activity was one of the reasons I was feeling so uneasy. Where was Oliver? He should have been visible on the pirate's deck, but there was no sign of anyone at all on board.

Vincent was at the *Omega*'s rear platform, supervising the rover's retrieval after its most recent dive. I hurried over to ask if he knew when Oliver had left.

He scratched his chin. "I wasn't really paying attention, but I think he left right after your team started the dive. I'm sorry I can't be more exact."

I thanked him and went back to the rail to see if there'd been any changes on the other boats, but there was no sign of life on any of them. I called Newton's SAT phone.

He agreed that it was odd that nobody was around on the pirate ship. "I didn't see them leave, but I spent a good hour below on the phone with Gus this morning. Maybe that's where they all are. Playing video games or something. Don't worry about Oliver. He's a big boy."

I knew Oliver wasn't a fan of video games, but maybe Newton was right, and they were all below deck doing something innocent. I'd give it a few minutes. "Thanks, Newton," I said.

"Don't worry, Honey. I'm sure he's fine. And by the way, I'll have some interesting news to report at dinner." We disconnected, and I went back to staring at the three boats that weren't part of our expedition.

After another fifteen minutes, I was beginning to panic. I was going to ask Vincent if I could use another of the *Omega*'s tenders to investigate, but as I turned, I saw motion out of the corner of my eye.

Four divers had surfaced under their own power near the pirate ship, and they were towing a fifth diver. They heaved the fifth diver into the Zodiac Oliver used. One of them climbed aboard and started the engine, aiming the small boat toward the *Omega*. Without my binoculars, I couldn't make out his face, but from the shape of the diver who was driving, I knew it wasn't Oliver. Which meant he was probably the injured party. I sucked in a panicked breath.

I ran across the deck to the transom "Liam! Maddy! Vincent! Get the doctor. Come quick. Someone's been hurt. I think it's Oliver."

Maddy and Liam had been sitting on deck under a canopy sipping lemonade and discussing RIO business, but they jumped up so quickly they knocked over their chairs, and the computers they'd been using tumbled to the deck. They ran across the boat and joined me in the transom, where we watched the Zodiac approach.

I held my breath and repeated silently. "Not Oliver. Not Oliver. Not Oliver." But in my heart, I knew it was him slumped on the Zodiac's floor. He wasn't wearing a RIO silver dive skin, but it was hard to miss his long legs and broad shoulders.

The Zodiac was racing toward us at top speed, bouncing over the waves and landing in the troughs between them with what must have been bone-jarring force, but the boat never slowed. It roared up to the *Omega*'s transom, splashing us all with its wake. We reached out to pull the body aboard before we'd even tied up the inflatable. The doctor put her stethoscope to Oliver's chest and trotted alongside Liam, who was carrying his limp body up the stairs to the main deck.

Oliver's lips were blue, and his eyes were shut. His face, neck and hands were covered in angry looking red welts. I couldn't tell if he was breathing.

Liam placed Oliver on the waiting gurney. "He's alive," Doc shouted as she turned him on his side. "You,' she shouted at the Zodiac's driver. "What happened?"

"I don't know. We were diving, and there were all these little jellyfish in the water. Kind of cute, ya know? Pulsing and floating, like those hippos dancing in that old movie. They were all around us, and we were watching them and poking at them. Then suddenly, Ollie here started shaking and jerking around. We didn't know what to do, so we dragged him back to the boat. I got him here as fast as I could. He's gonna be okay, isn't he?"

"Thimble jellyfish? He must have been stung by their larvae." I knew the tiny thimbles themselves were harmless, but the water around them was always full of their invisible larvae. Known as 'sea lice,' the larvae stings could result in a fierce itch and angry red welts. Usually the cute little thimbles—about the size of a small thumb—appeared in the late spring. Divers in the know either avoided diving during the spawning season or at least avoided diving where the thimbles were swarming. Their schools sometimes covered hundreds of square feet, and they could be found anywhere in the water column from the surface to extreme depths.

The doctor nodded at my words. "Yes. Looks like thimble jellyfish stings to me too. Severe reaction though. Epi," she shouted, and one of her team handed her a pen. She rolled Oliver onto his back, jabbed the pen into his leg and rolled him back to his side while the rest of us watched and waited for a reaction. Any reaction.

After a second, sea water spewed from his mouth. When the trickle of water stopped, Oliver groaned feebly. He lifted one of his hands to scratch at his face, but Doc pushed his hand away.

"That'll only make it worse," she said gently. "Don't worry. We'll take good care of you." She and her medical team rolled the gurney away to sick bay.

"What really happened?" I snarled at the pirate. "It's not thimble jellyfish season, and it usually takes hours for the stings to show up even when it is. What did you do to him?

The pirate stared back at me. "I told you the truth. Stefan was right about you. You're a raving witch." He turned away as though he were going to leave.

One of Doc's team had been cleaning up the sea water Oliver had ejected. "It looked to me like a severe allergic reaction, Fin," he said. "That can happen fast, with no warning. Lucky they had the presence of mind to bring him here fast. Has Oliver ever been stung before?"

"Not that I know of," I admitted. "But he may have been."

"We'll ask him when he wakes up. If it was an allergic reaction, he'll need to be careful diving when thimbles are around," he said. "In fact, he'd be better off to stay out of the water altogether when they're in season." He picked up his bucket and headed to sick bay.

Liam, Maddy, and I huddled together on deck. "One of us should tell Lily," I said.

"I can do it," said Liam. "I'll pick up Newton on the way and drop Stewie's dinner off. But what should I do if she wants to see him? I don't think we want her on board, do we?"

Maddy bit her lips. "No, we don't. But he's her twin brother. We can't be that heartless. If she wants to come to the *Omega* to see him, it's ok to bring her back. But we'll have one of the crew stay with her at all times while she's on board."

Liam nodded and headed to the Zodiac. He held out his hand to the young pirate. "Keys, please."

"I'm Noah," the pirate said. "Keys are still in the engine. Are you giving me a ride back?"

"With pleasure, Noah.' Liam said. "Get aboard."

Maddy and I stood at the rail and watched Liam pilot the Zodiac to the *Tranquility.* He tied up for barely a minute, and Newton jumped in. Stewie stood forlornly on the transom. He must have been hoping for a visit from Lauren. It looked like he wanted to go with Liam too, but it was clear from their body language that neither Newton nor Liam would allow him to get on the small boat.

As soon as Newton was settled on the middle bench of the Zodiac, Liam zoomed to the pirate ship and allowed Noah to disembark. Then he slowly putted over to Alec's catamaran. You could almost see the reluctance as he got nearer.

Alec had been sitting on the catamaran's canvas deck, reading, with Lily curled up beside him. They both stood when Liam approached in the Zodiac. It looked like they were chatting for a few minutes before Lily screamed. We heard her all the way over on the *Omega*. "Noooo. Oliver!! Hold on. I'm coming."

Within seconds, a woman raced out of the cabin of the mystery boat and ran to the deck. I was watching through my binoculars, so I could see it was Cara Flores, Lily and Oliver's mother.

"Maddy, I know who's on the mystery boat," I said.

She had her own binoculars out, so she already knew. "No wonder she didn't show herself. She must have known she wouldn't be welcome here."

Lily and Alec jumped in the Zodiac, and Liam made a stop at the mystery cabin cruiser to pick up Cara before heading back to the *Omega*.

Cara leaped from the Zodiac to the *Omega* before the small boat had even stopped moving. She raced up the steps to the deck and over to my mother. "Where is he? What have you done to my son?'

Maddy is always cordial, and she has a lot more patience than I do. She didn't smile, but her voice was mild as she said, "I believe he's awake. I'll show you the way to sick bay." She walked off, leaving Cara and Lily to follow if they wanted.

As she walked past me, Lily smiled her shining smile. "Hello, Fin. Long time no see. Maybe we can catch up after I see Oliver. It would be so nice to have one of our little chats."

I was too stunned to speak. The last time I'd seen Lily she'd been in police custody, and I knew that after what she'd done to Ray and me, she should still be in custody.

I heard my ex-husband's voice from behind me. "Thanks for not freaking out. She's really upset about her brother."

I whirled around. "And I'm really upset about her being here. And you. Even Cara. What are you three doing here? Lily should be in jail."

"She's out, and there's nothing you can do about it. Free as a bird. No evidence of wrongdoing on any of your trumped up charges."

I gagged. "She killed Ray. Tried to kill me. She confessed."

Alec smirked. "Nobody saw anything the day of Ray's death. As for her alleged attempt on your life, it's your word against hers. Her lawyer argued that the confession was made while in a state of nitrogen narcosis and under duress. Charges dropped. You lose."

My mouth opened in shock, but I couldn't speak because I was so angry. At Alec. At Lily. At the whole world.

Liam came over and took my hand. "Let's get you out of here."

"Don't you have some cars to park?" Alec said, a sneer in his voice.

Liam raised his free arm over his head as we walked away. I'm pretty sure he made a rude gesture. I was too dizzy to look up. But I could hear Alec laughing as we went through the door to the crew quarters below.

Liam walked me to Maddy's cabin and brought me inside. I sat on the couch. "I'll get you something to drink and go check on Oliver. Wait here where they can't get to you," he said. But before he could leave, the door opened and Maddy and Newton walked in. Newton was pushing a small cart laden with tea, lemonade, and water.

"Who's watching the bad guys?" I asked.

"Vincent sent Lauren as an escort for Lily and Cara, with strict orders they are not to go anywhere unaccompanied," Maddy said.

"Can someone explain the animosity to me? I get Alec and Lily, but what's up with Cara? Why does she hate everyone?" Liam looked puzzled.

Newton sighed. "I think that's on me. Cara used to work for me, and she and I used to be in a relationship—strictly consensual. But I made the mistake of telling her that I was in love with someone else." His eyes darted to Maddy, and he quickly looked away again.

"Cara didn't take well to that idea, but we kept working together for years afterwards anyway. Then she came up with this scheme to bilk Ray Russo out of some money. She thought he was rich, so she told him he was the twin's father. She chose him because of his connections—a way to hurt someone she knows I care about. Ray and Oliver look a lot alike, but I still don't know how she planned to finesse a paternity test. It didn't matter anyway. Ray knew it wasn't true, but he also knew the kids needed a father, so he took on the responsibility."

Newton looked at me before continuing. "That's the kind of guy he was. At first, nobody realized Lily was a whack job. After he died, Cara tried to extort money from Maddy, who kindly set up trust funds for the twins from her own assets. I guess Cara thought she deserved a trust fund too, but instead she got fired. It didn't go well."

"That's quite a story," Liam said. "Someone should write a book about it."

"Ancient history," Maddy said.

I rose. "Alec's on deck by himself. He'll go snooping around, asking questions. I've got to watch him."

Liam stood up too. "I'm going with you. You shouldn't be alone where he can get to you." He poured lemonade into two mugs, then put the lids on. "Let's go."

Alec wasn't standing at the railing where we'd left him. I looked around but didn't see him anywhere. I stopped a passing crew member. "You seen Alec Stone around anywhere?"

"The guy came over on the Zodiac? Yeah, I think he went over to the tank tent." He jerked a thumb over his shoulder to the far side of the *Omega*'s deck.

I caught a glimpse of Alec as he left the tank tent and headed down the *Omega*'s deck toward where we'd been using the lifeboat to enter and leave the water. Liam and I trotted across the deck to stop him.

Too late. He was standing beside the lifeboat we'd been using, looking down at the pile of dive gear on its floor. Scooters. Rebreathers. BCDs. It was easy to see what we'd been doing. We might just as well have given him a written copy of our plan.

"Clever," he said as we drew near. "But now we know." He

smiled, and if you didn't know he was insane you might have thought he was being friendly. Charming even.

I didn't say anything, but Liam said, "We thought you might be hungry. Would you like to get something to eat in the galley?"

"No, I'm fine," Alec said. "I'll just stroll around and wait for Lily and Cara."

Liam smiled, but he didn't let the smile reach his eyes. "Either come to the galley with me and stay there, or I can take you back to your boat. Those are your only choices."

Alec drew himself up, and I thought there was going to be a fight. Then he took a deep breath and exhaled slowly. "I'll wait on my boat then," he said. "It's more comfortable than this old tub anyway. Tell Lily she can reach me on the radio if she needs me." He stuck his hands in the pockets of his shorts and strolled across the deck to the Zodiac. Just before stepping aboard, he turned back to us. "Coming?" he asked, as though he were the one in charge.

Liam hopped down to the Zodiac and started the engine. The inflatable roared off.

I sent Maddy a text to ask about Oliver.

"No change," she sent back.

I returned to Maddy's cabin to wait for more news, but the stress of the day got to me, and I must have fallen asleep. I was immediately transported to the locked room on the wreck, in the time before it was a wreck. The raven-haired woman was seated in the same place, her wrists and ankles still bound to the chair with iron bands. The tattoos on her wrists glowed in the lantern light.

"See what you made me do?" she said, laughing, the sound like the crunch of broken glass under heavy boots. "It could have been worse. He could have died. And it will be worse unless you set me free. It'll be all your fault if he doesn't make it."

She was talking about what had happened to Oliver. I started shouting. "It's not my fault. It's not my fault…"

Newton's hand on my shoulder woke me up. "Of course, it's not your fault, whatever it was that you were dreaming about."

153

"Is Oliver okay?" I asked. "He isn't any worse, is he?"

"He's awake. Itchy, but otherwise, he's fine. The doc has him on steroids and she slathered him in cortisone creams. He'll be out in time for dinner, and he'll be able to dive tomorrow, as long as there aren't any jellies in the area. Liam's on his way back from bringing Lily and Cara to their own boats. We'll regroup here to figure out a new plan when he gets back."

I nodded. "It's a disaster. Alec knows about the rebreathers, the scooters, the decoy divers. The whole thing. By tomorrow, we'll be lucky if he isn't selling tickets to the inside of the wreck."

"Good. Since he knows, we can drop all the subterfuge. Don't worry. Everything will work out as it should." He sat beside me on the couch and put his arm across my shoulders so I could lean my head against it. "As long as we're together, all is right with the world."

But that's not the way the world works.

Chapter 27
A Witch

LIAM AND MADDY arrived at her cabin at the same time. I noticed Maddy had dark circles under her eyes, and I hoped my nightmares hadn't been keeping her awake. She sat beside me on the couch while Liam paced around the small space.

Newton seemed to be waiting for one of us to speak, and when we didn't act right away, he took control.

"Listen up, everybody. I figured out that Flowers Corporation is Cara's company. I haven't found out what its charter is yet, but I'll keep looking."

"And the reason we couldn't find any background on Noah Dylan is because, as we suspected, he doesn't exist. It looks like Stefan Gibb made him up, using the names of his three brothers. Noah. Dylan. Austin. I haven't confirmed that yet either, but it fits.

"He must've known we'd investigate the lease on the boat, and he thought the alias would throw us off. He obviously didn't expect us to ever meet his brothers, but as soon as I heard the names the pieces fell into place. What I don't understand is what he's doing here. He hasn't tried to interfere with the diving or the filming. What could his motive be?"

I thought for a few seconds. "Pirates don't usually find treasure on their own. They take it from its rightful owners. He may be waiting until he knows we have the treasure in hand before making his move."

"But he must realize that we know who he is. What's to stop us from turning him in to the police if he does take the treasure?" asked Oliver.

"It could only be one of two things. He'll take the treasure in international waters, or he won't leave anyone alive to report the theft," Liam said. "Probably both. We'll have to keep a close eye on him once we start bringing the treasure up. And on the way back to port."

Newton tapped his lip with a pencil. "This development changes everything. Divers, you should get back in the water as soon as you can. This afternoon for sure. Now that Alec and the pirates know we're not anchored over the treasure, they'll start a search of their own to home in on the wreck's location. If we don't get there first, they could snatch the treasure right out from under us."

Maddy yawned. "I don't think I'm up for a dive this afternoon. I'm exhausted. I didn't sleep well last night, and we've been working hard the last few days."

"Me too," said Liam. "And look at Fin. She falls asleep within a minute whenever she sits down. We all need a rest. And taking a day off will give Oliver a chance to recover. He's worked as hard as any of us. He deserves to be with us when we first see the treasure."

Newton slammed his fist into his palm. "There's no time to waste. Do you want to throw away all your work only to find the treasure gone when you guys get around to diving again?"

"Look," I said, trying to keep a reasonable tone in my voice. "We've been going a mile a minute trying to get to the treasure before Alec or the pirates found it, but there's no evidence they've gotten anywhere near the wreck site. We haven't even seen them dive, except at The Great Blue Hole and that one dive with Oliver. Since Alex saw the scooters, the only thing they know for sure is that the treasure's not directly under the *Omega* or even within easy dive distance. We're not going to be able to fool them anymore. If they want to, they'll find ways to follow us. Here's what I suggest."

"We all need a break, so let's take the afternoon and evening off. We'll take all the boats over to anchor above the wreck. We'll do a couple of easy, shallow dives, just for show.

I paused for a breath, "After the dives, we should have a cookout on deck. Make it a very visible and lively party, so they'll think we're celebrating because we already recovered the treasure. After that, we can keep diving the wreck as long as we want. They won't suspect a thing, or if they do, they may not realize we're anchored right over the treasure because we've been so careful not to anchor directly in its vicinity before this."

Liam nodded. "Good plan. It'll make the dives easier too, if we can go straight down to the wreck without the scooter ride."

Maddy looked thoughtful. "We should still use the rebreathers though, so they won't see any bubbles to show we're staying right under the *Omega*."

The three of us were quiet, not looking at each other and not smiling, even though we had all agreed to figure out a new plan.

Realization dawned. "You guys saw her too, didn't you?" I said.

"Saw who?" Newton asked. "When?"

"In my dreams, every time I sleep. The witch from the wreck." I hung my head. "Sorrow, betrayal, death by drowning."

Newton made a scoffing noise, until Maddy and Liam both nodded.

"You're serious? You guys are scientists. Businesspeople. Well, Fin's an artist too, so maybe... But whatever—you can't believe in witches."

I was trying to decide if Newton had insulted me by catego-rizing me as an artist rather than a scientist or businessperson. I liked to think of myself as good at all three areas, so I almost missed it when Maddy spoke.

"Ray had those dreams when he came back from that last treasure hunt. At first it was every night, but later it tapered off to just an occasional dream. Sorrow. Betrayal. Death by drowning. He used to mutter those words in his sleep. I scoffed at him when he told me about the witch...just like you're doing to us now."

"I see her in my dreams too," confessed Liam. "It's one reason I don't want to dive right now."

Newton stared at us for a minute. "You're all nuts, and probably suffering from too much nitrogen in your brains. So fine. Let's take the rest of the day off. Let's have a party, and invite all the pirates, thieves, nutjobs, and crazed killers in the area. Whatever. We'll move the boats in the middle of the night and go from there." He threw his hands in the air and walked out.

Chapter 28
A Party

IT WAS GETTING on toward dinner time, and the scent of hot coals wafted through the air around the *Omega*. The cook was firing up the grills for a barbecue dinner, and the aroma of the tangy sauce made our stomachs growl. Oliver was out of the infirmary, and all five of us had been taking turns keeping a surreptitious watch on the nearby boats. It was my turn, and I was surprised when Alec dove in the water and swam to the *Tranquility*, where Stewie was alone.

A few minutes later, my SAT phone rang. It was Stewie.

"I've been invited to dinner on Alec's boat. I'll be heading out in a few minutes. Just wanted to let you know where I'll be in case you need me." He hung up before I could say anything.

"I don't like it," said Liam, crossing his arms. "They have something up their sleeves, I'm sure of it."

"I agree," Newton put a hand to his chin and rubbed his silvery stubble. "Maybe we should invite them all to the *Omega*."

Three voices shouted "NO" in unison. Oliver's was the lone dissenting vote. "Good idea," he said. "Maybe we can find out what they're up to. One of us can stay with them all the time, and we can send them home early so it's not too much of a pain."

I didn't relish the thought of my sneaky ex hanging around but having him where we could keep an eye on him seemed better than having him, Lily, Stewie, Stefan, and the other pirates hatching a plan that we'd have no way of knowing about. And even though we'd tried to keep him isolated, who knew what details Stewie might inadvertently reveal. I nodded. "Okay."

Maddy and Liam nodded too.

"I'll call Stewie and pass on the invitation," Newton said.

A few minutes later, Lauren left in the Zodiac to pick up our guests and the chef threw more lobsters and racks of ribs on the grill. The party would be starting soon.

Lily was the first to climb aboard the *Omega* when the Zodiac arrived, and I was struck again by how beautiful she is. She was dressed in a bright pink baby tee and cut off shorts and she wore several gold chains and pendants around her neck. Her long, dark brown hair was brushed to the side, and her lustrous brown eyes glowed in the rays from the setting sun.

Several of the younger male crewmembers perked up when Lily walked by on her way to say hello to my mother. At least, the ones who didn't know her perked up. It was easy to be taken in by her. Heaven knows I had been.

Maddy jumped like she'd been poked with a cattle prod when Lily neared her, but she was polite in front of the crew as Lily air kissed her on both cheeks. Cara Flores, Lily, and Oliver's mother, boarded next, and she too was striking. She looked chic in her short sundress and bare feet, with her glossy dark hair cut in a spiky pixie. She greeted my mother and Newton politely but didn't touch either of them. Both Cara and Lily ignored me.

Alec, Stewie, and the pirates came aboard in a crowd. Alec and Stewie both wore cargo shorts and a Hawaiian print shirt, but the effect was quite different. Alec looked pressed and elegant. Stewie looked like he'd fallen out of bed after a three-day bender. His clothes were stained and rumpled, and he hadn't shaved for at least a week.

His most recent betrayals must have been weighing on his mind. I was worried that the enforced alone time was getting to him, and he'd be tempted to fall off the wagon. Since there was no alcohol on the *Tranquility*, if he made it through tonight, he'd be safe from that until we returned to port. Still, it hurt me to see him falling apart like this again.

To be honest, I was surprised he'd had the nerve to face us tonight, and I wondered how much his role in the lethal chain of events leading to Ray's death contributed to his self-loathing. But then again, since his budding relationship with Lauren might be the only thing keeping him afloat, maybe he'd decided to come to the party for the chance to spend the evening with her.

The pirates, wearing their black tri-corner hats, clumped together in a group, standing apart from everyone. Because the entire crew knew he'd been fired after Ray's death, it must have been awkward for Stefan to be back aboard the *Omega*, but he seemed at ease with his companions.

Oliver watched them standing in line at the bar. "I'm going to go over and thank Noah for saving my life. If he hadn't thought fast and brought me here, I might be dead now."

"I'll thank him too," I said, walking across the deck beside him. "That'll fulfill my social obligation, and maybe I can learn something about their plans."

Noah stepped forward when Oliver and I approached. "I'm glad to see you're okay, Bro," he said. "I thought for sure you were a goner."

"I would've been if you hadn't gotten me here so fast. Some crazy allergic reaction. Thanks," Oliver said. "I guess I owe you my life. Can I get you a beer?"

I stood with Noah while Oliver went to the open bar. "I want to thank you for saving Oliver. He's like a brother to me, and I never want anything bad to happen to him."

Noah turned red. "No problem. He's a good guy. I'm glad he's okay." We stared over each other's shoulders for a moment. "You want to meet the other guys?" He walked over to the three pirates. "That's Austin with the earring and Dylan with the parrot tattoo. You know Stefan, right?

"Yes, I know Stefan. Nice to meet you, Dylan, and Austin. Are you enjoying the diving here? It's a beautiful ecosystem. A lot of the area is a designated marine park, so the scenery is stunning."

The two men shrugged. "It's alright," said Dylan. "We haven't been diving much."

I nodded. "Please help yourselves to some food before the lobster is all gone." I waved a hand toward the buffet line and all four of the pirates trotted off to fill their plates.

Vincent played a mix tape over the *Omega*'s loudspeakers, and the late afternoon was filled with the sounds of Jimmy Buffett, Bob Marley, and other vacationland favorites. Some of the crew began to dance, and Liam glided over. "Dinner first? Or dancing?"

"I have a better idea." I took his hand and we jumped down into the Zodiac. Liam pushed us away a few feet before starting the engine to keep the noise down, but the party was in full swing. It's possible nobody would have heard us even if we'd taken off in a helicopter. We putted slowly to the *Tranquility* and climbed aboard.

I went below to grab a sweatshirt, shuddering when I passed Stewie's bunk and saw the mess he'd left. Newton had been staying in my cabin, and as I'd expected, it was pristine. I pulled a sweatshirt from one of the built-in drawers beneath the bed and headed back to the deck, grabbing a couple of sodas and a package of cookies I'd kept hidden in the back of a tall cabinet on the way.

Liam and I sat on the bow, enjoying the last rays of the dying sun, and sharing stale cookies and stories from our lives.

"Tell me about your marriage to Alec," Liam said. "I don't really know the whole story—only that he hurt you."

I swallowed a bite of cookie. "I led a sheltered life, spending most of my childhood aboard the *Omega*. I went away to college, and senior year, I met Alec. I was too naïve to see that he was only with me because he knew who my parents are. He was looking for a career boost, and he thought they'd give him his big break as an underwater photographer at RIO."

"But they don't operate like that, and although Alec is a pretty good photographer, he's not a great one. Maddy and Ray wanted him to earn it on his own, the same way they made me earn it. So, Alec started commingling our work, making it hard to determine who had taken the photographs. He submitted some of my best stuff—including that shot of Maddy facing down the great white—as his work. When I called him on it, he publicly accused me of trying to steal his work. People believed him. My photography career had just started, and the accusations tanked it."

Liam's arms tightened around my shoulders. "What a jerk. I can't believe he got away with it."

I sighed. "He almost did, but Ray forced him to tell the truth. That's how I got this contract with *Your World*. Carl Duchette, the editor in chief, offered it to me because he'd believed Alec and he wanted to make it up to me."

"Duchette's lucky to have you," Liam said, planting a kiss on my forehead. "But we should be getting back before they miss us. And the cookies are all gone…" He rattled the empty bag before helping me to my feet. "Shall we?"

We got in the Zodiac and reluctantly headed back to the *Omega*. I piloted the boat this time. Liam got out to wait for me on the platform while I tied up. I heard him stumble and swear softly. He pulled a small flashlight from the pocket of his shorts and shone it near his feet. I heard him gasp "Fin, get the doctor. As fast as you can, but not fast enough to cause a panic."

"What's the matter?"

He held out a hand to help me onto to the transom. 'Don't look. Just go. And fast."

I returned a few minutes later with Doc.

Liam held out a hand to each of us as we came down the steps. "Careful. It's kind of a mess."

As he spoke, I caught the stench of vomit on the air. I'd been moving so fast I hadn't noticed it when I left. "Were you sick?" I asked.

"Not me. Him." He shone a small flashlight toward the edge of the platform, where one of the younger pirates lay on his side in a pool of vomit. "I rolled him on his side in case he vomited again. I didn't want him to choke."

"His name is Dylan," I said, recognizing the parrot tattoo.

Doc was already at work, rolling Dylan over so she could examine him. She listened to his heart and breathing and checked his pupils. She opened her medical bag and pulled out some gloves and a vial of NARCAN®. She inserted the can's nozzle in Dylan's nostril and pressed the plunger.

He gasped and drew in a single ragged breath but was otherwise still. Doc looked at her watch. "Liam, will you bring the medical team please. With the gurney." Liam took the steps two at a time. I picked up Dylan's hand and squeezed. "C'mon, Dylan. You can do this."

Doc started giving CPR. When two minutes had passed without a breath, she gave him another dose of NARCAN®. The EMTs arrived and rolled him onto a board to carry him to the gurney. Once he was strapped in place, the whole crew took off at a trot toward sick bay.

I picked up the empty vials and wrappers. "Drugs?"

"Looks that way," Liam said. "The question is, did he bring them with him or get them on board?"

We found Maddy and told her what had happened to Dylan. She was upset, naturally enough. RIO had never had a drug problem before. We walked down to sick bay to check on Dylan. He was sitting up when we arrived.

"What did you take?" Maddy asked him when we arrived at his bedside.

"Nothing. I swear it. I don't do drugs. I'm into healthy living."

"Sure," said Maddy. "So how did you get drugged? Are you saying you think somebody slipped something into your food or drink?"

He looked confused. "I guess so. Maybe. That must be what happened. I told you I'm into healthy living. But I don't understand. Why would anyone want to drug me?"

Maddy turned to Liam. "Please let Vincent know it's time to shut the party down. And will you please take all the outsiders back to their own boats? I don't want Oliver alone with whomever brought those drugs aboard. I'll find out from Doc when Dylan can safely leave the infirmary and let you know."

She left in search of Doc while Liam took off to find Vincent. I went up on deck to look for Newton, but I didn't see him anywhere. I was surprised to see Cara chatting with Stewie and Lauren, and I was shocked to see Stewie take a sip from the can of beer in his hand. I'd address that issue later. Right now, I needed to find Newton and Oliver.

As I passed by the film lab, I saw a light on inside. Nobody should have been in there, so I went inside to see who it could be.

Alec was seated at the table, working with the lab's computer. He was clicking through the images we had taken on the wreck dives, displaying them on a nearby light box. I noticed he had a USB drive plugged into the computer, and he was downloading some of the best shots.

I flicked on the light switch. "What do you think you're doing?"

He hadn't heard me approach and the sudden burst of light and my loud voice startled him.

He recovered quickly. "Oh, hey. These shots are great. Beautiful work. You've really improved in the last year."

"You mean since the last time you took credit for my work? Yes, I've gotten better. I've worked hard at it. But I see you're still looking for shortcuts."

Alec stood and tried to block my view as he pulled out the USB drive and slipped it into his pocket. "I don't think I've had a chance to congratulate you on the *Your World* gig. That one spread can make your career if you do a good job on it." He started edging toward the door.

I stepped in front of him. "I know. And I'll take that USB drive, Alec. No way am I letting you steal my work again. I'm sure you understand, since you've just told me how important it will be to my career." I held out my hand.

Alec's face turned red, and he bit his lip. I remembered some of the rages he had thrown after Ray made him tell the truth about stealing my photos, and I wished we weren't alone, so far from the lights and people at the party. But I stood up straight and looked him in the eye, trying not to show fear.

After a moment, Alec dropped the drive into my outstretched hand. Then he walked past me, out the door and presumably, back to Lily and the party.

As soon as he was out of sight, I sagged into the chair he'd vacated and took a few deep breaths until I calmed down. I changed the computer's logon password and shut everything down. Then I put the drive Alec had used in my pocket and left the film lab to resume my search for Newton and Oliver. I didn't see them anywhere, so I headed back down to Maddy's cabin to see if she'd returned.

Newton and Oliver were sitting on her couch, sipping lemonade, munching popcorn, and putting together a jigsaw puzzle. They were laughing when I came through the door, and I bit back a stab of jealousy. Newton had never taken the time to play games or do puzzles with me. He hadn't even bothered to see me for more than twenty years.

I shook off the jealousy. Oliver needed a father figure even more than I did. At least growing up I'd had Ray, while Oliver never had anyone at all. Newton was trying hard to make up for neglecting me all those years, and we were making progress in our relationship. And he was kind to Oliver. That's what mattered.

"Hey, glad you're here. We could use your help." Newton held out a hand for me to join him on the couch. I glanced down at the puzzle they were working on. It was an underwater scene, with angelfish, parrotfish, a nearly invisible trumpet fish hiding vertically in the coral, a starfish, and a small blue crab. A stingray floated in the water above them, looking like a UFO in the sky. I laughed. "Haven't you seen enough underwater landscapes on this trip, Oliver?"

He grinned back and handed me the bowl of popcorn. "Not yet."

We munched popcorn and plugged an occasional piece into the puzzle, but it was clear nobody was trying very hard. I knew I had to tell Oliver what had happened to his friend Dylan, but I didn't want to ruin the cozy vibe we were enjoying. Soon enough, the popcorn bowl was empty. Newton rose to put it on the table near the door to remind him to take it back to the kitchen when he left. I thought now was as good a time as any.

"Oliver, I'm sorry I didn't tell you right away, but you were having such a nice time I didn't want to ruin it. But now I can't put it off any longer. Your friend Dylan is in sickbay. Drug overdose. I'm not sure how long he'll have to stay, but doc says he'll be ok."

He looked at me, clearly puzzled. "Dylan doesn't do drugs. He's all about health and living holistically. There must be some mistake."

"Maybe," I said. "Doc seemed pretty sure an overdose was the problem, but you can talk with him about it in the morning. I think she wants him to stay overnight."

"I'll go now," he said, rising.

"Not a good idea." Newton stood too. "Let's get back to the boats. I'm sure Liam is beat by now too, and you guys have an early dive scheduled for the morning."

When we walked up to the main deck, Liam was just returning from dropping off Cara and the pirates. Stewie, Alec, and Lily were the only outsiders still aboard *Omega*. Stewie was sitting on the floor with his back against a life preserver, fast asleep with his beer can still clutched in his hand. Lauren was nowhere around.

Alec and Lily were sharing a set of earphones and slow dancing to whatever song they were listening to, since Vincent had turned off the music long ago.

Liam joined us near the doors to the crew quarters. "I'm going to make the last trip to get everyone back on the boats where they belong. Then I think we should all turn in. We've had a few rough days, and we've got an early morning ahead of us."

"What about Dylan?" I said. "He needs to stay in sickbay." We had forgotten about the young pirate. "Can we just steal off in the middle of the night with him still aboard? What will his friends think when they wake up and see that the *Omega* is gone?"

Newton paced for a few steps, his hand on his chin, thinking it through. "Since you guys will be busy, I'll stay in sickbay with him and get him to send his brothers a text as soon as he wakes up, so they don't worry. If he wants to rejoin his friends, Vincent can have Lauren bring him over as soon as the doc gives the ok. But I think he should stay here with us where it's safe. It must have been one of that group who gave him the drugs, and he may not appreciate that. Whoever did it nearly killed him."

"Thanks, Newton,' I said. "I'd have stayed with him, but I need to spend the night on the *Tranquility* if we're moving the boats in the middle of the night. And Liam, you or Maddy need to be on the *Sea Princess*. Stewie can stay here on the *Omega* to sleep it off, and we'll sort him out in the morning. Everybody set? Know where you're sleeping, and what the plan is?"

Everybody nodded, so we took off to our assigned locations for a short night's rest.

Chapter 29
Treasure

THE SUN HADN'T EVEN THOUGHT about rising when my alarm went off the next day. I splashed some cold water on my face and brewed a pot of coffee, then sat down to listen for sounds of the *Omega* preparing for departure. As soon as I heard the clank of the anchor being drawn up, I untethered the *Tranquility* from her mooring. Liam was doing the same thing on the *Sea Princess*, and we waved and smiled at each other.

I climbed up on the flying bridge, started my engines and pulled away at a slow pace to minimize both engine noise and any wake I might create. I fell in beside the *Omega*, and we all took off for the wreck site.

I had no sooner anchored the *Tranquility* when I heard Lauren coming for me with the Zodiac. I hopped into the small boat alongside Liam, and we zipped back to the *Omega*'s dive platform.

Maddy and Oliver had already set out our tanks and gear, so it was a quick task for us to prep for the dive. All four of us were in the water within a few minutes, and the sun still wasn't fully up. Since it was still night in the undersea world, we carried powerful underwater flashlights so we could see where we were going as we descended along *Omega's* anchor line.

Vincent couldn't have put us closer to the wreck unless he'd actually dropped the anchor right through her, so we didn't have a long swim. Liam and Maddy went in first, carefully holding the guide ropes with one hand and their underwater flashlights with the other. Oliver and I went in next, and I could see he had learned his lesson about careful diving in an overhead environment. He kept one hand on a rope, kept his fins pointed up, and barely wiggled his toes for propulsion. I drew a star on my slate and showed it to him. Behind his mask, his deep brown eyes glowed with pleasure.

We swam down the stairway to the captain's quarters, and I hovered behind Maddy and Liam, filming them as they worked together to open the locked door.

People think it's silent underwater, but sound carries well. In fact, sound travels 4.4 times faster underwater than it does in air, which makes it hard for humans to perceive the direction of the noise. But there was no mistaking the direction of the loud crash when Liam pulled the locked door open.

Liam and Maddy were poised in the entry, their eyes wide. They both moved aside when Oliver and I approached so we could see the inside of the room. My training kicked in, so despite my excitement and curiosity, I kept the camera rolling even as my mind stuck on one scary fact.

The room I was seeing looked exactly like the room in my dream, except it was covered with about a hundred years of coral growth. The chair in the middle of the room was the same, and a skeleton remained shackled to it by iron bands on its wrists and ankles. The bones of the spine and lower legs had succumbed to gravity, and the skull, still wearing the tiara, had toppled into the body's lap.

The skull's forehead was encircled by the gorgeous, jeweled tiara, its gold diadem crusted with sapphires. Each point of the tiara was tipped with a diamond, and the metal was covered all over with rubies and sapphires. An immense diamond filled the tiara's center point, and it was surrounded by smaller gems, each of which would have been spectacular enough on its own.

The skeleton wore several jeweled rings on each of her bony fingers, and a massive emerald bracelet adorned one wrist. The other bore an equally fabulous bracelet of sapphires. The overall effect was eerie but magnificent.

Even more stunning was how similar everything was to my dream, right down to the design of the tiara. I wondered if I'd ever seen a picture of it in the past. Maybe Ray had shown it to me, although if he had, I'd long forgotten the occasion.

Liam and Maddy pulled back further so I could film the rest of the room before we went inside to search for more treasure. I did a slow pan, taking in every corner, the entire floor, and the ceiling. Then I swam in and did closeup shots of the chair, the skeleton, the loose bones, the rings and bracelets, and the crown on the skull. The iron shackles also got the closeup treatment.

The whole time I was filming, my outward demeanor was calm. I forced myself to focus on the task at hand, the way a pro should, even though inside my head I was screaming to myself "Get out of here before it's too late."

I needed to capture all these details to fulfill my contract. I knew it wasn't real, but a voice in my head kept repeating, "Set me free and you can have anything you want." It took all my willpower to resist. I turned to see that Liam and Maddy had withdrawn up the stairs to the main cabin, pulling Oliver along with them.

Maddy pointed at her air pressure gauge, and I nodded. It was time to surface. I shut off my strobe light and swam after them, relieved to be heading back to fresh air and sunlight on the surface.

Once back on board the *Omega*, we had a quick snack and some water. I changed over the batteries in my camera and strobe to fully charged ones. Liam and Maddy attached catch bags to their BCDs for the treasure they would collect on the next dive.

Oliver, wide-eyed, sat quietly to one side. I hoped his mind wasn't troubled by thoughts of the skeleton below the way mine was.

We cut our surface interval to forty-five minutes. It was still within the bounds of the dive algorithm our dive computers used to monitor our bottom time, but it didn't include the safety margin we usually liked. Given the need to retrieve the treasure before the pirates made their move, we felt the risk was worth it. The sun had just fully crested the horizon when we began our second dive of the day.

We went right to the room I thought of as the cell, and Liam, Oliver, Maddy and I each took a separate quadrant of the room to examine the detritus and junk on the floor to see if there were any salvageable relics.

My segment was the left rear side of the room, so I had my back to the skeleton. I felt the hairs on the back of my neck stand up when I turned my back to the gruesome sight. I started by scanning the walls to see if any valuable artifacts might be hanging on them. The ceilings were low, and the room was small, so this step didn't take long. Then I started a detailed search of the floor. Rather than swim around randomly seeking treasure, I set up a mental grid of small overlapping strips of the area that I would search in order to make sure I didn't miss any areas. I hovered mere inches above the floor and examined every crevice and cranny. The floor was encrusted with coral and silt, so it was possible that the growth could hide small treasures if we weren't careful.

I used my dive knife to scrape away the coral from any likely-looking mounds or unusual shaped growth patterns I came across. On my third try, I found a gold doubloon. It was dirty and crusted, but it looked like a perfect match for the one Ray had given Maddy on their wedding day. I put it in the pocket of my BCD.

A few sections further on, I found another doubloon, and then a third. I was about half done with my segment when I heard a metallic clicking sound. Oliver was tapping on his tank with the edge of his knife to get our attention. He pointed at his pressure gauge, and I nodded. Each of us left a marker on the area we were examining and swam out of the room. I used one of the doubloons as my marker.

The sense of relief I felt when I exited the wreck was like an elephant had just removed his foot from my chest, and I took a slow deep breath to steady myself. From the volume of bubbles around us, it looked like we'd all had the same response. We slowly ascended along the *Omega*'s anchor line, did our safety stop, and then climbed aboard.

Because we'd cut our surface interval to the bare minimum after our first dive, we decided to take some extra time before we went back below. None of us had eaten much today, so we went to the galley for breakfast.

Newton and Dylan were sitting at a corner table. We waved at them as we walked by but didn't stop. After we'd loaded up our trays with food, we found our own table and sat down to eat. A few minutes later, Newton and Dylan stopped at our table.

"I wanted to thank you for saving my life yesterday," Dylan said. "I don't know what happened, but I swear to you I don't do drugs."

Oliver took a sip of his juice. "I believe you."

Dylan seemed stunned. "You do?"

As Oliver nodded, Newton said "And I already told you I believe you. Trust us. We'll find out who did this to you." Newton placed a comforting hand on Dylan's shoulder, and I had to tamp down another wave of jealousy. My father was so caring to everyone else, but he hadn't bothered to see me or even call me for more than twenty years. I wondered what I could have done to drive him away. Even though he and Maddy had told me the story behind why he never came to see me when I was a child, it still felt like our long estrangement was somehow my fault.

"Is Doc letting you go back to join your friends today?" I asked. "Do you need a ride?" I realized as I said it that it sounded like I was trying to push Dylan out, so I added, "Although you're welcome to stay as long as you want."

I saw Liam's lips twitch as he tried to hide his smile. He knew how much trouble I had trying to keep my feelings about Newton straight, and he could tell I was wrestling with the jealousy dragon.

Maddy chimed in. "Someone will take you back whenever you want, but please feel free to stay with us for at least another day. We don't want to jeopardize your health, and we have plenty of room."

Dylan nodded, pleased by her warm invitation. "Thanks. I think I will stick around another day. This place is pretty interesting. But right now, I have to get back to sick bay. Doc told me she needs to check my vitals every half hour." He grinned and walked away.

"I never saw anyone so pleased to have their vitals checked," said Maddy.

"I don't think he gets a lot of attention from his family in real life," Newton said. "But he seems like a good kid."

Liam squeezed my hand under the table.

We finished our breakfasts and went back on deck to prepare for another dive, but before we could get too far, we heard boats approaching. Alec, Cara, and the pirates were coming.

Chapter 30
Alec

THE THREE BOATS anchored in a line, about a mile away from us, with the pirate ship closest, then Alec's catamaran, and then Cara's cabin cruiser. The pirates wasted no time in hoisting the Jolly Roger again once their ship was secure.

Alec stood on the catamaran, his arm around Lily's shoulder, staring across the water at us. We decided to postpone our dive until the visitors were more settled and we were under less scrutiny. It was still early—not even ten in the morning yet.

We had no sooner agreed to hold off on our next dive when Alec dove into the water and began swimming toward the *Omega*. "Great," I groaned. "Just what we need. More Alec." I quickly filled the team in on how I had discovered Alec in the film lab. "I don't think he'd gotten to the treasure pictures yet, but he certainly saw the wreck."

"I knew we should never have let him aboard," said Liam.

Newton nodded. "I agree. It was a bad idea. Sorry."

We watched Alec's approach. He was an exceptional swimmer, and he swam the mile from his boat to the *Omega*'s transom quickly. Nobody offered him a hand when he climbed aboard, but

Stewie rushed forward with a warm towel, causing me to grind my teeth in annoyance. Even if he had no personal loyalty to Maddy or RIO, Stewie didn't seem to realize we paid his salary.

"Need anything else, Alec? Some water? A snack?" Stewie said.

"Nope. All good. I want to talk to Fin for a minute though."

Liam stood. "You can talk to me if it's about RIO or the photo montage. I'm in charge of the budgets for both, and I can guarantee you we have no funds for a washed up...I mean, additional... underwater photographer."

Alec's jaw tightened. "I said I wanted to talk to Fin. I never mentioned money or wanting a job, so butt out." He jerked his thumb over his shoulder toward the deck. "Can we go somewhere private?"

I stood up as tall as I could and glared at Alec. "Nope. You can say what you have to say right here, right now, in front of these people."

"Okay," he said. "You should know you have a drug problem on the *Omega*, which means it's someone on the RIO staff distributing them."

Maddy sucked in a breath as though she'd been punched. RIO was her life's work, and it would kill her to think someone on the team would betray her like that.

I patted her back for reassurance and looked Alec in the eye. "Funny. We suspected you were the source."

Alec's face reddened. "I don't do drugs. After all we've been through together, you should know that."

"Obviously, I didn't know the real you at all, or I never would have married you." He was still standing, and I looked up at his angry face. "Where are you getting your information anyway?"

"I can't tell you that," he said.

"Can't or won't?" Liam said.

"I'm not talking to you. I came here because I care about Fin and Maddy. Do whatever you want with the information. I've said all I'm going to say." He walked to the transom and dove in.

Chapter 31
Hurricane at Sea

THE DAY HAD dawned sunny and bright, but while we waited out the rest of our surface interval after Alec's departure, huge piles of angry storm clouds rolled in, obliterating the blue skies and brilliant sunshine. The wind picked up, and the gaily colored pennants we had hung on the boats all stood out stiffly in the gusting air. The pirates' Jolly Roger was flying taut on the mast where it hung, contrasting with the usual slow dance it performed in the playful ocean breeze. The typically gentle Caribbean waves grew large, and the ocean water turned a dark impenetrable blue.

Vincent came by to talk to Maddy about storm preparations, and the two of them walked off together to make plans. Liam called after her "I'll take care of the *Sea Princess* for you."

She flashed him a smile of thanks.

"It looks like it's going to get bad. I need to check out the *Tranquility*. Will you drop me in the Zodiac?"

"I'll do it," Oliver said. "Then I'll bring it back here and tether it where it'll be safe."

"I'll go with you, Fin. I can help you batten down the hatches.

Or whatever." Newton grinned at me. My father was not a true seafaring man, but he was trying hard.

The first raindrops were plinking into the ocean as we dropped Liam at the Sea Princess, and Oliver scooted quickly to drop me at the *Tranquility*. The waves were growing wilder, threatening to wash us off the Zodiac. "Stay here and ride out the storm with me," I said to them.

"Thanks," Newton said climbing aboard. I could feel his relief at not having to make the storm-tossed ride back to the *Omega*.

I helped Oliver tie the Zodiac to the *Tranquility*'s stern, and we let out a long lead so she could be free during the storm. Meanwhile, the rain had become a torrent, so heavy and thick it was like someone had dumped a bucket of water on my head. I couldn't see anything beyond the falling water, so Oliver and I went below to check if I had enough foul weather gear for the three of us. While we were down there, Oliver decided to use the head.

I came up from the lower level to see Newton standing on the deck, getting drenched. His hands were in the pockets of his shorts, and he was staring transfixed at the angry ocean, oblivious to the rain. "Newton, get below! You never know…"

A huge wave washed across the *Tranquility*'s stern. When it ebbed, the deck was empty. Newton was nowhere to be seen. In that moment, I realized how much I loved my father, and I despaired. *I'll never find him in this storm. He can't swim in this.*

I screamed for help, knowing no one could hear me. I dropped the rain gear I'd been holding and raced up to the main deck. I searched the water's surface for any sign of my father, but I saw nothing.

Liam's back was turned as he tended to the *Sea Princess*, and the roar of the storm was too loud for him to hear my shouting. If I was going to try to save Newton, I'd have to do it alone. And I was determined to save him or die trying.

I grabbed a line from the storage locker and tied it around my waist and wrapped the other end around one of the cleats built into the gunwale. I draped a life ring over my arm and dove into the water, which had somehow turned icy cold in the sudden storm.

Newton had been swept off on the side of the boat away from Liam and the *Sea Princess*. Even if Liam turned this way, once I'd jumped in, he wouldn't see anything amiss. The hull of the *Tranquility* was between us, blocking his view. Oliver hadn't come on deck, so he'd have no idea what had happened. It was me against the ocean, but I was determined not to lose my father again. I'd die myself before I'd let that happen.

"Newton," I screamed. "Where are you?" A rogue wave lifted me up just in time to see him going under again. I swam as hard as I could in his direction, but it was nearly impossible to make any headway in the rough seas.

My best bet was to swim underwater, because sometimes the water is calmer even a few feet below the surface. Although there was usually a wicked surge in a storm like this, you didn't get tossed around quite as much underwater as you would on the surface. I wished I'd been wearing my scuba gear when Newton washed overboard. It would have been so much easier to find him. Even just my mask or fins would have been a help, but it was too late now for regrets. There was no time to go back for them. I took a deep breath and dove, kicking with all my might. My open eyes stung from the salt water, but I barely dared to blink in case I missed him.

I was down at about ten feet when, out of the corner of my eye, I saw a flash of a light color amid the angry dark blue of the roiling water. I whipped my head around, thinking it might be a shark, but it was the seat of Newton's shorts. He was hanging limp and unmoving, still sinking, and letting the water toss him at will.

I kicked toward him with every ounce of strength in my legs. My lungs were ready to burst when at last I managed to grab his belt. I swam for the surface, but the higher I rose the more it seemed like the ocean was determined to push me down. I swallowed hard, willing myself not to breathe. I would not lose this battle.

But I was on the verge of losing consciousness myself. There were pulsing black spots in front of my eyes when at last my head broke the surface. I sucked in a huge breath and pulled Newton up so his head was above the water. Somewhere in the struggle I'd lost my grip on the life ring, so I slipped the knot in the rope around my waist to loosen it and pulled it over Newton's head and down his torso, so we were both inside the loop. I shifted him around me, so we were back-to-back, his head resting against mine. I pulled the knot tight and started swimming.

The roar of the wind made it impossible to hear anything, and the waves were so high they blocked my view of everything around me but water. I wasn't even sure I was swimming toward the boats, but I had to hold on. My father's life—and now my own —depended on it.

Another surge lifted me, and I caught a quick glimpse of the *Tranquility* dead ahead. I struck out with renewed hope, clawing my way through the churning water. It felt like forever before my fingers touched the edge of the boat's transom. I crawled aboard with my father's body still tied to my back. Staggering under his weight, I pulled myself forward into the relative serenity of *Tranquility*'s cabin.

I fell to my knees, gasping, but I didn't have time to rest. Newton wasn't moving. I turned him on his side, and a large quantity of sea water spilled out of his mouth. He wasn't breathing.

I flipped him to his back and began chest compressions. In my head, I let the old Bee Gees' song "Stayin' Alive" play on an endless loop. Not only is it a great hopeful theme for times like this, but it also has the perfect rhythm for chest compressions.

My eyes were streaming tears, stinging from the salt water, sorrow, and fear for my father. My arms burned from the hard swim and the exertion of the compressions. I knew I couldn't keep this up for long. Where was Oliver?

"C'mon, Newton. Don't leave me again. I need you," I whispered. "Please."

I felt a flicker under my hands. Newton turned his head and spewed out an astonishing volume of sea water. He gasped and took a deep breath, then tried to sit up.

"Stay there a minute," I said, rolling him onto his side. A sharp spasm brought forth more water, and when he finished, his color was no longer that sickly bluish green that struck terror into my heart. I helped him sit up, resting his back against the built-in daybed in the *Tranquility*'s cabin. I draped a blanket over his knees, then I sat down and shifted close to him, so my back was also to the daybed, my shoulder touching his.

Just as Newton leaned back, the door to the head opened and Oliver popped out and walked slowly up the stairs. He was sporting a large dark bruise on his forehead. "Thanks for checking up on me. I've been passed out on the floor in there while you guys are hanging around here all cozy."

"Yep. That's what we've been doing," I said. "What happened to you?"

"I must have fallen when one of those big waves hit. I just came to. I can't believe you didn't check on me before this. How long was I out?"

We both shrugged. "No idea. We've just been hanging around. Went for a swim. Newton decided he wanted to learn to swim, right dad?"

"Yes, it seemed like a good idea at the time."

Oliver looked incredulous. Hurt bloomed in his eyes.

Newton was quick to put the pain to rest. "I'm sorry we weren't paying attention and you were injured. It won't happen again."

Just then the boat gave a huge lurch and settled back down. The storm was over as abruptly as it had started. The sea melted back to its usual warm inviting color; the waves were no bigger than the length of my thumb; and the sun burst through the cloud cover. It was a gorgeous day in the tropics. And we were all safe.

I helped Oliver over to the gunwale where he sat on the bench, then I went back to help Newton to sit in one of the captain's chairs. No sooner were they settled than Liam emerged from the cabin of the *Sea Princess*. He was wiping a wrench on a rag, but he waved when he saw us looking safe and sound.

I saw Liam pick up his SAT phone a second before mine rang. "Just checking in on you. It was a wild time, huh? I was taking on water for a while, but it's all good now. You guys ok? Any problems?"

"We're good. I'll fill you in later. Right now, I'd like to get us all back on the *Omega*. Let's wrap up this treasure hunt and go home."

I spared a glance to our three stalker boats to make sure they were all okay. Alec waved when he saw me. It looked like the pirates were playing cards on their deck. There was no sign of life from Cara's boat, but that wasn't unusual. I didn't feel she was my responsibility anyway, so in the absence of any obvious sign of distress, I decided to call it good.

I made sure everything was ship shape on the *Tranquility*, then bundled Newton and Oliver into the Zodiac. I putted over to pick up Liam, and we sped to the safety of the *Omega*.

Vincent reached out to grab the line when we approached the *Omega*'s transom and tied us off to an open cleat. I'd never been so happy to be on the stable surface of *Omega*.

Maddy gathered us all into a group hug as soon as our feet touched the deck. "I was worried sick. That storm came out of nowhere. No warning whatsoever from the weather service. You could have been killed."

"You don't know the half of it," I said.

She stepped back and for the first time noticed Newton's pallor and soaking wet clothes and the dark lump on Oliver's forehead. "What happened?"

"Dad decided to let me give him swimming lessons as soon as we get home," I said. "And Oliver is taking up yoga to improve his balance. It's all good. Nothing to worry about."

Chapter 32
Death by Drowning

LATER THAT DAY, Liam and I were leaning against the *Omega*'s gunwales. He had gray circles under his eyes and his usual cheerful energy was obviously depleted. I too was exhausted. The last thing I wanted to do was dive again today, but I didn't want to spend another night with my dreams invaded by the woman wearing the tiara. "Let's go down there and bring everything back up. I have enough shots for the montage and plenty of video footage for that part of the documentary. I want to get it over with and go home."

"Me too," he said. "Let's not make a big deal of it. We can go alone. Maddy and Oliver are as beat as we are, so it'll be a good break for them. We'll grab the tiara and the bracelets and then we can get the heck out of here."

I nodded and rose wearily to my feet. I waved down a passing crewman to tell him we were diving. "You don't need to tell anyone we're going, but if we're not back in ninety minutes, let Maddy know, ok?"

He nodded and walked away whistling a happy tune. Hearing him, I thought I'd never be that happy again.

Liam and I headed to the dive platform and put on our BCDs,

masks, and fins. We made our usual giant stride entries and descended. I'd been worried that the storm would have roiled the bottom, filling the water with sand and other particles that would ruin the visibility, but the water was clear. We had at least one hundred fifty feet of horizontal visibility all the way to the wreck.

As we peered into the opening, we were dismayed to see that the water inside the wreck was silty and dark. It would be close to impossible to see once we went in. It was a dangerous situation. I considered the risk and knew I would never recommend that anyone else do this dive under these conditions.

On the other hand, I wanted to get this whole expedition over with. I was trained to dive in dangerous situations. I had mapped the entire wreck, and I knew it well by now. There were guide ropes throughout the area that would lead me to the exit if I couldn't see. I could always keep one hand on the rope so I wouldn't get disoriented. I wanted to do it, but not at the cost of endangering Liam.

I looked at him, and I could see his eyes behind his mask. He looked serious, and I thought he'd probably just finished the same analysis I'd done. We nodded at each other and kicked slowly inside.

We made it through the main cabin in just a few kicks and headed down the low-ceilinged stairwell to the captain's quarters. If anything, the visibility here was worse. I swallowed and moved forward, toward the room with the woman's skeleton and the Queen's Tiara.

We made our way slowly toward the center of the room, where the skeletal remains sat on what I thought of as her throne. My left hand was raised above my head to clutch the guide rope, and my right hand extended in front of me to feel for obstacles. Although Ray had trained me to dive in zero visibility—even going so far as covering the lenses of my mask with black tape during training dives—I didn't like it. It was daunting. There was no question

184

about it—swimming forward into nothingness is about as menacing as it can get.

My hand touched the arm of the chair. Feeling ghoulish, I slipped an emerald ring off the finger bone and placed it in my bag. I reached for the jeweled bracelet that encircled her wrist. I was going to unclasp it for removal, but I realized that her wrist was free of the iron band that had held it to the chair for so many years. The bracelet was not there.

I assumed we had somehow knocked her hand loose during an earlier dive, and the storm had finished the job of setting her free. The bracelet must be on the floor. From an inch away—which was all the visibility we had—I signaled to Liam that I needed to let go of the rope. He held on to the lift strap on the back of my BCD as I searched the floor around the chair legs with both hands.

I touched something that wasn't coral. Soft. Fleshy, yielding. I recoiled and screamed into my regulator.

The sound of my scream had to be unnerving, but steadfast Liam never let go of me or the rope. I took a deep breath to steady myself and put my hand back down on whatever it was. I felt smoothness, like a dive skin, and then the rough canvas-like feel of a BCD. I swallowed fear.

This was a diver, or more specifically, the body of a diver, because there were no bubbles signaling that whoever it was had breathed recently. The body had not moved or flinched when I touched it, so I had to assume someone had died here.

I felt around until I found the diver's BCD lift strap and grasped it. I rose in the water. Once again, from an inch away, I signaled to Liam that we should leave. He lifted my free hand to the guide rope, and we began slowly making our way out of the wreck, with me towing a dead body behind me.

It felt like it took forever for us to get out of the wreck. Liam exited a fraction of a second before I did. He turned to me in case I needed help, but I swam out unaided. I was so happy to see the open water I could have cried. Only when I had fully emerged did Liam see that I was towing a body.

The body was that of a male, and the Queen's Tiara was firmly clamped to his head, even after the swim through the wreck. His mask was off, and his regulator floated freely in the gentle current. I rolled him over and recognized the parrot tattoo on his neck. It was Dylan, the pirate who had nearly suffered from the fatal overdose of Fentanyl.

Liam looked at me, and I saw my own sorrow reflected in his eyes. We had started out disliking the pirates and thinking they were trying to mess up my project. I still didn't like Stefan Gibb, and I'd probably never be able to forgive him for the part he'd played in Ray's death, even though the bulk of the blame lay elsewhere. But we'd come to know and like Dylan and his brothers Noah and Austin. They would be devastated by his death.

So would Oliver, for that matter.

Liam gently took one of Dylan's hands and I took the other. Together, we swam back to the *Omega*. We decided to forgo the usual three-minute safety stop at twenty feet. It seemed ghoulish to hover there, holding Dylan's lifeless body, while everybody on the *Omega* went on about their business, unknowing. We were at the ladder when Liam reached over and removed the crown from Dylan's head, putting it in his catch bag for safe keeping.

I surfaced first, and the crewman I'd tasked with notifying Maddy if we didn't return on time was pacing across the dive platform, looking at his watch with a frown.

"We're back," I said. "Thank you for taking my request so seriously. Would you please do one more thing for me? Would you tell Maddy and Doc that I need to see them here as soon as possible? Thank you."

The young man saluted, which would have made me laugh under any other circumstances. Right now, I didn't feel like laughing.

The doctor was the first to arrive. "Not more jellies?" she said.

"Worse. We found a body."

She nodded. "This voyage has been cursed. Who is it?"

"Dylan," I said. I saw the glisten of tears in her eyes before she turned away.

"Where is he?"

"Liam has him. They're on the ladder."

"I'll send for the gurney." She pulled out her radio and alerted her team.

The medical team with the gurney arrived quickly. Maddy and Newton were just behind them, running as fast as they could. Apparently, no one had told them there was no need for haste.

They were so relieved when they saw me alive and well that they wrapped me in a group hug. By now, the medical team had pulled Dylan's body out of the water and strapped it to the gurney. They covered him with a sheet and rolled away at a stately pace.

Liam climbed up the ladder and put his gear away. He walked over to join us, but stood a little to one side, probably not wanting to intrude on what looked like a private family moment. Maddy saw him, and to my surprise, she reached over and drew him into the family hug. Newton stepped over to make room for him. A few minutes later, Oliver joined us, tears running down his cheeks.

"I have to tell his brothers," I said at last.

"I'll do it," Oliver said. "I know them best."

"You sure, mate?" Liam said. "It's not an easy thing to do."

Oliver squared his shoulders. "I'm sure." He walked over to untie the Zodiac. "Might as well do it now."

Maddy and I each raised an eyebrow when Newton silently climbed into the Zodiac with Oliver. They nodded at each other, then sped away.

They were gone for nearly an hour. On their return, Oliver walked by us without a word, his head down. I reached out to touch his shoulder as he passed, but he shrugged me off and kept walking toward the crew quarters.

"I'd like to be alone tonight," said Maddy. "I'm going to bed early."

I nodded. "I can sleep on the *Tranquility*, since Stewie's staying here with Lauren now."

I packed up the Queen's Tiara, her emerald bracelet, the rings, and the doubloons I had found during the grid search, and asked Vincent to let me keep them in the ship's safe overnight. When I had everything safely stowed, I returned to the deck to rejoin Liam and my father.

None of us felt like eating, and we weren't up for conversation, so the three of us silently climbed into the Zodiac. Liam dropped me at the *Tranquility*, and he and Newton putted back to the *Sea Princess*.

Even though it was still early, I went to bed. Exhausted but unable to sleep, I tossed and turned. When I finally did sleep, I dreamed of the woman in the wreck.

She was indignant. "Don't make me hurt you too. I just want what's mine. Bring back my crown and my bracelet. You've seen what I can do. I don't want to hurt anyone else. And I want you to set me free. If you don't do as I command, you'll really see what I can do."

"No." I said over and over as I tossed and turned. "Please don't hurt anyone."

I awoke before dawn, feeling like I'd spent the night in a boxing match. I looked it too, with big dark circles around my eyes and my hair sticking straight up in unruly tufts. I took a quick shower and went on deck to start my day.

Since it was so early, I was surprised to see Liam and Newton on the deck of the *Sea Princess*, sipping coffee. They waved when they saw me. Newton filled an extra mug with coffee while Liam untied the Zodiac. Then they headed over to get me.

Newton looked like his usual self—he was a handsome, distinguished silver fox who'd been named *Human Magazine*'s Most Eligible Bachelor for eight years running. Liam looked like me—

ragged and disheveled, with black circles around his eyes and a gray pallor to his skin. Most of the time he was a glowing advertisement for the benefits of healthy living, so I was surprised to see him this way. I raised my eyebrows when I saw him, but he turned away without saying anything.

Newton handed me the RIO-branded stainless-steel mug of hot coffee, and I took a sip through the hole in the plastic lid, relishing the warmth and the hit of caffeine. I nodded my thanks. Liam steered the Zodiac toward the *Omega*, and our day was off to its start.

We grabbed a corner table in the galley for breakfast. We'd just begun eating when Oliver slid his tray onto the table and sat down with a grunt. "Man, I'm so beat."

He looked as bad as Liam and I did, his eyes sunken and hollow and skin so pale he could have been a corpse. Maddy joined us a minute later and sat next to Newton. Normally, she looked much younger than she was, with clear glowing skin and bright shiny eyes. Most days, she moved with boundless energy, but today, she looked drained and worn out. I had never seen her look her age before. It was frightening, and the contrast was even more pronounced next to Newton, the only one of us who didn't look like a Halloween version of himself this morning.

I realized that the four people at the table who looked like death warmed over were the people who had been diving on the wreck. I wondered if there was something sinister at play or had we simply been driving ourselves too hard.

Chapter 33
Stefan

THE DIVE TEAM was standing on the *Omega*'s rear transom, getting ready to go back to the wreck to collect the remainder of the treasure. None of us were hurrying into our gear, and we kept stopping and staring off into space. Newton watched us for a few minutes before speaking up.

"I don't think you guys should dive today. Your hearts aren't in it. I'm not a diver, but I know enough to recognize that's a recipe for disaster. It's just too soon after Dylan's death. Why don't we all take the day off. We can watch old movies or play cards. I bet we could even go to the mainland and tour some of the old Mayan ruins. What do you say?"

"I wouldn't mind taking the day off from diving." I was amazed to hear myself saying those words, because I rarely ever wanted to sit out a dive opportunity. "I can take pictures of the ruins to add some variety to the *Your World* montage. If Carl doesn't want them, I can always use them later."

"I'll go too. I could use a good hike," said Liam.

"Me too," said Maddy. "I've never felt so worn out. A change will do us all good."

"It's settled then. The only question is do we take the *Sea Princess* or the *Tranquility*?" Newton asked.

"Let's take the *Tranquility*. I don't feel like being captain today," Maddy said.

"It's a deal," I said. "Liam, Oliver, and I can take turns piloting her."

"If it's ok with you, I'd rather stay here today. I'm not feeling very sociable, and I want to try to get some sleep," Oliver said. "You guys go. Have fun."

Oliver's refusal to join us worried me. He was a sociable guy, and he loved being included as part of our family for outings and events—possibly because his actual family was so dysfunctional. On the other hand, if he felt half as beat as I did, I could understand wanting to stay behind to sleep and take a day to himself.

"You sure, Oliver? We can all stay here and go together another day if you want."

Everybody nodded their agreement. We loved Oliver and didn't want to leave him behind if all he needed was a long nap.

"Thanks, but I don't want to spoil your fun. You guys go without me. I'll be fine."

"You know," Maddy said, "I could use a nap too. I think I'll stay behind as well."

The two of them got up and walked away.

"Then I think we should wait for another time when we can all go together," Newton said. "I have work to do anyway. Will you drop me on the *Sea Princess* when you leave, please? It has more workspace than the *Tranquility* does." He stuck his hands in the pockets of his shorts and walked off whistling.

Liam and I looked at each other. I'm sure we were each thinking the same thing.

"Let's take an easy day," I said. "No diving, no hikes, no touristy tours. Maybe a picnic? Just the two of us?"

"Perfect," he said. "Let's get the cook to make us a lunch." He stood up and held his hand out to me.

Fifteen minutes later, we were ready to go, with a lunch lavish enough to feed a small army. We thanked the chef, then stowed the basket on the Zodiac. I texted Newton, and he strolled up a minute later and jumped in the small boat. We dropped him off, then continued to the *Tranquility*.

We climbed up to the flying bridge and I started the engine. We chugged slowly away, careful not to create a wake that would disturb the nearby boats. Once we were well away, I gunned it.

It was exhilarating to feel the sun on my shoulders and the wind in my hair. I loved the underwater world, but since we'd found the wreck, I'd felt claustrophobic and uneasy while diving. The feeling grew more and more intense with each subsequent dive, and I was happy to take a day off from diving to be with Liam.

We didn't have a specific destination in mind, but the area was full of tiny islets and temporary sand bars, so we just cruised along until we found a likely spot. I held the boat steady while Liam jumped in and dragged the anchor close to a tiny sand bar, just big enough for the two of us.

The sand bar wasn't on any map, and I knew it would be gone with the tide, but it felt right to stop here and decompress. Liam too seemed to feel an easing of the malaise that had plagued him this morning. His color was already better and although the circles around his eyes were still intense, there was a spring in his step.

He spread a blanket on the sand, and I put the picnic basket on one corner to keep it from blowing away in the breeze. Then Liam and I stretched out side by side to soak up some of the ample sunshine. We held hands. I felt easy, relaxed, and at peace. I shut my eyes.

The next thing I became aware of was someone shouting my name, then a splash of cold water across my face, and a shadow blotting out the sun. I opened my eyes to see dark skies and heavy clouds instead of the sunshine and clear blue I'd been expecting. I was still lying on the sand, but now my feet and legs were in shallow water, and the corners of the blanket floated around me.

The picnic basket was headed out to sea, and when I stood up to grab it, I saw Liam trying to climb aboard the *Tranquility*'s transom. The anchor was adrift, the line swinging out behind him. The boat was heaving in the increasingly heavy surf.

I waded out to join Liam in trying to tame our wild, runaway boat. As I neared it, I tossed the basket aboard then veered off to the left to try to catch hold of the anchor line. I lunged as it passed by and managed to grab it. Liam splashed over, took a deep breath, and ducked under the rising water to reset it in the sand, while I tried to unlatch the ladder on the transom so we could climb aboard.

The latch was feeling stubborn and refused to come undone. I could see Liam wasn't having any luck either as he tried getting the anchor to catch on the shallow sandy bottom.

I gave up on the ladder and braced my arms on the transom, then I pushed up with my arms and kicked as hard as I could to lift myself out of the water. I slung one leg onto the transom, then stood up holding onto the folded ladder's edge. I raced to the cabin to start the engines, signaling to Liam to get clear as I passed him still struggling to set the anchor line.

He immediately let go of the anchor, got out of the way, and waited in the shallow water for me to get the boat under control.

The engine whined once. Twice.

The third time, it caught, and I held the boat in place with a low idle. I raced aft to lower the ladder, and Liam climbed aboard.

Together, we pulled in the anchor line and lifted the ladder into its travel position. When Liam turned on the depth meter, I saw that the water below us was barely deep enough to keep the *Tranquility* afloat. I raced up to the flying bridge and took a meandering route out of the area of shallow shoals and hidden sandbars before we accidentally ran aground.

When the *Tranquility* reached deeper water, we dropped anchor and fell into each other's arms. "What happened?" I asked Liam when we'd caught our breath.

"You fell asleep almost as soon as we arrived, and I must have been more tired than I knew because I dropped off too. I guess the anchor worked its way loose. I woke up just in time to see the boat heading for deeper water, so I shouted your name to wake you and tried to grab the anchor to stop the boat before we were left stranded in open water. I'm sorry. I must have messed up setting the anchor, and no matter what, I should have stayed awake to watch over everything."

"It's no more your fault than it is mine. I should have chosen a better spot for us to stop."

He took my hand. "Either way, we're safe, and we make a good team." He looked at the sky, glowing above us like a perfect porcelain bowl. "It's so beautiful out here. Almost as beautiful as you. And although I'd like to talk about your beauty all day, right now, I'm starved. Do you think the food in that basket is still good?"

I laughed. "Sweet talker. Well, there's only one way to find out about that food." We climbed down the ladder and retrieved the picnic basket to see what we could scavenge to eat.

We sat on the *Tranquility*'s bow, eating our lunch, and talking quietly about our lives. I loved hearing Liam's stories about growing up in Sydney, and he seemed equally enthralled by stories of my childhood spent mostly aboard the *Omega*.

"It's your turn to tell me something about your life before we met," I said.

"You're right. It is. Well, let me see what I can remember…" he rubbed his chin with one hand like an old man, making me laugh.

"I grew up in Sydney, as you know. My father was an executive with a global trading company. At twelve, I fancied myself a surfer dude. As you can imagine, my father and I were destined to irritate each other."

I laughed. "Go on…

"He was very fastidious. Liked everything just so—kind of like Newton, but nowhere near as easygoing about it all. And I had this dog, Cherry."

"Cherry was a stray I'd found at the beach. I begged my family to let me keep her. At first, they were dead set against a dog. But besides being half-bald, she was starved and scared silly, so they came around. Of course, I had to promise she'd be no trouble."

He paused to smile at the memory. "And one day my dad was getting ready to go on a business trip. He had a box of leather goods—samples he was taking with him, and he left the box on the floor in the front hall. Cherry found it, and she gnawed on every single piece in the box. Every keychain, wallet, slipper, glove—all ruined."

"Uhoh," I said. "Cherry must have been in big trouble."

"You'd have thought so, but my father was a great salesperson. He took the samples she'd gnawed and presented them to all his clients as the very latest fad. He called it the chewed look. They bought it. Placed big orders. And you know what—the look became trendy for a while. Biggest fad in years. Dad got a big promotion out of it for having been clever enough to think of it. He never told his company what really happened, but after that, he loved Cherry. Loved her until the day she died." His voice grew soft when he mentioned Cherry's death, and I could tell she'd meant a lot to him.

I nestled into his shoulder, and we sat like that, just enjoying our time together, but before we knew it, the sun was touching the horizon and it was time to head back to the boat. I felt better than I had since we'd found the wreck, happy and relaxed. Liam seemed to feel lighter and freer too as he tied us to the mooring ball where we'd left the Zodiac.

We stowed our belongings on the little inflatable and stopped by the *Sea Princess* to pick up Newton. When we arrived at the *Omega*, Maddy was waiting for us on the dive platform.

She still looked tired and worn, and I felt guilty that we hadn't forced her to take the afternoon off with us. She'd obviously needed a break as badly as we had. On the other hand, our morning had been a little more hair-raising than restful, and the afternoon had given Liam and me a chance to get to know each other and tighten our growing bond.

She rushed over to help us tie off the Zodiac. Once the boat was secure, she looked out over the *Omega*'s gunwales and said, "Uhoh. Company coming."

We all looked in the direction of the boats that had dogged our heels this whole trip. A small skiff with three people in it was headed our way. I groaned.

When the skiff neared the *Omega*, Liam reached out and grabbed the line Stefan Gibb threw to him and wound it securely around one of the cleats designed for the purpose. Then he held the boat steady while Stefan, Austin, and Noah came aboard.

Stefan walked right up to Maddy. "Good evening, Dr. Russo. We've come for my brother's body. We'd like to take him home."

I gasped. "Dylan was your brother?"

He gave me a sour look. "You didn't know? We're all brothers. I'm the oldest. Austin is the youngest. Noah and Dylan were in the middle. Not that you care." He turned back to my mother. "We'd like to take him now, please."

Maddy nodded. "Of course, you can have him. But you may want to let him stay on the *Omega* until we get back to port. We have his body in a refrigerated compartment we use for our research. Do you have a way to keep his body cold while you travel?"

The three brothers flinched when she said the word 'body.' They glanced at each other, shuffling their feet, and looking uneasy. It was obvious they hadn't thought this through.

"No, I have to admit we hadn't considered that. We just don't like leaving him here with strangers. We need to be with him."

My mother nodded again. "I understand. Would you like to stay on the *Omega* until we return to Grand Cayman? You can bunk with the crew, and you'd be able to see Dylan whenever you wanted to."

I knew this kind and thoughtful offer must have stressed

Maddy out. Like me, she put part of the blame for Ray's death on Stefan, who had left his post at a crucial point. But she was a compassionate woman, and she recognized that the brothers were in pain because of Dylan's death. She knew it must have cost Stefan Gibb a lot to come here to ask for his brother's body to be returned.

"Thank you, Dr. Russo. That is very kind of you. Especially considering he got the drugs that killed him on your boat." He looked toward his brothers, who all gave a faint nod. "We accept your generous offer. I know where the crew quarters are. Should we go there now?"

I bristled at Stefan's assumption that my mother had been involved with the drugs that caused Dylan's overdose. "How dare you imply that RIO or my mother had anything to do with dealing drugs. If you really think that, then you should get off the boat right now. Maddy has been nothing but kind to you despite the role you played in Ray's death."

Maddy put her hand on my arm. "It's okay. Stefan is grieving the death of someone he loved. We both know what that's like."

She turned back to Stefan and his brothers. "If you want to go back to your boat to gather your things before you settle in, that's fine. I want you to be comfortable here. Come aboard whenever you like. When you're ready to see Dylan, let me know and I'll take you there, so you know the way." She turned to walk away.

Newton watched her departure. "There's nobody like her in all the world." I could hear the longing in his voice. I nodded, pretending I hadn't heard the sadness.

"Let's find Oliver, grab some dinner, and go watch a movie on the *Sea Princess*. We can make popcorn. It might cheer him up a little. Dylan's death hit him hard." I knew both Liam and Newton liked Oliver a lot, and I was sure they'd want to help him through the hard times he'd been experiencing lately.

"Where is he, anyway? He's usually here to greet us when we get back," Liam said.

"Don't know," said Newton. "Let's split up and see if we can track him down." They took off to see what they could see below decks.

I looked around on the main deck and didn't see him, but I bumped into the *Omega*'s captain. "Hey, Vincent. Have you seen Oliver around?"

He paused for a moment to think. "I saw him getting ready to dive a little while ago. I just assumed he was going with you. That was about …" he looked at his watch, "…a half hour ago. Is his dive on the manifest?"

I'd already checked, and Oliver had not signed up on the list of unscheduled dives. "Thanks," I said over my shoulder. I was already on my way to the dive platform. If Oliver had gone diving, then he'd gone alone. I didn't want to think of him alone in the wreck, lost and afraid the way Dylan must have been. I had to make sure he was alright.

I struggled into my dive skin, connected my regulator to a fresh tank, shrugged my buoyancy control device high on my shoulders, fastened the Velcro cummerbund, and stepped into my fins, all in under a minute. I stepped off the dive platform and started my descent along the *Omega*'s anchor line. As I descended, I looked around in all directions to see if I could catch sight of Oliver or his scuba bubbles, but I saw nothing.

I swam toward the wreck as quickly as I could. As I swam, I tried to calculate Oliver's air consumption and nitrogen uptake in my head. He used his air faster than I did, and he was down about eighty feet, so he'd be using air at a rapid rate. If he was in the wreck, he wouldn't be swimming hard, so that would slow his air consumption, unless he was scared or in a panic— that would increase his need for air.

In my mind I kept seeing the roiling silt that had obscured everything inside the wreck the first time I'd brought him there. If he'd forgotten his training, even for a second, he might have stirred it up again. He might be inside, lost, alone, and unable to find his way out. Running low on air. Scared. Breathing faster with each passing moment.

I alternated between telling myself Oliver had plenty of air left so he'd be fine—and steeling myself in case I was too late, and he'd already run out of air. The truth is that so many variables affect air consumption while diving that even if you have all the starting data—which I didn't—you can't calculate it in your head. That's why safe divers constantly check their air pressure gauges and depth meters, and that's why we use dive computers that continuously recalculate safe dive limits based on actual dive conditions. If we don't have a computer, we use tables that can approximate safe dive times at various depths.

I was breathing faster than normal because of my fear for Oliver. I knew he was smart, and he learned fast. He'd had excellent training. He'd be fine. Or at least I told myself that, over and over.

I didn't see him around the outside of the wreck as I approached, and there were no bubbles or any signs that anyone was diving nearby. Swallowing my fear for him, I swam hard to the opening in the wreck's hull and peered inside.

As I'd feared, the silt had been disturbed and there was no visibility. I didn't see anything to tell me Oliver was inside. I reached up and grabbed a guide rope and inched into the opaque interior of the ship.

I kept my knees bent as I crept forward so my fins were away from the bottom, and I propelled myself with the merest twitch of my toes to move ahead. I waved my free arm off to each side as I penetrated the wreck, hoping that if Oliver had lost contact with the rope my seeking hand would find him so I could pull him to safety.

I reached the stairwell to the captain's quarters without making contact. Despite listening carefully for the sound of his bubbles, the wreck was as silent as a tomb. I slowly drifted down the stairs and made my way across the room to the door to the small compartment where we'd found the skeletal remains of the unknown queen and her magnificent tiara.

The water in here wasn't as silty as it was in the outer chambers, and I could just make out a bulky shadow on the floor in front of the queen's remains. It could be a diver, or because the visibility was so bad, it could have been almost anything. But whatever it was, it wasn't moving. I pulled a folding titanium dive knife out of my BCD's pocket, reached behind me, and tapped its edge lightly on my tank to get the diver's attention. No movement.

I swam to the area in front of the chair and got as close to the form as I could without letting go of the guide rope. Looking down, I could almost make out the outline of a diver slumped on the floor, the hose of his regulator out of his mouth, floating free. Even through the murk, I knew it was Oliver. I couldn't reach him without letting go of the guide rope which, if I had trouble getting a firm grasp on him, might mean we'd both be lost in the impenetrable haze of the cabin's water.

It's not a good idea to use a line to attach yourself to the guide ropes because it increases the possibility of getting tangled up and trapped, but I had to save Oliver, and I didn't have much time. I pulled a short retractable line out of my BCD and attached the carabiner on one end to the guide rope and the one on the other end to a D-ring on my BCD. Then I dropped down to Oliver.

I flipped him over and confirmed he was unconscious. I checked his pressure gauge, and his tank was empty. He'd used all his air. I had no way of knowing how long he'd been here without breathing.

I stuck my own primary regulator in his mouth and pushed the purge button to clear any sea water out. Then I turned the flow regulator up to max, which would push more air into him even if he wasn't consciously trying to breathe, putting my spare regulator —known as an octopus— in my own mouth. Oliver and I were now sharing the limited air in my tank since he'd sucked his own tank dry.

I lifted him under his arms and rose awkwardly to the slightly clearer space near the room's ceiling. I'd need every inch of visibility I had to get us out of here safely, and the silt floating in the water wasn't quite as thick higher up.

I needed both hands to hold onto Oliver, so I had to leave the line attached to the guide rope so I could follow it out without getting us lost. Unfortunately, Oliver was tall enough that his fins dangled near the floor, stirring up more silt as we passed. The water grew thick with it, and visibility lessened with each foot we covered.

As we neared the top of the stairwell, I tried moving forward and to the right, because I knew the exit was in the right-hand wall. The line attached to the guide rope pulled me up short. As I'd feared, the line's carabiner was hung up on something and we were caught.

I couldn't let go of Oliver without the risk of him drifting away, but I needed my hands free to untangle the carabiner so we could continue making our way out. For a minute, I was stymied, on the verge of panic. I was conscious of our dwindling air supply, and I knew there was barely enough air left for us to make it to the surface, never mind leaving any margin for safety stops or another unexpected hang-up.

Then I had an idea. Instead of holding him under both arms, I slid one of my hands along Oliver's arm and grasped his hand. Then with my other hand, I unhooked the carabiner attached to my BCD and attached it to Oliver's. He was floating free from me, but I would be able to find him in the murk by following the line.

Once I knew he was secure, I followed the line attached to Oliver back to the guide rope. One handed, I detached the carabiner from the guide rope and, still using one hand, reattached it to my own BCD while keeping my other hand on the guide rope. Oliver and I were now tethered to each other. I reached up with both hands, found the guide rope and started swimming. My forward motion came to a screeching halt, and Oliver's inert body bashed into me, startling me.

I almost screamed in frustration. What was wrong now?

It took a few minutes to realize that I hadn't untangled the snarl in the carabiner line that had caught us up in the first place. I backed up a few feet and disconnected the line from my BCD while holding onto Oliver. I reached up with my other hand, found the spot where the retractable line had snagged on a knot in the guide rope and tried to untangle it. When the tangle didn't yield immediately, I wanted to scream with frustration. Oliver didn't have time to wait while I unraveled a knot. I hadn't seen any bubbles from his regulator to indicate he was breathing. I had to get him out of there, and I had to do it fast. I was afraid it might already be too late.

I looked ahead. The silt had begun to settle in the main room while I had been working on getting Oliver out. The water was still roiled, murky and turbid, but I could see a faint hint of brightness ahead and to my right. I hoped it was the opening to the outside.

I debated what to do for a split second, but really, I had no choice. I disconnected Oliver from the line, pulled him close to me, held the regulator in his mouth with one hand, purged it of water again, and swam as fast as I could without kicking up the sand and silt on the bottom of the boat. I reached the opening in the wreck's hull at the same time my pressure gauge entered the red zone.

I burst out of the wreck and swam as fast as I could toward the surface, still holding Oliver. My air tank was empty, but I knew the residual air in the regulator hoses would expand as we rose because the ambient pressure decreased with decreasing depth. I wanted to save any remaining air for Oliver in case he was still breathing, however shallowly, so I spit out the octopus regulator.

Since the air in my lungs had been compressed, it would expand as the water pressure around me decreased, keeping me from feeling air starvation. As I rose, I let a slow, gentle stream of air exit my mouth to reduce my risk of inducing an air embolism.

I was moving so fast that the compressed air in my lungs could easily expand beyond the ability of my lungs or their tiny, delicate alveoli to tolerate. If Oliver was breathing at all, he was breathing compressed air that would automatically balance the pressure in his lungs with the ambient pressure. If he wasn't breathing, air expansion wouldn't matter much anyway. When I popped out of the water, I spit out my regulator. "Help me!" I called. "I need help."

I pushed Oliver's body onto the dive platform and clambered up after him. Still wearing my tanks and fins, I rolled him onto his back and began chest compressions. After a few minutes, I rolled him onto his side, and he expelled seawater. I rolled him back and jumped up to grab one of the emergency oxygen tanks we keep aboard in case of accidents. I attached it to his face and began compressions again.

Another few compressions and he gasped. More seawater escaped from his mouth, and I held the oxygen mask away from his face as it came up. He coughed a few times, then subsided. His eyes fluttered open, but they were blank and unseeing. At last, he inhaled on his own.

I'd just gotten him re-situated when Lauren appeared. "What happened?"

"Never mind that now. Please just get the doctor."

She turned and hurried away. I crouched beside Oliver, holding his hand, and whispering over and over, "Please wake up, Oliver. Please be okay."

Doc arrived at a run, followed by her team of EMTs and the gurney. She took one look at Oliver and barked, "Get him to sickbay. Now. You too, Fin."

The team strapped Oliver to the gurney and sped off. A group of sailors who had come running when they saw the medics helped me to lay down on a body board and then they carried me to sickbay.

I wasn't even all the way through the infirmary's swinging

doors when one of the EMTs rushed over and stuck an oxygen mask on my face. I took one very deep breath, then pulled it away from my mouth so I could speak. "Oliver?"

"He's breathing on his own. Great work, Fin." He smiled at me, and I felt a wave of joy. Oliver would be okay.

Chapter 34
In the Infirmary

DESPITE MY PROTESTS that I was fine, the EMTs put me in the infirmary's last cubicle. After she finished with Oliver, Doc took her time checking me out. She was concerned about the effects of my rapid ascent, especially after the heavy diving schedule I'd been doing for the last week. Lung barotrauma and 'the bends'—formally known as decompression sickness—were both very real possibilities, at least in her mind.

I didn't agree. "I'm not sick," I said, pulling the oxygen cannula out of my nose. "Really. I'm fine." I reached for the blood pressure cuff to remove it.

She pushed my hand off the pressure cuff and gently replaced the cannula. "Don't even think of removing the IV. You're only fine when I say you're fine."

"And not a moment before." Maddy had entered the room just in time to hear Doc's pronouncement.

"At least let me get out of bed. I'm okay to sit in a chair. And I have to retrieve the rest of the treasure. I'd like to do it today."

Maddy came to the foot of my bed. "Liam and I will do it as soon as Doc finishes with you here. You need to rest."

She and Doc stood side by side, arms folded, looking stern and formidable.

I sat back against my pillows, knowing when I was outnumbered. "Can I at least have something to read?"

"I brought your book. Here you go." Maddy handed me the volume of Ray's ship's logs I'd been reading. "Liam said this is the one you're reading now."

I took the book from her hand, but I didn't open it yet. "Thanks. How's Oliver doing?"

"He's sleeping, and his lungs seem fine. Pulse ox is good. He'll be here overnight." Doc turned away, taking Maddy with her. "I'll be back in a while to check on you. Don't get out of bed until then." She looked back at me over her shoulder as she walked.

I saluted her. "Aye, aye, Captain Doctor. Or is it Doctor Captain?"

She and Maddy laughed as they exited my cubicle.

I sat up and opened the logbook. I loved reading Ray's logs. He was an engaging writer, observing everything around him and describing it with keen insight. His youthful escapades, when he and his friends Stewie and Gus had traveled the world seeking treasure and adventure, were always fun to read. I'd finished several of the books so far, and I was almost up to the time when he'd met my mother. I couldn't wait to read about how they'd met and what his first thoughts were about the petite, blonde dynamo he'd ended up marrying.

I was riffling the pages looking for the spot I'd left off when I heard voices in the hall. Maddy and Doc were talking quietly outside my cubicle.

"You're sure she's okay?" my mother asked.

"Yes, I tested her blood twice to be sure. No drugs," Doc replied.

"But Oliver? You're sure about him? I can't imagine he took drugs. He's such a good kid."

"Tested him twice, too. No question. Fentanyl, just like his friend. Found a needle mark on his hip. Funny place for an injection, but it's easy to keep hidden. Anyway, he's still sleeping. Not a good sign. We won't know more until he wakes up."

I stood up, but I had to hold onto the bed rail for support because I was so dizzy. I was determined to see Oliver and make him wake up even if it killed me. He couldn't be taking drugs. Not my almost-brother.

Slowly I took a step forward, but I had to stop when my head spun. I paused a moment, then took another step. I finally reached the guest chair on the far wall, and I plunked into it to catch my breath.

A few minutes later, Doc came in. "I told you not to get out of bed," she scolded.

It was hard to look contrite but before I could say anything she spoke.

"Luckily, I came by to set you free. Everything checks out, and you're fine. As soon as I remove your IV, you can go."

When my IV was out, I thanked Doc for her excellent care. Then I gathered the dive skin I'd been wearing when they brought me in and grabbed my book. I was ready to go.

The *Omega*'s infirmary dressed its patients in hospital scrubs instead of the backless johnnies used by regular hospitals, so I was good to walk back to Maddy's cabin.

"Okay if I stop in to see Oliver on the way out?" I asked.

"He's still sleeping," Doc said. "Let him sleep."

I was surprised he was still asleep after all this time, but if he was, I guessed he needed the rest. "I'll come by later then. He should be awake after dinner, right?"

"Give it till morning," she said, biting her lip. She didn't meet my eyes.

That scared me. What was wrong with Oliver?

Chapter 35
Lily

I STOPPED by the film lab on my way back to Maddy's room to see if I could figure out if Alec had downloaded any images that weren't on the USB drive that he'd given me when I caught him in the lab during the party. I wouldn't put it past him to have prepared a dummy drive to put me off his tracks until it was too late for me to do anything about his thievery.

I was sitting in the chair, feeling weak and tired, vowing to myself to return to my bed for a nap as soon as I finished here.

A voice from behind me broke my concentration.

"Have you seen my brother?"

I turned and saw Lily standing in the doorway, carrying an ancient Monopoly game box. I recalled that in the past, the twins had enjoyed long Monopoly marathons.

I switched off the computer. "Wrong room. He's in the infirmary, sleeping. I don't think the doctor wants him to be disturbed."

Lily gave me that stare—the one that said I was too annoying for words. "I'm his twin. He won't find me disturbing." She turned to leave.

"Lily, let him be. He nearly died today. He needs his rest."

"Nearly died? What have you done to him this time?"

"Nothing. He went diving, and he had drugs in his system. Let him sleep. He needs to rest now."

She paused but didn't turn around or leave. She stood stock still, until I thought she'd turned to stone. Slowly, she twisted back to me, a ghastly smile on her face. "You're right, as always. I'll wait here with you for a few minutes until he wakes up. Maybe you'll play a game with me while we wait."

She put the Monopoly box on the table beside the computer. "I notice you're wearing hospital scrubs. Were you hurt or are you taking up medicine in addition to all your other talents?"

I reached for my cellphone, but she grabbed it out of my hand. "Don't bother the doctor. I'll get you anything you need."

I was trapped here. She had my phone, and she was between me and the door. I was too depleted, tired, and weak from my ordeal earlier today to think I could best Lily in a battle right now, so I'd have to find a way to get out of here without a fight. "I'm kind of tired myself," I said, faking a yawn. I hoped she'd take the hint and leave, but in my heart, I knew I'd never be that lucky.

"Okay. I won't stay long, but I do want to clear the air between us. I feel like there was a terrible misunderstanding. You must know I never meant to harm you." She held the tantalizing cellphone just out of my reach.

"Sure, Lily. I believe you." I didn't, and we both knew it. "But I need to rest now. I'll go back to my cabin. Maybe you can come back later. We can chat then."

"No, why don't you let me take care of you. Would you like some water?"

"No, I'm fine. Really. Please go. I just want to take a nap."

She smiled, but her smile radiated evil. "Have some water first." She poured water from the carafe on the table onto the pages of Ray's logbook which was still beside the computer. "Oops. Sorry," she said. "I'll get you a towel." She didn't move, just stood there watching me.

I blinked back tears. I loved Ray's logbooks, and they were one of the few things I had to remember him by. This one was surely ruined. I grabbed some lens cleaning cloths from a nearby stack and blotted up the water, hoping not to smear the ink too badly.

Once I'd mopped up most of the water, I carefully placed the open book on the edge of the table on the side away from her. I scrambled away, putting the table between us.

I'd have to get past Lily to get away from her, but at least now I had a little bit of room to maneuver.

Lily quickly walked around the table, so we were on the same side again. "I only want to talk." She took a step toward me.

"Sure. Let's go out on deck for some fresh air while we talk." My heart was beating so fast it's a wonder I didn't set off an alarm. I took a step toward her.

I was surprised when she took a step back. I walked toward her, taking slow, deliberate steps. For each forward step I took, Lily took a step backward. Could it really be this easy to get rid of her?

I fixed my gaze on her eyes and tried not to blink. I kept my slow, steady advance going. We were only a few feet apart.

I took a step toward her.

Pause…

Step.

Pause…

Step.

Pause…

The tension was too much for her. Lily turned and fled, dropping my cellphone as she ran. I sagged with relief and sat down to let my heart rate return to normal.

Chapter 36
Confirmation

I WENT BACK to Maddy's cabin and opened the pull-out couch into a bed. When the couch was open there wasn't a lot of room to wander around, but I wasn't holding a party in there. And although I would never admit this to the doctor, I was beat. An early night was just what I needed.

I snuggled under the covers and opened the logbook I'd been reading to assess the damage. As I'd feared, a lot of the writing on the page the book had been opened to was smeared, but some of it was still readable. I held the book close to my face so I could see better and tilted the page toward the light.

To my surprise, the stiff paper separated into two pages. They'd been glued together, and a slip of the lightweight paper known as onionskin, drifted out of the now open slot, settling like a snowflake on my lap.

I unfolded the tissue-thin sheet and saw Ray's handwriting sprawled across the page. This is what I read:

Fin, after I'm gone, please don't go looking for the Queen's Tiara. You know me—I don't believe evil manifests itself in places or people. But still, there's something at the site where that treasure lies that feels malevolent, and I don't ever want you to be exposed to it. If you do find it, you'll see what I mean. Or maybe not, and it's all a figment of my imagination.

But if you do go and you find something wicked there, do your best to resist it and destroy the site if you can, so no one else will fall under its influence.

Your loving stepdad,

Ray

PS. Don't worry. Your mother's gold doubloon did not come from that stash, even though that's what the "legend" says. Truth is, I pawned my dive watch to buy it from a jeweler in Curacao. Please don't tell her. It would ruin her image of me and break her heart.

I folded the paper carefully and slipped it back between the now-dry pages. Then I leaned back against the pillows to think.

It was obvious now that it had been Ray who welded the door shut and affixed the plaque proclaiming the ship's tiny interior room held something foul. As he'd said in his note, Ray didn't believe in supernatural occurrences or that evil manifested itself except through the deliberate actions of misguided, cowardly, or clueless people. But something at the site had scared him so much that he'd left a fortune in gold and jewels behind, at a time in his life when he was dirt poor.

The wreck was a deep dive, at eighty feet or more, and like my present team, Ray probably dove multiple times a day over several days. Fatigue would have set in, and his nitrogen load would slowly have increased, even if he observed recommended surface intervals between dives to allow his body to off-gas the excess. All this to say—he could have been suffering from nitrogen narcosis, and the "evil" he thought he saw and felt was nothing more than the product of his own mind.

That was exactly the conclusion I'd come to about the heebie-jeebies suffered by my present-day dive team. Maddy might have known about the 'witch' in the back cabin from old conversations with Ray. After all, they'd been married for more than twenty years, and she'd said he had nightmares about it. Who is to say that her mind hadn't inserted those images into her dreams each night after we arrived at the site?

I might have overheard the stories as a child, and my subconscious only dredged them up now because the stories were about the wreck.

As for Liam, Oliver, and me, we'd read the plaque before we entered the room. We could have been narc'ed from all the diving we'd been doing at depth. We were primed to see something malicious, even if all we really saw was a poor woman who'd been left to drown in a sinking ship.

Sure, there'd been accidents on the wreck, but wreck diving can be dangerous, and neither Oliver nor Dylan was an experienced wreck diver. Their problems might have started with diver error and escalated from there. Dylan had been on drugs, making the situation even worse for him.

Our fears didn't mean the woman locked in the room was a witch or that the room was manifestly evil. The accidents were flukes—problems caused by bad luck or bad timing.

I reached up to shut off the light and tried to sleep, but the words in Ray's note kept running through my mind.

"Destroy the site if you can."

Not legal. Maybe not even moral, if the site held historical significance. But I was going to do it if I could. Crazy or not, I wanted that horrible, cursed wreck so far down in the deep that no one would ever find it again.

Having reached a decision, my fretting was at an end. At last, I fell asleep.

Despite my concern for Oliver, I slept more deeply than I had since we'd started the hunt for the Queen's Tiara. I didn't even wake up when Maddy came in that night. Nor when she got dressed and left in the morning. The only way I knew she'd been there was because her bed had been slept in.

I got dressed in a bathing suit and a pair of shorts, stuck my feet in some flip flops and went in search of breakfast. And coffee. Definitely coffee.

Chapter 37
Investigation

LIAM AND NEWTON were in the crew galley sitting at a corner table. They'd finished their breakfast and were lingering over coffee. I loaded up a tray with eggs, toast, juice, and coffee before joining them.

They stopped talking as soon as I sat down, and the silence was uncomfortable. "Talking about me?" I asked.

Liam gave me the side eye. "Not exactly. We were trying to figure out who is pushing drugs on the *Omega*."

"Actually, at all of RIO. It seems to be rampant." Newton sipped his coffee, trying and failing to look nonchalant.

I almost spit out my mouthful of toast, but I managed to contain myself. I finished chewing before I asked, "And you suspect me?"

They both gaped at me. "Not you. Oliver," Newton said at last.

"It's not Oliver," I said. "Couldn't be."

Liam put down his cup. "Could be. He had drugs in his system and barely made it out alive. His friend Dylan ODed after diving with him. He's the only person that's traveled between the *Omega*, the pirate ship, Cara's boat, and Alec's catamaran. If not Oliver, then who?"

Newton pushed his plate away. "Look, I know you like the kid. Heck, I like him too. We all do. But he's had a tough year and maybe that skewed his judgement. And if not him, then who could it be?"

I thought a moment. "He's not the only one who's traveled between the boats. Stewie's been to them all. Alec's been to them all. Lily has. Stefan Gibb and his brothers have. Even Lauren's been to all of the other boats a couple of times." I folded my arms. "It's not Oliver."

They stared back at me in silence until a few minutes later Maddy sat down with a cup of coffee. "Oliver's awake. I'm going to talk to him about…you know."

"Not without me," I said. "He needs someone there who believes in him."

She nodded. "Right. Let's get to it."

We all rose and headed to the infirmary. Doc was in with Oliver when we arrived, so we waited outside the curtain. We couldn't see, but the thin cloth did nothing to hold back the sound.

"You're sure?" Doc said. "You swear you didn't take something? You can tell me anything, you know that. I won't be shocked."

"I don't do drugs. The last thing I remember is talking to Lily and Lauren about diving. She wanted to see the wreck. I didn't think it was a problem since we'd finished the recovery operation and all the salvage is in the *Omega*'s safe. We geared up. She was checking my gear when I felt a bug bite my hip. We jumped in the water. That's the last thing I remember."

Maddy and I both drew a sharp breath when he said Lily had been there. What Oliver thought was a bug bite could have been a needle spike. I knew Lily was crazy, but even I couldn't believe she was mean enough to needle spike her own twin brother with fentanyl before sending him alone into the ocean.

Doc must have heard our shocked gasps because she pulled open the curtain. "I know you two better than to think you were deliberately eavesdropping, but since you were standing here, I assume you heard. What do you think?"

"Oliver, did Lily dive with you?" I asked.

"I don't know. I can't remember," he said, staring at me. His eyes pleaded for me to have faith in him and his sister.

"I believe Oliver didn't purposely take drugs, but I do think Lily is behind all the drug problems we've been experiencing." I reached out and took his hand.

Maddy nodded. "Possible," she said. "Oliver, was Lily around the day Dylan ODed?"

He looked stricken. "Yeah. Yeah, she was. We were all hanging around on the pirate ship, listening to some tunes and just chilling. She was sitting off in the corner with Dylan. They were sharing her Air Pods, listening to tunes together. Alec and Lauren were talking, then I guess Alec got fed up with Lily flirting with Dylan—but he was just a kid, no reason for Alec to be jealous. So anyway, Alec took her back to the catamaran. The other brothers and I went diving. Dylan stayed on the boat, but I guess he got bored and went diving by himself. He passed out during the dive. You know the rest."

So, it could have been Lily needle spiking Dylan. Or it could have been Alec, annoyed at Lily's flirting. Or one of Dylan's own brothers. Stewie had been on the *Tranquility*, which was anchored close enough to the pirate ship for him to swim. Even Lauren had been there that day. We were no closer to learning the truth about who had been the culprit. I just knew in my heart it wasn't Oliver.

"But it could also have been Lauren. Or Stewie. Everyone was there that day." Oliver clearly didn't want to implicate his sister. Who could blame him for wanting to protect her? They were twins, after all.

I was trying hard not to let my fully justified dislike of Lily prevent me from keeping an open mind on this topic. Her past misdeeds didn't mean she was guilty of every bad thing that had happened in my life from that point on.

221

I looked at Maddy and Newton, and I could see they were wrestling with the same issue. I couldn't figure out how we were going to find evidence of who was responsible for the rash of drug use and needle spikings we'd been dealing with, because all the suspects were people we knew. But we would get to the bottom of this. It might take some time, but we would do it.

Just then Vincent walked into the cubicle, followed by Lauren. "Maddy, Fin. You're needed on deck. The Belize Harbor Master is here to talk to you."

Chapter 38
Harbor Master

NEWTON HAD BEEN LEANING against the back wall of Oliver's cubicle, but he straightened up when he heard Vincent's words. "I'd better go with you. Liam, as RIO's CFO, it would be a good idea for you to be there too. I think I know what this is about."

I had no idea what it was about, so I just followed everyone out of the cubicle. Oliver started to get out of bed, but Doc stuck her head back in. "Not you, Oliver. It's too soon for you to go wandering around."

Oliver looked like he was going to protest, but then he settled back in bed. That worried me because it meant he wasn't feeling in tip top shape. I resolved to check on him as soon as we found out what this unexpected visit was about.

There was a small delegation standing with the Harbor Master on the *Omega*'s deck. Newton walked over and shook hands with the man who appeared to be the leader. Newton introduced himself and the rest of our team. When the hand-shaking ritual was over, Newton asked, "So what's up? Why are you here?"

The Harbor Master cleared his throat. He spoke in English, so we all understood him. "I have been informed that your team has found a wreck nearby and taken salvage from it. The government of Belize would like you to surrender the salvaged items."

"Not so fast," Newton said. "The international law of salvage recovery says the salvager owns the recovered items if the property has been clearly abandoned."

The Harbor Master nodded. "Indeed, that is so. But the Belize Wrecks and Salvage Act makes an exception for wrecks owned by national governments. Those wrecks are never considered abandoned. The wreck below us is claimed by the government of Belize."

Newton pulled out his SAT phone and did a quick search. He pursed his lips. "Aren't we in international waters?" he asked Vincent.

Vincent looked at Lauren. She shook her head.

Newton thought a minute. "If your government claims the salvage, you must know what we've found. Can you describe the items?"

"I don't know exactly what you recovered, but we know that the ship contained an extremely valuable tiara set with diamonds, rubies and sapphires. An emerald bracelet. Several gold rings set with various precious and semi-precious stones, and a small but unknown quantity of gold doubloons."

Newton looked at the rest of the group and we all nodded. The Harbor Master's list included everything we'd brought up. It was also exactly what the fables said was there.

Newton nodded. "Okay, we're willing to cede the recovered items to your government, but we'd like the famous photographer Fin Fleming to take pictures of the ceremony marking the return. We'd also like to claim the salvage recovery fee contained in the act. Is that acceptable?"

The Harbor Master nodded. "Agreed, provided you return the artifacts immediately." He turned to me. "Can you be ready to film in five minutes?"

"Yup. I'll just get my camera." Vincent followed me for a few feet but soon veered off toward his office to retrieve the recovered items from the *Omega*'s safe.

As I walked away, I heard Maddy say to the Harbor Master "There was a young man who died while exploring the wreck. He wasn't part of our recovery team, but we'd like the reward to go to his family. I think they may need it more than we do."

"Very honorable," he said. "I will see that it's done."

I returned and set up my video camera. While I filmed, Vincent handed Maddy the wooden box that held the recovered relics. She ceremoniously handed it to the Harbor Master, who handed it off to one of his aides. While the aide held the box, the harbor master opened it. I aimed my camera at the interior to get a close up shot of the jewels lying on the ebony velvet lining. They glittered in the harsh sun.

When I nodded to him that I had all the footage I needed, the Harbor Master thanked us for being so cooperative. We repeated the hand shaking ceremony, and he returned to his cutter. As soon as he was aboard, his crew started the engines and the boat departed.

"Thank heaven that cursed stuff is off my boat," Maddy said. "I never want to see or hear about the Queen's Tiara again. And if the reward helps Stefan and his brothers come to grips with Dylan's death, at least those relics finally brought some good into the world." She made a motion like she was wiping something unpleasant off her hands, then she turned around and went to the infirmary to let Oliver know what had occurred.

I was thrilled that the Harbor Master had removed the jewels from the *Omega*. Maybe now they'd stop haunting my dreams.

Chapter 39
Reaction

As soon as Maddy told him about the deal she'd struck with the Harbor Master, Oliver broke into a huge grin. I'd thought he'd be upset that we had given the hard-won treasure away so easily, but Oliver was happy that Dylan's family would receive the reward.

"Good," he said. "I'm glad we got rid of those jewels. Every time I looked at them my skin crawled."

I'd had the same feeling, but I would never have been brave enough to voice it. Once again, I was proud of my almost brother and his level-headed maturity. He really was a good kid.

Now that the treasure hunting portion of our expedition was over, I could concentrate on getting the remaining footage necessary for the RIO documentary.

Maddy and I went to Omega's film lab and sorted through the video I'd already captured. Despite the considerable time I'd spent on filming the wreck and the treasure hunt, I'd also managed to capture a lot of footage of the scientists and oceanographers collecting specimens and samples from the water and the ocean floor. The unmanned rover had hours of film of the terrain well below our normal dive depth, and we had the film of the Great Blue Hole. We were almost there.

Maddy leaned back and rubbed her back. "We just need a few shots of damaged coral along the barrier reef, maybe some trash on the ocean floor to tie in with our Save Our Seas theme. We can wrap this up in another day or so."

"I agree. I know just the spot."

She and I shut down the lightboxes and headed up to the dive deck. We picked up Liam on the way. The plan was for Maddy and Liam to dive along the barrier reef, pick up some of the trash we were sure to find, and call it a day.

We stowed our dive gear on the Zodiac and Liam took us to a spot we had noted on an earlier dive, where the coral was starting to bleach. It was a great spot for the documentary because it made it easy to contrast the healthy coral with the dead coral just a few feet away. On the way back, we planned to dive near the pirate ship to film the trash pile we were sure had grown beneath their boat. We'd brought several bags to carry the trash we removed so we'd leave the area pristine.

We made short work of filming the coral, then headed back toward our tiny fleet. Liam tied the Zodiac to the *Tranquility* because we'd planned to do our trash pickup from my boat. We geared up, then did giant stride entries off the dive platform.

As we descended along the anchor line, I noticed another line running horizontally from the anchor line, on a pulley like a clothesline. I pointed it out to Liam and Maddy. They were as puzzled by this as I was.

The pulley line was stretched in the direction of the pirate ship's anchor line. There was another faintly visible line heading off from the anchor line, and I guessed it led to either Alec's catamaran or Cara's boat. I handed Liam my video camera and signed that he should film Maddy doing the cleanup on the bottom, while I followed the line. He nodded as he took the camera, and they descended toward the bottom.

I swam along on my back, looking up at the unauthorized line. I'd expected it to stop at the pirate ship, but it missed their anchor line by a few feet and went straight to the anchor line of Cara's cabin cruiser. Dangling beside the pulley line was a Styrofoam cooler, held shut with a bungee cord. When I saw that, I was sure I'd found the source of the drugs. Now I understood their distribution method. I wished I'd kept the camera with me because I would have liked to have proof.

This cooler held the drug stash, and Cara was the distributor. She must have been using the pulley to send drugs to Stewie when he'd been sequestered on the *Tranquility*. He had easy access to the *Omega*, and he must have been selling the drugs to the *Omega*'s crew during his frequent visits.

This was far more important than a few shots of Maddy cleaning up the ocean floor, at least for right now. I had to find the two of them to get my camera back from Liam so I could film the proof.

I turned to follow the line back to the *Tranquility* but came face to face with Cara holding a large, sharp dive knife. She'd been just about to cut my air hose. As it was, she only managed a small nick. I watched a tiny stream of bubbles—my precious air racing toward the surface.

You'd think she'd have learned from the recent attempts on my life that I could handle myself underwater, even without a ready source of air. We weren't down very deep, and I could easily reach the surface with just the air in my lungs. Plus, despite the slow leak in my hose, I still had plenty of air in my tank, so I wasn't worried about running out of air any time soon anyway.

I never worried about anything to do with diving.

I was, however, worried about the knife in her hand.

Even though I might be fine without air for a while, that knife gleaming wickedly in her hands could do all sorts of damage if she managed to reach an exposed part of my body. I reached out and grabbed her wrist, trying to wrest the knife away from her.

Cara was a tiny woman, petite and feminine in appearance, but like her daughter Lily, she was a lot stronger than she looked. She pulled her arm out of my grip while dropping down a foot or two in the water. I let her go, realizing too late she now had a clear shot at my vulnerable abdomen. She struck hard with the knife.

I don't think she had accounted for the tough tensile strength of my BCD's cummerbund, because her thrust barely made it through the tightly wrapped fabric. I felt the knife break my skin, but the blow was nothing like the rending gash we'd both been expecting.

I grabbed her wrist, and again she pulled free, this time nicking the fragile skin on the inside of my wrist. She drew blood, and I sucked in a surprised breath at the pain. Blood was flowing freely from my wounds, and I knew it would only be a few minutes at most before the presence of blood in the water drew every shark for miles around. I needed to end this fight quickly.

She looked into my eyes and grinned a nasty grin, before dropping down even further to grab my lower leg. She kept swimming down, pulling me deeper as she went. I watched her through the blood swirling from my wrist and belly. I assumed she was hoping to get me so far down that I wouldn't be able to make it back to the surface in my weakened condition. I guess it didn't matter to her whether the cause of my death was drowning, blood loss, or the ministrations of circling sharks.

But I don't give up that easily. I knew I couldn't let her plan succeed. I kicked with all my might, and she lost her grip on my leg.

She rose through the water, slashing wildly with the knife. As she came within reach, I reared back and smashed her in the face with my knee. She lost her mask and regulator a millisecond before she lost consciousness.

The knife fell from her hand and drifted toward the bottom. I caught the loop on the back of her BCD and swam for the surface. I hooked her body to a D-ring on the *Tranquility*'s dive platform, high enough that her head was above water, before climbing the ladder.

Once I was on the dive platform, I shrugged out of my gear and then went to find a rope to tie her hands with.

After her hands were secured, I pulled her fully onto the boat and dragged her onto the deck. Her nose was bleeding, and her eyes were already blackening. I didn't feel good about having hurt her, but at the same time, this woman had just tried to kill me.

I left her lying on the deck and went below to get the first aid kit. My wrist was bleeding steadily, although luckily, she hadn't hit the artery. I wrapped it in gauze to staunch the bleeding.

Next, I pulled off my ruined dive skin and examined the gash in my belly. It stung like crazy, but that was probably as much from the immersion in salt water as it was from the wound. I stuck a gauze pad over the puncture and sealed it with surgical tape. Then I shrugged on a t-shirt to cover the gap in my bathing suit.

I'd no sooner settled the shirt over my hips when I heard Maddy calling from the ladder. "Fin, are you on board? We looked around below and didn't see..." her voice trailed off, and I assumed she'd caught site of Cara, lying on the deck with her nose leaking blood.

"It's okay. I'm fine." I walked up the steps from the cabin to the main deck.

Maddy saw the bandage on my wrist and as any mother would, she rushed over to tend to her child.

I smiled at her. "I'm fine. Just a little nick."

She clasped me in her arms with all the might in her tiny yet powerful body.

We heard Liam clamber aboard. "I found this dive knife right under the boat. It looks brand new. Did either of you lose it?" Then he caught sight of Cara lying on the deck and looked up at Maddy and me holding each other fiercely. He crossed the deck in a couple of hurried strides and wrapped us both in his strong arms. "Are you two okay?"

"All is well," I said, hugging him back. I breathed a sigh of relief. "All is well."

We radioed Vincent to have him ask the Belize Harbor Master to send law enforcement to the *Omega*. By the time he understood what we wanted, Cara was awake. She started screaming that I had sneaked onto her boat, attacked her, and tried to kill her by holding her underwater. Since she was still wearing full scuba gear—except for her mask—this story was implausible at best and ludicrous in the extreme. We loaded her into the Zodiac and Liam putted to the *Omega*.

As soon as we'd tied up, I asked Vincent to send someone over to the *Tranquility* to keep an eye on all the boats while we waited. He nodded. "Lauren, please secure the *Tranquility* and the other boats until relieved by the Belize Harbor Master or me."

"Aye, Captain," she said. "I'll leave the Zodiac here and swim over. It's not far and you may need the small boat."

"Good plan," he said.

Lauren wiggled into her dive skin and dove. She was a strong swimmer, and she crossed the distance to the *Tranquility* quickly.

Doc came hurrying up. "I heard you were injured," she said. "Again." She sighed as she looked me over. "Can you walk to the infirmary?'

I nodded, and we walked away so she could dress my injuries. After examining the wounds, she said, "You were lucky, as usual. Both cuts are superficial—little more than scrapes, although I bet there was lots of blood. I'll give you some antibiotics and put on some bandages, but you should be fine."

When Doc said antibiotics, I knew she meant a shot, not a pill, so I steeled myself for another poke from a sharp object.

She gave me the injection, rubbed some ointment on the punctures Cara had made, and handed me the tube of ointment and a small bottle of pills. "Use both twice a day. Take the pills with food. No alcohol. See me tomorrow."

"Thanks, Doc." I said, tucking the bottle in the pocket of my shorts before heading out of the infirmary.

Before the door shut, she called after me. "Fin?"

I turned back.

"I'm glad you're okay. Take care of yourself."

About fifteen or twenty minutes later, I was back on deck when I noticed the pirates had removed their tri-corner hats and they were hauling down the Jolly Roger they'd been flying so proudly during the entire expedition. Less than a minute after they'd taken the flag off the line, the authorities from Belize arrived. From the timing of these separate events, I realized the pirate brothers must have been monitoring our radio communications all along.

The authorities separated us so they could question us individually. My session was the last to finish, so everyone else was assembled on the *Omega*'s deck when I emerged from Vincent's office with the maritime detective.

Several of his team were gearing up to dive. They'd asked Liam to dive with them to show them exactly where the pulley lines were connecting the boats, and he was helping them load their tanks onto our Zodiac. He powered the boat on and made the short hop back to the *Tranquility*. He tied up, then all the divers did backward roll entries into the water.

Newton, Vincent, and the Harbor Police Detectives stood together off to one side, barely speaking. Newton didn't understand Spanish, and the detectives seemed uncomfortable using English for what amounted to small talk. The trio looked tense and unhappy in each other's company.

Maddy and I were pacing the *Omega*'s deck, waiting for the divers at the *Tranquility* to surface. We both looked at our dive watches in surprise when the group popped up after no more than ten minutes under water.

Lauren and the divers all climbed into the Zodiac. Lauren was sitting at the engine, and I could see Liam in the bow, talking to the men. They were having nothing of whatever he was saying. Reading the body language, I could tell both sides were upset. After a few minutes, Liam threw his arms in the air and Lauren started the engines for the trip back to the *Omega*.

The law enforcement types hopped out of the Zodiac while Lauren was still tying it to the big ship. She put the Zodiac's keys in the pocket of her shorts and stepped onto the dive platform. She stood off to one side to watch whatever came next.

The officers strode over to their leader. They spoke quietly in Spanish for a moment, then the leader gestured for us to join him while one of his team bent to untie Cara's hands and help her onto their boat.

"We found nothing. No ropes, no pulleys, no cooler. Miss Fleming, it appears to us that you concocted a wild story to cover up your vicious attack on Ms. Flores. Your wounds are superficial, and they even look like they may have been self-inflicted. You are lucky we do not arrest you for assault, but it seems that, contrary to what we said earlier, both boats where the skirmishes took place are just over the line into international waters—so your crime is outside our jurisdiction. But be forewarned. If you ever come to Belize again, we will be watching."

He turned, and he and his team boarded their own boat and roared off. They dropped Cara back at her boat and then they moved off to a position where they could watch us without interfering in our operation.

"What happened over there?" I asked Lauren.

"Dunno," she said. "They dove, stayed down a few minutes, came up, and left. I came back on the Zodiac with them, as you just saw. They didn't talk during that trip. We boarded the *Omega*. After that, I heard what you heard." She shrugged her shoulders and walked off.

Chapter 40
Apology

NEWTON, Maddy, Liam, and I were sitting on the *Omega*'s gunwales, wondering how we'd ended up being the bad guys in a situation we'd never asked for.

"How could they believe her over me?" I asked the universe at large.

Newton started the list of what he considered contributing factors to the lack of credibility the Harbor Master had seen in our claims. "She's tiny. Looks delicate. Bleeding. You had her tied up. You're famous."

"I'm not famous," I said. "Maddy is."

"Okay, you're famous-adjacent," he said. "And he must have known that you and Lily had an unresolved conflict where she seems to have come out on top. He probably thought you were seeking revenge."

"I don't do revenge," I said. "I retreat. Or I compromise. Revenge isn't worth the price you pay."

"I know that, and I agree with..." he broke off. "What's going on now?"

We all looked across the sunlit waves to where one of the pirates was in the process of launching the tiny rowboat they used as a tender. He began rowing steadily, heading toward the *Omega*.

I groaned. "It looks like Stefan Gibb. What does he want?"

"We'll soon find out," Liam said, patting my hand. "But just relax. We're all here with you and we're on your side."

I smiled at him and watched the rowboat's steady approach. Stefan tied up at the transom and stepped aboard. He stood on deck and looked around until he spotted our small group amidship. I could see him take a deep breath as though steeling himself for a dreaded task. Then he straightened his shoulders, removed his black pirate hat, and walked slowly toward us.

He stopped in front of Maddy. "Dr. Russo, may I have a word?"

She didn't smile, but when she spoke her voice was pleasant enough. "Sure, Stefan. What's on your mind?"

He took another visible breath and swallowed before he spoke. "I owe you a major apology. When I worked for you on the *Omega*, I abandoned my post during the documentary filming last year. I justified it in my own mind because I told myself that Fin here said the task was completed. But the truth is, I wanted to see Ray make that dive, just like everyone else aboard. I was selfish. And because of me, someone took the opportunity to tamper with his guide rope, and he died." His voice cracked, and he swallowed hard.

"His death was at least partly my fault. I live with that guilt every day. Ray was a good man, and I admired him. I am very sorry for your loss." His voice cracked on the last word.

"And I apologize to you too, Fin. I knew I was in the wrong, but I lashed out and made you feel like it was your fault. It was no such thing. You did everything you could have to make sure Ray could dive safely. I was the one who screwed up."

The huge block of ice that had taken residence in my heart when Ray died cracked and began to melt away. I'd blamed myself, and I'd beaten myself up every day since he'd died. I was by no means completely over my guilt, and I knew I too had made mistakes back then, but I felt much better than I had since that awful day.

"Thank you. It means a lot to me to hear you say that." I tried to smile, but tears spilled out of my eyes instead.

"I'm not done yet," he said. "I deliberately tried to embarrass you that day at Nelson's. I should never have made that videotape, and I should never have played it." He turned back to Maddy. "And you. Since the first day I worked for RIO, you were kind and generous. Even now, after all I did to hurt you and your family, you helped Dylan when he ODed, and you made sure that my brothers and I were comforted and taken care of. Those are the acts of a truly admirable person, and once again, I've repaid you with betrayal."

"What do you mean, Stefan? What betrayal?" Maddy looked frightened and a little bit scared.

"First off, I called the Belize officials and told them you'd recovered the treasure."

I nodded. "Makes sense. I wondered how they knew exactly when we'd finished the recovery. But why?

"Spite," he said. "Second, the woman you know as Lauren Forster is a loan shark and a drug dealer, and I owed her money." He looked at Newton. "I borrowed the money to put my brothers through college."

Newton nodded. "Admirable."

"But after a while, Lauren was pressuring me to repay her. I couldn't keep up with the interest. I met Cara Flores at a bar, and for some reason, I told her about my predicament. She offered to pay Lauren off if I'd help Lauren to get a job on the *Omega*. She didn't care about making money from the drug sales."

"Cara only wanted to discredit Maddy and RIO. Out at sea, she knew she'd have a captive market for drugs. I coached Lauren on the job requirements and how to pass the interview, so she'd get hired as First Mate. It's my fault there are people in your organization using drugs. My fault Dominic died, and my fault Dylan died."

I could see the tears in his eyes, but he kept talking. "When I heard the police were coming, I suspected Cara and Lauren had planted something on the *Tranquility*. I swam underwater, saw the cooler and the pulley, and removed everything so you wouldn't be implicated. That was the first step in turning my life around, and this apology is my second step."

Maddy had tears in her eyes. "Thank you, Stefan. If there's anything you…" she broke off when Newton gave her a little poke in the ribs.

We both knew she'd been about to offer him his old job back, and we both knew that wasn't a good idea right now. Probably it never would be, but Maddy was so soft hearted she'd never see that.

I stood up straighter. "Thank you. Your apologies are accepted. I know I speak for my mother too when I say we're glad you're trying to turn your life around. It will be hard work but keep at it. It'll be worth it in the long run. Is there anything you or your brothers need before you return to your own boat?"

He looked at his feet, his hands working nervously at the rim of his pirate hat. "No, thank you," he said. "We're fine." He turned and walked back to his rowboat without another word. The last I saw of him he was making his way slowly back across the waves to the pirate ship.

Chapter 41
Night Dive

O<small>LIVER</small> and I were still working on his advanced diver certification, and later that afternoon he asked if we'd be able to finish it up on this trip. So far, he'd checked off deep dive and wreck dive, but he needed one more specialty dive to complete the required three. I suggested we try a night dive. Oliver was excited by the idea.

Night diving can be scary. If you have any fears while underwater, night diving may not be for you. First off, it's black as the inside of a lump of coal down there, even with a full moon. No light at all penetrates the water. All you see is what's in the beam of your flashlight.

On the other hand, at night you will see entirely different sea life and distinctive behaviors even from the fish that you see during the day. Nocturnal creatures come out to hunt at night. Night dives are the best times to see normally shy creatures like the octopus, if you're lucky enough to catch one in the beam of your flashlight.

You can see colorful parrotfish, asleep in a cocoon of mucus they spin to mask their smell and sight from predators. Other fish burrow into the sand or hide in coral grottoes. Sharks may sometimes form a small group for protection while sleeping. Other fish simply hold still, facing into the current so they have a continuous flow of oxygen over their gills.

Oliver and I both already had small handheld underwater flashlights in our BCD pockets that we used for peering into small spaces or illuminating coral during a dive so we could see the true colors. But these small flashlights would only be the backup lights for the night dive.

Instead, we would both carry much larger, more powerful handheld lights that could cast a beam for several feet through the inky water. These lights were so powerful that we couldn't keep them turned on above water for more than a few minutes, because they would overheat and burn out. They worked well while we were diving, because the water conducted the heat away quickly, keeping them operating as long as the battery lasted.

We practiced using glowsticks to orient the flashlights without aiming the beam directly at each other's face, so we wouldn't blind our buddy underwater, and we practiced using hand signals in front of the flashlights so our buddy could see what we were trying to communicate. Sounds simple, but it's a lot to remember when you are floating in pure, black nothingness.

After I went over the safety procedures one more time, and we agreed on our dive plan, Oliver and I put on our gear. I attached small glowsticks to our buoyancy control devices, so we could keep track of each other under water without blinding the other diver with the brilliant beams from our flashlights.

When I judged Oliver was ready, I hung a powerful beacon off the *Omega*'s transom to aid in navigating our way back to the boat. Oliver and I did giant stride entries off the transom and began our descent.

No amount of conversation and discussion can prepare you for the utter blackness of a night dive, although there were tiny sparkles of phosphorescence around us. The phosphorescence came from tiny organisms in the water. The irritation of currents or collisions with other organisms caused the tiny creatures' lights to glow.

Phosphorescence occurs during the day too, but it isn't easy to see. On a night dive, it's like what I always imagined floating through outer space would be like.

We swam down to the top of the reef and spent a few minutes watching the coral polyps feed. Many people think of coral as rock, but it's actually tiny living creatures. They pull microscopic nutrients from the water as it moves over them. Although some corals feed during the day, most are nocturnal, so it's best to dive at night if you want to see this activity.

We dropped over the edge of the reef and swam about ten feet down the wall. I made sure we did this just so Oliver would get a taste of hanging over the deep at night, when the murky blue becomes solid black, and your imagination can run wild.

Once I was sure Oliver could handle himself, we went back up and over the rim to spend the rest of our bottom time on the reef top. I'd given Oliver the responsibility for monitoring our dive time and navigating back to the *Omega*. In a few minutes, he held his hand in front of the beam of his light and signaled it was time to ascend. I followed him as he used his compass to effortlessly navigate back to the boat. Although he didn't appear nervous, I think we were both happy to see the flashing strobe I'd set to guide us through the return leg of the dive.

We hovered at fifteen feet to do our mandatory three-minute safety stop, another unnerving part of night diving. There you are, hanging in the blackness. There's not much to see, because the reef is too far away for the flashlight beam to penetrate. It's you and your imagination, and many first-time divers who make it through the rest of the dive, freak out at this point. But Oliver stayed steady. At the end of the three minutes, he signaled for me to go up the ladder first. He followed behind me.

When we'd both removed our gear, I hugged him. "Congratulations. You did great."

Maddy, Newton, and Liam were waiting just off the transom to offer their congratulations, and it was easy to see that their support meant a lot to Oliver. Doc was there too, chiding me for diving and getting my bandages wet. She'd come prepared with fresh gauze, and she made quick work of changing the sodden mess on my wrist. She gave me a large adhesive pad to replace the bandages on the wound in my belly and told me to change it myself when I got dressed again.

Chapter 42
A New Sorrow

Later that evening, Liam and I decided to take some private time aboard the *Tranquility*. We dressed in our dive skins and swam over, a bundle of snacks in a waterproof pack on Liam's back. We were sick of taking the Zodiac back and forth, and anyway, we wanted to leave it with the *Omega* in case they needed it for anything. Strictly speaking, I was pretty sure Doc would not have wanted me to get my bandages wet yet again, but I was sure that what she didn't know wouldn't hurt me. She could scold me in the morning if she found out.

After we'd clambered up the ladder onto the deck, we moved to the bow of the boat to enjoy the moonlight. We settled with our backs against the cabin wall and stretched our legs out in front of us. Liam put his arm around my shoulders, and I rested my head against his broad chest.

Despite the horrifying events of the last several days, it felt right and good to be sitting with Liam this way. I thought that maybe we were ready to take another slow step toward deepening our relationship into an actual romance.

We'd asked the cook to pack enough snacks for two, and he

outdid himself by making us a complete dinner. When we unpacked the waterproof packet he'd prepared for us, we found two perfectly prepared filet mignons, parslied potatoes, and a green salad with his secret recipe Greek dressing. He'd also packed a variety of sodas and juices, rather than the margaritas I knew Liam had requested, so I guessed that Doc already knew about our plan and had dictated the drinks menu. Trust her to pretend not to know what was going on while still doing everything in her power to take care of her patients. I smiled, thinking about what a good friend she'd been to Maddy, Ray, and me over the years.

We adjourned to the *Tranquility*'s cabin to reheat and enjoy the dinner. Liam started a playlist of soft music from his phone, and while we ate, the sun set, and the stars came out. We chatted; we laughed. It was magical.

After we'd cleaned up and repacked the dishes and utensils to return to *Omega* later, we went back to sit on the bow and enjoy the warm evening breezes. I lit a scented candle and placed the sturdy holder on the end of the bow, attached to the boat by a small piece of rope wrapped around a cleat. Then we settled back against the cabin wall and resumed the positions we'd been in before dinner.

While we were sitting there, we saw Lily and Alec come up on the deck of his catamaran. They shared a passionate kiss, then Lily dove into the ocean and swam to her mother's boat. A few minutes after she'd climbed aboard, we heard the clank of the anchor being hauled in and the engines started. The boat's running lights came on, and the cabin cruiser left the area.

After that, the sound of the catamaran's engines broke the stillness, and Alec too left the area. The pirate ship was still and dark. It seemed that the brothers had made an early night of it.

"Alone at last," Liam whispered in my ear.

I sighed with delight. The evening was perfect.

"Tell me more about your childhood," he said. "I love hearing about what it was like growing up on the *Omega*."

I told him my childhood had been wonderful because it had

been. What child wouldn't love spending their days learning to swim, and dive, and fish, and captain a boat—all the amazing things my stepfather Ray Russo had taken the time to teach me. Who wouldn't love seeing themselves on TV, getting asked for the occasional autograph, showing the world how much she was loved by her family and the scientists and crew of the *Omega*? I hadn't known I was missing anything from a more typical lifestyle until I left for college.

That's when I discovered I had no friends my own age and no idea how to make them. That people would always remember me as the kid who lost a tooth on camera or who squealed when a stingray brushed her head with his velvet wings. The person who tripped and fell often, who tore her shorts, and who made a face when she ate raw fish.

All the misadventures that my parents had captured on film and later broadcast around the world. Those disasters lived on in reruns, so that people rarely realized I was now an adult—and a very accomplished one at that.

"But on balance, it was all good," I said. "I wouldn't have changed a thing.

He smiled and kissed the top of my head.

"Tell me more about your life back in Sydney," I said.

"A terrific balance of culture and outdoor life. I had a mother, a father, and a nanny. I went to private schools. When I was home, I wore dorky clothes, but when I was at school, I could break out the jeans and tee shirts like the other kids wore. I got into the usual, age-appropriate troubles growing up but nothing serious. College. Master of data science from Macquarie. Founded Oh! Possum. Sold it. Went to the Caymans to find myself. Found you instead."

He smiled and kissed my head again. "I feel like I'd been searching for you my whole life."

I was still trying to uncurl my toes from the pleasant rush his words had created when he said, "But I have a wife."

I paused a moment, a cold stillness entering my soul. "No prob-

245

lem," I said carefully. "We're grownups. I had a husband. You had a wife. Now we have each other." I shut my eyes and inhaled. The last words sounded so sweet to my ears.

"Not had. Have," he said. "Not an ex-wife. A wife."

My world came crashing down. I shivered but moved away from his warmth. "You're married?"

He sighed. "Not exactly. I was. I am. I don't know anymore. The trouble is, I still love my wife. But I love you too."

I shrank back another inch. "You should have told me sooner."

He nodded. "Yes. I should have. Amelia's the reason I've been taking our relationship so slowly. I want what you and I have together, and I know we can't go on like this. It isn't fair to you."

"I don't imagine your wife is crazy about the situation either. Or does she even know?" I tried hard to keep my voice even, but it cracked with bitterness at the end. I was mortified to show him how much he'd hurt me.

He tried to pull me close, but I resisted. I guess he could tell I wouldn't relent, because he gave up on trying to get nearer to me.

"I don't know what she knows. It's a long story. I came home from a business trip one day. I'd been gone for a few weeks. The house was empty. The doors were open. Amelia didn't answer her phone. None of her things were gone, or at least, there was nothing I recognized as missing."

"I'd been working a lot. Away a lot. I wasn't very good about calling to let her know where I was or what was going on. I thought at first she was giving me a taste of my own medicine by leaving me wondering where she'd gone." He bit his lip.

"Days later, she still hadn't come home or answered her phone. Her voicemail was full. I called her friends—the ones I knew—but she'd lost touch with them. None of them had heard from her. I didn't know any of her more recent friends, or even how she spent her days when I was away. We'd grown so far apart it was like she was an entirely different woman than the Amelia I'd married. She'd vanished."

"I finally called the police. They thought she'd been a victim of foul play, and they suspected me of hurting her because I hadn't called them right away. I put up a huge reward for information, hired a small army of private detectives, and eventually, a witness came forward who claimed to have seen Amelia at a gas station a few days after I'd called the police. They confirmed it was her on security footage. A forensic accountant traced the debit card she'd used to one of several bank and investment accounts she'd opened before her disappearance. She was using a different name and making regular withdrawals in small amounts—the kind you'd make to cover normal day-to-day living expenses."

"The police tracked her down and confirmed she was alive and well, told me they'd talked to her, and she didn't want me to contact her. They dropped the case and left me hanging. I moped around the house for months, hoping she'd come home. Lived like a hermit. I couldn't bring myself to file for divorce. I thought for sure she'd come to her senses and come back to me."

He inhaled, a slow, unsteady breath. "And then, without warning, she came home one day. Said she'd missed me. Not the new me, the big tech executive in the fancy suits driving the fast cars. She said she wanted the simple guy she'd known when we first met."

His hand was shaking in the dim glow of the candlelight as he brushed the hair out of his eyes. "I was devastated. Told her I'd do anything, be anyone she wanted if she'd just come back to me. She said she didn't think I could live simply anymore—not the way we had when we were first together. I swore I could."

"We argued all night, and finally we agreed that we would stay apart for a year. My test during the year was to live simply. No cars. No fancy clothes. Living on my wages from an entry level job. I swore I could do it and that I'd be back to make it up to her. Her task was to decide if she'd ever really loved me."

He paused and took a sip of juice. "We agreed to meet up in a year to see how we'd done and if we still wanted to be together. If we did, we'd put more effort into the relationship to see if we could make it work. The next day, I flew to the Caymans, where nobody knew me. Got a job as a valet at the Ritz—something no one would expect the CEO of Oh! Possum to be doing."

He laughed without a trace of humor. "And then I met you and I knew I'd found the person I was always meant to be with. But I have to keep my promise to Amelia. The year is almost up. I've gotta go back to keep my promise. If we work things out, you'll never see me again. If we don't, I'll be at your door begging you to give me a chance."

"You never told me any of this," I said with bitterness.

"I didn't tell you any of this," he agreed. "And I was wrong to keep it from you. But now I have told you."

"But I'm your second choice," I said bitterly.

"No, you're not. That's what I'm trying to tell you. I have to go back to keep my word, but I promise you I will move heaven and earth to get Amelia to give me a divorce so you and I can be together. I swear it. I'll fly to Australia as soon as we get back to port."

I was choking on my tears, and I could barely speak. My relationship with Liam was only the second serious relationship of my life, and both times I'd been badly betrayed. I was crushed, and my faith in my own judgement and in myself was shaken. I could not wait to be alone to lick my wounds.

"Okay," I said. "But in the meantime, I don't see married men. Call me when you get back with those divorce papers. You'd better go now."

Liam nodded. "I'll be back. I swear to you, I'll be back." He dove off the bow and swam back to the *Omega*.

Chapter 43
Return to Port

I was lying on the daybed feeling sorry for myself when I heard the roar of the approaching Zodiac. "Ready for breakfast?" Oliver called.

I rose wearily. "Be right there." I threw on a bathing suit and a clean tee shirt, then went up on deck.

Oliver wisely didn't say a word when he saw me, and I wondered if he'd already heard from Liam that we'd broken up. He waited until I was seated, then putted over to the *Sea Princess* to pick up Newton.

As usual, even when he was dressed in his most casual clothes, Newton looked like he'd just stepped out of the pages of *GQ*. "Morning," he said, as he took a seat on the middle bench. "Looks like nice weather for our last day."

He didn't ask where Liam was, so I gathered that the family had been alerted to our change in status. Once on the *Omega*, I grabbed a coffee and half a bagel and went straight to the film studio. Maddy, Newton, and Oliver joined me in a few minutes, coffee cups in hand. Our goal for the day was to make sure we weren't missing any crucial or exciting shots for the documentary.

I'd cued a rough cut of the film, and when they were all seated, I started it. Everybody had something to take notes with—Oliver and I used our iPads while Newton and Maddy had notebooks and pens. We watched for an hour and fifteen minutes. "Ready for a break?" I asked. "Then we can go through it again slowly."

Maddy stood. "I'll ask the chef to bring coffee and juice here. That'll save time."

I surmised she was trying to protect me from running into Liam by keeping me confined, but before I could respond, I heard the distant "thwop" of helicopter blades, and I knew he'd departed without saying goodbye. "Sounds like it's safe to go on deck now," I said, trying to keep a brave face. "And I could use the air."

As we walked, we talked about what we'd seen and decided that the documentary was already complete—no missing shots necessary to flesh out the story. We didn't have to go over it again. Now my job was to cut it down to the required running time without losing vital detail. "Since we don't have to spend the day editing, let's do one last dive while we're here," I said. "Who knows when we'll be back."

But when we arrived on the deck, I was surprised to see two tugboats anchored directly over the wreck site. Two teams of divers from each boat were wrestling with steel grappling hooks on the ends of heavy cables, getting them into position to heave overboard. Once the hooks were in the water, they dove, pulling the grappling hooks below with them.

"What are they doing?" Oliver asked.

"I think they're trying to rid the world of a curse," I replied, pulling out my camera to film the activity.

We watched for an hour until the divers returned to the surface.

As soon as the divers were safely aboard, the tugs took off, both pulling in the same direction, straining as though towing a great weight. The boats stopped again in a spot that I estimated was over the deepest part of the nearby ocean trough. The divers jumped in, but they surfaced more quickly this time. I guessed they had gone down to make sure the wreck was far enough away from the reef and its wall to eliminate damage to the coral and sea life.

The tugs strained forward. I heard a groaning roar from below the surface. The water frothed. Fish jumped. My guess had been right.

They'd dragged the wreck off the edge of the reef wall and released it over the deepest part of the drop-off, where it would never be dive-able again. Unless they'd removed her while we were below decks, the skeleton of the woman in the chair would also be consigned to the deep.

I felt a deep welling of relief that she was gone. I knew that whoever she was, she wasn't a witch. Her malice had been a figment of our collective imaginations, but she had haunted me and filled me with dread.

When the turmoil in the water subsided, the sailors on the other boat reeled in the cables and the two tugboats chugged off.

"Everything must be settled by now. Is it safe for us to dive again?" Oliver asked.

"I think so. I'd like to get some shots of the spot where the wreck was," I said. "It'll make a great ending to the *Your World* story."

Maddy, Oliver and I helped each other into our gear and did giant stride entries off the dive platform. I sank slowly beneath the water and surveyed the coral landscape below. The water was turbid, filled with debris and specks of coral and sand, but life was already returning to the area. I watched a leatherback sea turtle pass a few feet from my face. A graceful manta cruised along the wall. The usual school of jacks hovered under the *Omega*; parrotfish chomped on the coral; and the tiny reef fish scurried about their business. Everything seemed normal.

We dropped down to about eighty feet and swam along the reef to the former location of the ship we'd been exploring. Instead of the coral encrusted wreck, the area was now a sand chute, with fine grains of sand and coral slowly sliding down the slope. A grey reef shark swam down the chute and out into the blue, passing no more than three feet away from us. Oliver turned to look at me, his eyes wide behind his mask. I smiled and gave him the okay sign.

He and Maddy swam slowly along the sand chute while I filmed them. I was pleased to see that the coral was as vibrant and beautiful as it had been before. It was remarkably undamaged by the wreck's removal, and the sea life population seemed to have completely and easily forgotten the wreck and the noise it'd made when it was removed.

I saw a gleam in the sand below, and I dove down to check it out. A gold doubloon we hadn't recovered during our salvage operations must have fallen from the wreck during its removal. For a moment, I was tempted to keep it.

Then an image of the woman from my dreams flashed into my head, a thin smile on her face.

I knew she wasn't a witch, but there was no question that all of us—hardheaded scientists and businesspeople—had been adversely affected by her presence. So had Ray, the bravest man I ever knew.

Whether she was a figment of my imagination or a witch who defied time and the boundaries of the physical world didn't matter. I knew I wanted no part of her or her treasure.

The wreck's setting had been undeniably creepy, with shadows, dim lighting, and a skeleton sitting in the middle of an empty ship. We'd seen no other bodies or bones while we'd been searching for the treasure, which said the woman had probably been left aboard to die, her hands bound to a chair with iron fetters, and the chair attached to the deck with steel bolts. For whatever reason, she'd been sent to the ocean's bottom all those many years ago. It was only sheer luck that Ray had found her, and only happenstance that led me here after his death.

Our fears and nightmares were just the effects of a bunch of overtired, narc'ed up divers, ignoring their surface intervals and letting their imaginations run wild. We'd had a couple of restless nights and we'd all let that color our whole perception of this woman and the expedition. Our growing fatigue and a series of easily explainable, natural, and logical events had sent us over the edge, and we'd let our imaginations run wild. There'd been no true witch here.

After my photo montage came out, I knew divers would be coming here in droves, hoping to see the wreck, or the body, or scavenging in case we'd missed some bit of treasure. Whatever their reasons, people would come.

I hoped there'd be nothing for them to find, and that the woman's remains were gone forever. If I left this doubloon here and someone happened upon it, people would think there was more treasure to find.

But if they never found anything at all, they'd soon tire of diving this spot. It was an undeniably beautiful reef and a vibrant wall, but no different than a hundred other reefs in the area, except it was more remote and harder to get to. Without the legend of the treasure, the site would fade from prominence. I didn't want anything to ruin this once-again beautiful, peaceful spot.

And I wanted no part of the treasure myself. Call me superstitious if you must, I felt like the treasure brought bad luck. I'd seen the curse come true.

Sorrow—Dominic's death.

Betrayal—First Stewie and then Liam.

Death by drowning—Dylan. And almost Oliver.

I couldn't risk more malevolence dogging my life.

So instead of slipping the shiny doubloon into the pocket of my BCD, I swam quickly off the edge of the reef until I was out in the deep blue, hovering over the drop off. I let go of the coin, and watched it drift slowly down to the ocean floor where I hoped it would stay forever.

Chapter 44
Arrival

SINCE WE ALL agreed we had more than enough footage and photos for the documentary and my photo montage, we decided to head back to RIO without waiting for morning. With Liam gone, there was no one else to captain the *Sea Princess*, so Maddy moved back onto her boat while Newton moved into her suite on the *Omega* with Oliver. I, of course, was alone on the *Tranquility*.

I radioed over to the pirates to let them know we were moving out and asked if they wanted to see Dylan one more time before we left. They declined, so I asked for instructions on what to do with his remains once we arrived back on Grand Cayman.

I told them Maddy would take care of the funeral expenses, and they could have whatever they thought Dylan would have wanted. They named a prominent funeral home in Georgetown, and I agreed to have Dylan transported there as soon as we docked. With that settled, the RIO group was good to go.

I started the *Tranquility*'s engines but shut them off again when my SAT phone buzzed.

It was Vincent "Have you seen Lauren? Is she there with you?

No one has seen her since last night. Even Stewie swears he doesn't know where she is."

"Nope. Sorry. I haven't seen her." I realized we hadn't told Vincent about Lauren's part in the drug scheme.

"Her bunk is cleaned out. All her stuff is gone. Stewie is inconsolable and not making any sense. Not that he usually makes sense, but right now he's worse than ever."

I thought a minute. "Lauren was the drug connection. I bet she left with Cara last night."

"What? You'd better come over here and explain it to me. I'll send the Zodiac for you."

I waited for Oliver to arrive with the Zodiac. He stopped at the *Sea Princess* to pick up Maddy on the way over. When I sat down, she leaned over and gave me a hug. "It'll all work out. You'll see."

Obviously, she was referring to Liam. I felt a rush of tears threatening, so I said nothing.

Newton, Maddy, Oliver, Stewie, Vincent, and I all crowded around a corner table in the galley. Vincent called the meeting to order.

"We're all worried about Lauren, given the problems we've had with drugs on this trip. She could be lying somewhere hurt and alone. We need to do everything we can to find her."

I nodded. "I agree we need to find her, but I doubt she's hurt and alone. Oliver, when you told us about your dive, you said 'she' dove with you. We all assumed you meant Lily, but you were talking about Lauren, weren't you?"

He nodded.

"Then Lauren was the one who tried to kill you, and I think she left last night with Cara. The two of them were working together to get drugs onto the *Omega*."

Vincent looked affronted. "That's ridiculous. I vetted Lauren myself. Her credentials were impeccable."

"I agree. They were." I held my iPad up so everyone could see the screen. "This is the real Lauren Forster, and her credentials are indeed impeccable. But as you can see, she looks nothing like the Lauren we knew."

Vincent's face turned red. "Maddy, I'm so sorry. It never occurred to me to check her social media. Her documents seemed legit."

Maddy patted his hand. "I understand. I wouldn't have thought of it either."

I didn't think that was true, because I knew she must have checked out Liam online before offering him the CFO job at RIO. That job was too critical to the institute's success to hire someone without real expertise, even if he was her daughter's boyfriend. But if she'd known Liam had been the founder of Oh! Possum, that probably meant she'd known all along about his wife Amelia. I couldn't believe she hadn't told me.

"Explain, please," said Newton.

I sat up straight before answering. It was important to get this right. "Lauren traveled regularly between the *Omega*, the *Tranquility*, Cara's cabin cruiser, and the pirate ship. She went back and forth in the Zodiac several times a day, bringing Stewie his meals and ferrying us all to and from the *Omega*. I think she and Cara had worked out a system.

"I believe that each day Cara put the drugs in that cooler I found, and when Lauren was on the *Tranquility* with Stewie, she used the underwater pulley to reel it over. She pulled it up, removed the drugs, then sent the cooler back to Cara's cabin cruiser.

"It would have been quick and easy to lift the cooler, remove the drugs and replace them with the money, so it wasn't likely that Stewie would notice her doing anything odd, especially after she got him drinking again. And she was far enough away from the *Omega* that we wouldn't see anything suspicious. Neither the drugs nor the cash take up much space, so she could have concealed them in a pocket of her cargo shorts or in her backpack. She wasn't worried about us seeing her with a lot of cash anyway. There's nothing illegal about carrying cash, although it would be odd out here with nowhere to go and nothing to buy. And she never had a large quantity of drugs on her, so it would be easy to dispose of anything incriminating if she found herself in a tough spot.

"I think Dylan caught on to her, so she gave him a needle stick. I'm not sure if she meant to kill him or just scare him, but either way, he got a lethal dose."

Oliver looked pensive. "But why did she drug me? I had no clue she was dealing."

"I don't know for sure, but I believe she gave you the needle stick to keep Lily or Cara in line. One of them might have been trying to end the game, or maybe they were looking for a bigger cut of the take. Doesn't matter why. You're their most vulnerable spot, so you became her tool to keep them in line. Thank goodness she didn't give you the same dose she gave Dylan, or we might have lost you too." I reached over and took my almost-brother's hand.

We all sat quietly for a minute, thinking about how close we had come to losing someone we loved. Then Vincent said, "So now what? We can't have drug use at RIO or on the *Omega*. How do we figure out who Lauren's customers were?"

Newton said, "I'll handle that. I'll get Gus to have drug tests delivered to the marina at RIO—enough so we can test the entire crew and research staff before we let them disembark. When we get the results, then it's up to you, Maddy."

She nodded. "If anyone tests positive, I'll have to let them go. Vincent is right. We can't allow drug users to stay on."

Stewie looked uncomfortable for a moment. "Uh, what about beer? Are you testing for beer too? Because I admit to having had quite a few beers when I was with Lauren."

"We'll cross that bridge when we come to it," Maddy said, but I could see she was as worried as I was that Stewie might have been drugged so Lauren would have an easier time retrieving the drugs and delivering the cash.

I didn't for a moment believe he'd been personally involved in dealing. He was lazy but he wasn't stupid. And he was, in his own way, loyal to Maddy and RIO.

Newton looked pensive for a moment. "We'll have to find Lauren, but I think we'll leave that to DS Scott. In fact, it might be a good idea to have him meet us at the dock when we return. That way he can question people while they're still surprised that we know about the drugs."

Maddy said, "Whatever you think is best, Newton," which was so unlike her that we all just stared.

After that, we were ready to head home. There was nothing to keep us here, and since we now knew about them for sure, we were all uncomfortable about drugs on the *Omega*. Rather than wait for morning, we decided to weigh anchor and make for port.

There was no rush to outrun treasure hunters on the return voyage, so even though we were nervous about the drugs, we took our time. Instead of traveling at top speed to the limits of our fuel supply as we had on the way out, we traveled slowly. We stopped often so the researchers and oceanographers could take water or sea life samples, exactly as we had always done on previous expeditions.

Oliver and I dove together during these intervals, and I remembered how nice it can be to dive for the sheer joy of diving. We were still working on his advanced diver certification, and I watched Oliver's skills improve with each dive. He might not have been Ray's biological son, but he was quickly becoming his equal as a diver. Soon he was letter perfect on every skill, and I was proud of him.

And I missed Liam with all my heart.

After three days of travel, we docked at RIO.

Gus met us at the dock with a pile of drug test kits. Doc took charge of them and required everyone to provide the necessary samples before they could board the launch to reach shore.

As the crew finished their tests, they got aboard either RIO One or RIO Two, the launches we used to ferry passengers and crew to the *Omega* and back.

Stewie and Oliver each captained one of the small boats, making multiple trips to help the entire crew disembark. I watched Stewie carefully to see if he was upset about Lauren, but he was his usual jovial self, so I guessed his heart wasn't exactly broken by her betrayal.

When most of the crew was off the *Omega*, I docked the *Tranquility* in my usual slip in the marina, and Oliver ran over to help make her fast. After he'd secured the boat to the cleats on the dock, he coiled the remaining line neatly, exactly the way I'd taught him.

Exactly the way Ray had taught me.

After securing my boat, I went inside to say hello to Rosie and to check my office. The office was dusty, but otherwise unchanged. I carefully didn't look down the hall toward Maddy's corner office, or glance at the closed door of Ray's old office—the office Liam had used during his short tenure with us. I went to the lab to reconnect with Rosie.

When she recognized me, Rosie flashed that lovely pink color, and I gave her a clam as a welcome home gift. I could see she wanted to play, because she slinked over to her pile of objects and started pulling them out, displaying each one as though waiting for me to show her the matching card. When I didn't, she must have been disappointed in me because I wasn't smart enough to play this variation on our usual game where I held up a card and then she matched the objects to the image on it. I smiled at her, but my heart wasn't in it. I didn't feel like playing. I couldn't help it.

I went back to my office, grabbed the canvas bag I used instead of a purse, and trudged to the parking lot where my Prius awaited. I wanted to go home.

But when I got there, I was too stressed to settle down and too tired to do anything useful. I cried myself to sleep in the wee hours of the night.

Chapter 45
Final Dive

THE NEXT MORNING, I got up early and wandered around the house. I still couldn't relax. I kept seeing Liam in every corner and in every item I touched. I decided the only cure for loneliness was a solo dive.

I drove to the beach at Rum Point, my favorite dive spot, and shimmied into my dive skin. After carrying my tank to the water's edge, I attached it to the BCD and lifted the whole assembly over my head and slipped my arms into the BCD as I lowered it onto my back. I cleaned my mask to prevent fogging, and waded into the water backwards, wearing my fins.

I surface swam to the ropes and ducked under before I sank down to the bottom. I swam along the sand path to the drop off at the edge of the wall, enjoying the sight of the garden eels as they snapped into their burrows at my approach. I smiled at the brilliant colors of the parrotfish chomping on the bright corals with their big buck teeth. The thousands of tiny, varied reef fish with their brilliant reds, yellows, purples, and blues darted about on urgent fish business.

Nothing had changed except me. I kept flashing back to the

times Liam and I had been diving here, holding hands as we drifted along the wall. The memory was bitter-sweet.

As I hovered over the blue, a small remora swam up and put her face very close to my mask. She stared at me, looking deep into my eyes. She must have liked what she saw, because after a long stare, she swam over my head and positioned herself over my tank. I'd often been the object of remora affection, and it always made me smile. I had no idea why they liked me, but I was honored when one chose me as a safe haven. I continued swimming slowly along the reef, peering into the crevices and grottoes formed by the coral, the remora at my back. I saw a slipper lobster and a sweet little octopus living in separate caves, side-by-side like neighbors in a coral condo, and I laughed at the image.

I remembered Liam's smile, and I thought about how much he would enjoy the fanciful image. Then I remembered he was out of my life, and my laughter withered.

I thought about the scar on my face. I'd had the surgery to minimize it, and although it had healed nicely and was much less visible, it was still there. Would I ever find someone else like Liam who looked past it to the real me inside?

"Stop it,' I told myself. I was going to have to get used to being on my own again. And I would do it. Ray raised me to be strong and resilient, self-sufficient when I needed to be. Right now, I needed to be self-sufficient, and that was that.

By this time, I had just a little bit more than half a tank of air left, which meant I'd reached the turnaround point of the dive. I reversed direction and let the current carry me back to the sand chute. As I crested the edge of the reef, I saw Suzie-Q flitting past some bright red fan coral on my left. She saw me, and immediately reversed direction.

I didn't want to spook her, so I pretended I hadn't seen her and swam past without stopping. When I saw the buoys of the ropes that marked the swim area at Rum Point, I flashed back to my collision with the Jet Ski, so I swam inside the area before surfacing.

I switched to my snorkel and swam to shore on the surface. When I was in a few feet of water, I put my regulator back in my mouth and sat on the bottom to remove my fins. I attached them to a D-ring on my BCD, rose, and waded to shore. I had my whole life ahead of me, and whether I was with Liam or someone else—or even no one at all—I would make the most of it. Ray would have wanted it that way.

Also by Sharon Ward

In Deep

Dark Tide

Killer Storm

Or see the entire series Fin Fleming series by following the link.

If you enjoyed Sunken Death, you can continue reading about the adventures of Fin and the gang by following the links above.

Also, nothing helps an author more than a positive review, so please give In Deep (and me!) a boost by leaving a review. Here's the link:

Sunken Death

And if you'd like to subscribe to my totally random and very rarely published newsletter, you can sign up here.

Acknowledgments

I am so lucky to have a supportive team of fabulously talented writers who help me stay focused and who so generously offer their time and expertise to help out.

Endless thanks to Andrea Clarke, Mary Beth Gale, Stephanie Scott-Snyder and Kate Hohl. You guys are the best. I owe you a lot. I'll pay you back in pictures of Ryan Gosling and Alexander Skarsgard.

Michele Dorsey, my fellow traveler in the world of self-publishing. Thanks for the hours of discussion.

The wonderful authors who helped me along the way and blurbed this book. Hallie Ephron, Edwin Hill, Hank Phillippi Ryan, Brenda Buchanan, Stephanie Scott-Snyder, and C. Michele Dorsey. Buy their books.

My writer friends at the Miss Demeanors blog. Thanks for letting me join you at www.MissDemeanors.com .

Jack, thanks for being so supportive. I know it's not easy to be such a perfect husband, and I'm grateful for everything you do.

And Molly, thanks for the pokes when I've been sitting too long.

About the Author

For years, Sharon Ward has been a successful freelance writer specializing in technology, manufacturing, and supply chain—even before the supply chain became the topic of the year. Before that, she worked at some of the most successful tech companies in the world, including Microsoft and Oracle.

Her real love, though, is diving. As a PADI certified divemaster, Sharon helped local dive shops with their training classes and has hundreds of dives under her weight belt.

Wanting to share the joy and wonder of the underwater world, she wrote In Deep, her debut novel, released in August 2021. Sunken Death is the second in the Fin Fleming Series. The third adventure, Dark Tide, will hit the shelves in the spring of 2022.

She lives in Southern Massachusetts with her husband Jack and their long-haired miniature dachshund Molly.

Printed in Great Britain
by Amazon

22801836R00162